Protecting Paige

Deby Eisenberg

Also by Deby Eisenberg

Pictures of the Past

For Mom, Dad, and Steve
Always with me on the journey . . .

"When the past dies, there is mourning,
but when the future dies,
our imaginations are compelled to carry it on."

—Gloria Steinem

Chapter 1
Sole Survivor

I went to live as a ward in my uncle's home in the year 1962. My uncle was the celebrated photographer, Maxwell Noble. You probably will know of his work, even if you do not recognize the name. His pictures were covers of the most famous publications of the decades; his photo essays filled the pages of *Look* and *Life* magazines. Along with the great names like Margaret Bourke White and Alfred Eisenstaedt, he defined the field of photojournalism, covering all areas of the human-interest spectrum, from simple, engaging scenes of everyday life to the cruel depictions of man-made and natural disasters. Perhaps he would not have made a name for himself in the modern era, when it is necessary for journalists to be "embedded" with the troops. But even today, he would be the one to best document the aftermath of any tragedy, to give names and faces to the overwhelming numbers of any catastrophe.

Yes, my famous uncle could personalize anything on a grand scale, although he had to struggle to relate to one small girl craving his attention. You may be thinking that I blamed him for that, but only because you don't know the story yet. It wasn't like that at all. Actually, he was my savior. He arranged for me to be taken care of properly, even though he distanced himself from that task.

Barbara Walters would be credited with handling Uncle Maxwell's most insightful and illuminating television interview in the 1970s, an hour-long dialogue and photo montage that actually helped establish Ms. Walters' reputation as a prime-time host. And because she so tastefully handled the delicate details of Maxwell's past, details that others in the press might have presented as merely salacious and scandalous, my uncle allowed himself to become more of a public figure in the future, moving from behind the camera and emerging as the subject of the lens on many more occasions.

I say the word *ward* so easily now, although I know that often it is a harsh, ugly, and disturbing creature in itself. Bearing the negative connotation of the "four-letter word" that it is, certainly it was correctly stated for many of the famous *wards* of literature that populated any Dickens novel. I was obsessed with words even at the early age of twelve, and in my desire to learn the etymology of so many, *Webster's Dictionary* became a close friend. You see, prior to that year when this word *ward* invaded my life—along with *murder, death, gun, blood, suffering*, and *orphan*—my world was filled with a softer, more poetic palette of sounds. *Twilight* and *fireflies* and *soft brushes* and *bubble baths* and *gardens* and *petticoats* and *kisses good night* and *hot chocolate*—this was the language of my youth until that point. Later, I understood that it was truly the word *innocence* under whose umbrella all those other terms would fall. But you can understand that concept of innocence, especially as a child, only when that protective shade is blown from your hands by the strong winds of fate—when you no longer have that shelter from the storm.

While I was first drawn to the library of my uncle's home because of Mr. Webster's dictionary, it was certainly the enormous globe that held my attention. I could set the world spinning and then stop it with a point of my finger, and Uncle Maxwell would have a story to tell of his adventures in those regions: England, Spain, Finland, Brazil, Kenya, and Antarctica. Only years later, not even as a teenager, but only when I had become a mother, did I realize that half of those stories were fascinating fabrications meant to entertain and distract me. But imagine—to have even experienced the other half.

And now I will reveal my name: Paige Noble. That name may be familiar to you—if not initially, then when I remind you of the infamous murders of three members of the Noble family on Chicago's South Side in the early 1960s. Even if you were not born then, you would have undoubtedly seen documentaries on the incident, or references back to it through the decades whenever similar tragedies occurred. In an era of innocence, even before the first Kennedy assassination, our story brought an entire nation to tears.

It was my father's mistake, a lack of judgment, perhaps naïveté, that on the long drive from our Winnetka home on the North Shore to visit the Museum of Science and Industry, for one of our numerous family excursions, he did not stay on the main highway as we neared our destination. And we became trapped in that classic scenario—in the wrong place at the wrong time.

Gradually, over the following days and months, I would learn of the gang initiations that involved young teenagers *proving* themselves with the shooting of random people, a part of life in the racially divided and depressed areas of major US cities. (Understand that this would be information that a twelve-year-old girl could collect or repeat but could not process until well into adulthood.) The epidemic of violence this fostered would prove more potent and long lasting than the polio scare of the 1950s, for no Dr. Salk vaccine has been invented to eliminate it even to this day. And so a trio of high schoolers, including fifteen-year-old Darren Barker, accompanied by two older members of the Street Guardians, savagely, without conscience, fired eight shots into the open windows of our Oldsmobile 98, after my dad pulled to the curb of a side street in their neighborhood. The shots instantly killed my mother and brother, mortally wounded my father, and grazed me with enough show of blood that I was left for dead.

Now I ask you to further process the fact that the mother of this Darren Barker came to my bedside at the nearby Michael Reese Hospital just one day following the tragedy. Imagine the security breach by today's standards. But then there were no really secure checkpoints in a medical complex, no surveillance cameras. Still, her intimate attention might have unsettled me further, even made me scream, had I not been moderately sedated, had my memory been more intact, had she not been wearing a nurse's aide uniform, had she properly identified herself as more than just a concerned caregiver. I would have screamed because now, for the second time in one week, I was being confronted by a Negro person. Yes, we said "Negro" then—we now know to say "black" or "African American." But this woman came with no weapons, no anger, and no fury. She came with tears, with cookies, with a teddy bear. I didn't understand it at the time. I was an injured child—a victim—but I was also a witness. In the end, it would turn out, I was the only witness—the sole survivor.

Sometimes when I would wake up, it was such a slow process that "wake" was too strong and active a verb. What was happening was a slow, slow drifting back *into* consciousness, and there was some memory of the reverse having occurred, a drifting slowly, slowly *out of* consciousness. But I didn't know why I had that feeling, and I didn't know where I was. I blinked my eyes open in stages, first a crack open and then a quick closing, reacting to some sort of glaring light. And then I tried again, and they opened a little wider, and there were blurry outlines of things as my eyes tried to focus. And finally, my eyes were fully open, but squinting and searching for something familiar. Where could I be? This was not my bedroom. That window was not our window. Those sheer drapes, those venetian blinds, slightly broken, slightly askew—they were not part of my mother's orderly home. Then I saw that the light was so bright coming through the window because it was a full morning sun reflecting off the lake. This was like the view out of my friend's window on a Sunday morning after a sleepover. Oh, how I would just die for twin canopy beds like she has in her bedroom. "Just one canopy bed, please, *Maman*," I would beg whenever I had slept over. But my mother would always answer in a whisper when we spoke about the Beckman family— "very wealthy"—as if she were saying something secret or malicious. In our nice, affluent suburb, there were still levels of elitism, and Sherry Beckman "lives on the lake" (whispers again).

But I was not on the twin bed in her room, dreaming in the beautiful fluff of comforters and pillows I loved, looking out her window through meticulously pleated pink satin drapes. The floor was not the plush raspberry carpet that was a treat to my feet on a chilly winter morning. This floor was a cold-looking, yellow-spotted linoleum tile. This bed was white-sheeted with guardrails like those on a toddler's bed. I scouted the room further, and just that slight movement of my head alerted someone sitting in a chair near the foot of the bed to stir. She leaned out of an unnaturally uncomfortable sleeping position and came at me with, "Honey, you awake now, girl? You just wait a minute. Now, where is that buzzer? Where is that buzzer? You just wait a minute—I will get you someone, honey."

But before she could even find that buzzer she was searching for, there was a rush of people to crowd her out, and suddenly she was hidden by their white coats and carts of medical devices. It was then, when I moved my arm to direct them away, that I realized that a tube or wire was attached to my arm, and my movements or heartbeat or something about my bodily activity had sent an immediate alert to this entourage. I was not quite yet in the moment. I was distracted by this woman, this stranger, who spoke to me briefly, who I could now see was content to just stand behind this barricade of people. I had never seen her before, but I had an idea why she may be there. I wanted to ask her something, but then it was too late. My eyes closed again, involuntarily, and I was ready to slip, slip, slip back into sleep.

But then someone took my hand, slapping it more than gently, urging me back to the room. "Stay with us, Paige." Slowly, I opened my eyes and saw a man, still slapping my hand and then pressing on my cheeks. "Paige, Paige, wake up. That's a good girl." My mild, slow emergence from that deep sleep, initially so peaceful with that one welcoming face, was now transformed into a consuming fear and desperation.

"Maman, Daddy, Maman, Daddy…Roger." I thought I was screaming, but my voice was only a whimpering, hoarse whisper. And then that man stopped slapping me, grabbed a penlight from his coat pocket, and shone it directly into each of my eyes. I blinked furiously and pushed his hands away.

"Paige, I am Dr. Levinson. I want you to know you will be all right. You are in a hospital, but we are taking good care of you. You have been sleeping for a while, but you will be okay. You have some injuries, but you will be fine."

"Maman." Now I knew my voice was above a whisper. "I don't understand. Where is everyone? I don't understand what is going on. Where—where is our car?"

Our car, yes. It seemed odd I should ask that, but that was my last memory—my family in the car, driving to the museum. And that last memory, little did I know, would be one that would have to last for a lifetime.

∾

My emotional distress and confusion, which had been my main focus initially, I suddenly realized had masked a newly emerging reality. I was in pain. My head was throbbing, and when I went to touch the source of that pain, my right hand to my right temple, I could feel a mound of gauze and then a moist spot. When I took my hand away and looked at my fingertips, I was horrified. They presented a shock of bright red blood. Immediately, I reached back to the source and followed the bandaging farther up my scalp. And then something else did not feel right, did not feel normal. I was touching my bare scalp above my hairline. I was thinking I could feel my brain. Finally, I looked at the man, the doctor whom I had tried to will away. I started to cry.

"What's wrong with me? Where is my family?" I could feel my heart racing. I was so agitated that I reached to pull a tube from its stand, and while the doctor reacted to hold that hand with a firm grip, I turned to the feel of another hand, a soft hand at my opposite side, gently soothing my arm and then pushing back my hair and comforting my cheek. It was the creamy black hand of the woman I had seen, and somehow that slight motherly touch relaxed me enough that I could listen to the doctor. But then, as I turned back to him, a new woman was by his side, dressed in a normal woman's suit, but with a gray hospital jacket.

"Paige," Dr. Levinson said, "we have been waiting for you to wake up, and we are so glad you have. You will be fine; I can tell. Your speech is perfect. The bullet has grazed your head, just deep enough that we need you observed. I want you to meet Miss Diane Welton. She is our social worker."

"The bullet," I whispered. "What do you mean, the bullet? Like from a gun?" I could see the surprised expression on the doctor's face. He leaned back so that Miss Welton could continue.

"Paige, I am Miss Welton, and I am happy to meet you and be here for you. I think we understand now that you do not remember what has happened. I want you to know first of all that you are not alone. Every one of us here just wants to help you."

"But I want Maman. Just bring her here."

"Paige," she said, and I was already wising to this technique of their repeating my name to keep my attention. "You are twelve years old. Am I right?"

"Yes."

"Well, twelve years old is not a little child, so I am hoping that you will be able to understand this—what I am going to tell you, Paige dear." She motioned for the doctor to move a bit so that she could sit squarely on my bed and take my hand. "There has been a very sad event for you and your family." She looked intently into my eyes to make sure I was following her words. "While you were all riding in the car, your father had to get off the highway. And on a street, a street very near this hospital, some men with guns shot into the car. Your mother, your father, and your brother, Roger—I am sorry to tell you this—they were all killed. Your mother and your brother were already deceased before the ambulance arrived. Your father was still breathing, but he did not make it through the night."

"I don't understand what that means," I remember saying, although I did understand, but I wanted her to have the nerve to repeat it.

"Paige, your father has passed away, has died, as well."

At first I was just silent. I was taking it all in. But it was too much to absorb. "No, no. Oh my God, no…. Why are you saying this? Where are they? Make them come back. Don't say that…." This much I remember vividly, crying, almost screaming, not buying her "You are twelve years old" routine, like twelve is grown up, like you wouldn't have the same hysterical reaction if you were twenty years old. And that is when I think they gave me something to sedate me, a shot of some sort into my arm, or maybe into the tube leading to my arm. I was floating again, back into that more blissful state of innocence.

Chapter 2
You Will Not Be Alone

Drifting in and out of sleep for the next few days, when I opened my eyes, I would almost always find the woman from the chair as my constant bedside companion. "Honey, don't you worry. I won't be going anywhere until I leave for my overnight shift at the nursing home. If you don't mind, I will just be watching over you. I am Gladys B." It seemed like she started to say her last name, but she left me with only the "bu" sound of the initial letter. "Well, you just call me Gladys. And you just call me whenever you need me, no matter what I'm doing sitting in the chair." Sometimes she would speak to me continuously in a very quiet, almost stream-of-conscious, rambling style, about the weather or the day or the show I was watching on television. Other times, she seemed only to meld silently into the background when nurses or doctors came to assess my vital signs and readjust the mechanics of the machines at my bedside. Those white-coated professionals would very quickly, patronizingly, ask how

I felt, and then they rather dismissively acknowledged my nods or winces, as if their clipboards and monitoring strips would provide all the important information they needed, and I was just a superfluous agent.

I began to think that I was having an out-of-body experience in that frightening place surrounded by strangers, and only the calming manner of Gladys kept me from hysteria. I had presumed during that time that she was a hospital employee (although I was confused when she said she'd be with me until her night shift at the nursing home started). Only later did I find out that the staff thought she was our maid from back home in Winnetka.

Sometimes I heard Gladys going on like she was praying or pleading to me when she thought I was sleeping. That scared me, so I wouldn't open my eyes or stir. Here was this woman speaking to the haze of the preteen person I was during those first days—reaching out to me in some way with an inexplicable intensity. I didn't understand. I felt weak and powerless, yet she implied that I was in charge of something. Was something being asked of me? A few times I saw her rock in her chair, her hand cupped over her mouth, mumbling something like, "Don't let them kill him." These were her words. "He is my boy, my baby. It is my fault—but I tried to give him dreams. He had no real father—he had no role model. He could only follow the men on the street." She would often fluff my pillows, gently lifting the back of my head to rearrange my position so that my wound would not be irritated. And when she would finish this routine with a quick shoulder rub, I would sneak glances of her surprisingly weathered hands. Even when I opened my eyes, I wouldn't speak. I would watch her looking out the window or reading a newspaper or book, and when she would look up and see me, I would skirt her gaze, so we rarely made eye contact. And soon she would continue speaking again, but so sweetly. "Paige, you get better now. Just you rest. Let time heal your body." She was interacting with me as if she were conversing with someone in a noncognizant, comatose state, without pausing for responses. I didn't really understand what was happening. I had not yet gained the experience of years, the adult maturity that allows you to interpret the actions of people, to analyze the complexities of unexpected emotions and project a story behind them. But maybe it was better. With the gullibility of childhood, I was certain that this person was genuine, loving, and deeply saddened, that she posed no immediate threat.

Finally, when we were alone after an especially painful probing for reflexes and responses, I found my voice. And my words, again so inappropriate by today's standards, left her with only a quizzical look.

"Do you know Sally?" I asked. "Did Sally send you?"

She was by my side in a second—taking and stroking my hand in a most intimate manner, soothing my forehead with fingertip massages and brushing back my somewhat butchered sweep of bangs. "Honey, I don't know a Sally—but I am here for you."

"But Sally told you to come," I insisted. When I saw this tender Negro face with the consoling voice I had been listening to, I associated her with the one other Negro woman I knew—Sally, our cleaning lady. Every

Friday at our home in Winnetka, a sweet woman would work tirelessly to make our house "spic-and-span" (her favorite phrase) for the weekend and would leave us with the best home-cooked fried chicken meal I would ever have in all of my life (as it turned out). So I just assumed that Sally had sent this woman to my side now. I was remembering more than one Friday when I was home sick, and Mother knew that she could continue with her various routines. Sally would take my temperature, feed me aspirin, and wrap me in three blankets until, within hours, my fever would break. Then she would treat me like a princess. She would insist that I clang a spoon on a glass when I was ready for orange juice or needed the television channel changed.

But now there was this other woman by my side, and her presence was certainly a comfort. When I looked around the room, I did not see Maman or Daddy or my brother—yes, at that time I began to cry and call for them again. But then Gladys B. did not have the heart to speak directly to me. "Press the buzzer, darling. Press the buzzer, sweet girl." And then she would not look at me. She moved from the bed, and I watched her turn her face away to gaze through the diaphanous draperies, which were slightly swaying with the breeze of the heating unit. And when I was once again told the life-altering truth, that my mother and father and brother were not just waiting in the corridor, not just taking a break for cafeteria food—that they were gone, never coming back, that they had died and that I was alone—then finally she turned back to me, when I whispered "Gladys."

At the time of the "event," we were on the last leg of the over-an-hour journey from our northern suburb of Winnetka to the museum on the south side of Chicago. Unlike many families from our area, who might make this excursion every few years at best or leave the tour for their children's school field trips, for us, this was a quarterly or at least semiannual occasion. You see, my father, Dr. Mitchell Noble, a scientist and an engineering professor, had actually helped design many of the exhibits at the world-renowned destination.

When the doctor and social worker had again detailed to me what had happened to my family, that we had pulled off the main highway and become victims of a horrific and inexplicable crime, they imagined that I blocked out the episode. But I knew I could explain it. So immediately I absorbed all of the guilt. Although I had no recollection of the time leading up to the encounter, I took the blame. "Oh no, it is my fault, my fault, my fault," I repeated so hysterically that I was once more sedated and they were reluctant to question me again. I was always nagging my dad on long car trips to "Please, please, pull over. I have to go to the bathroom." So for another day, I tormented myself with the knowledge that although I did not remember doing it on that fateful Saturday, I obviously caused the whole chain of events that led to the mass murder of the no-longer Noble family. Finally, the next morning, the social worker proved her worth by actually listening to my fears, reviewing all notes from the authorities, and assuring me that lane closures from a three-car pileup ahead had caused my father to pull off the Outer Drive and seek an alternative route, heading west on Twenty-Third Street, until a documented flat tire had caused him to pull over on a side street. And an almost tearfully empathetic young intern, who was originally from my same suburban town, said that most likely I remembered nothing because I had simply fallen asleep on the long ride.

❧

My first attempted conversation with Gladys was that afternoon. I awoke from a nap and actually felt almost no pain or anxiety. Until then, every time I woke up, there was the same confusion. *Where am I? Why am I here? What has happened to me?* And that always led to *Where is Maman?* Oh, even this time, I went through the list in my head. But before I erupted in my daily crying spells, I heard sobbing that wasn't my own. It was coming from the slumped-over figure in the rust-colored leather chair that Gladys was occupying. I couldn't think of what to do or say. I couldn't figure out a way to maneuver to her with the limitations of steel bed guards and my own attachment to a dripping line of something from a plastic pouch that was attached to my arm. So I called to her. And when she looked up, I offered her the best treat I had on hand: the freshly baked, delicious chocolate chip cookies that Gladys herself had brought to me when she arrived.

"Why are you crying? Can you come closer to me? I have some really good cookies that might cheer you," I said. And although my voice was still not at its full strength, she seemed to have heard me.

She turned toward me, her face soaked from her own tears, and she wiped her eyes. I now saw that she had been reading something that looked like a letter, written on a sheet of school notebook paper. But she didn't seem to want to share its contents with me. She neatly folded it up and put it in the pocket of her white uniform, attempting a slight smile. And then she walked over to my bedside.

"Honey, what makes you so sweet and smart? When the stomach is satisfied, the body can heal. You must have heard me say that. You must have been listening each day when I thought you were sleeping. It is the food aromas that please us. This, my mother taught me while she was teaching me her recipes." Gladys did take a bite of her own treats, but she didn't yet tell me what had disturbed her. She gave me a soft kiss on my forehead, quietly retreated to her corner chair, and closed her eyes again. I understood that she just needed some time alone, that she was troubled by her own problems. This knowledge was surprisingly a bit comforting to me. Not that I wished her any sorrows, but it lifted me in some way, empowered me a bit in my very helpless state, knowing that anyone can be sad and that maybe we can help each other.

By the end of the week, there was a constant parade of my neighbors and the families of my schoolmates. The thing about our family that was not so obvious to everyone was that we pretty much kept to ourselves. There was not one family that my parents would call their "best friends," although so many women tried to get close to my mother. No one really knew us intimately, knew our background, knew if we had close relatives. My parents, mainly my mother, always seemed to set boundaries on relationships. I didn't blame the others. I knew they each presumed someone else was stepping up to take charge of my situation.

One of my first visitors entered the room with "Paige, darling. Let me give you a hug. We are sooo sorry." It was Mrs. Deloitte, Blanche Deloitte, from next door. She walked unsteadily on heels that were too high for balance, and her short skirt and low top, as always, seemed a size too small. I knew she was often the object of ridicule in our very conservative village.

"Your parents, your brother…Oh, that smart young man. Honestly, we can't stop crying at our house," she continued. Just like my mother, she had a strong accent, and I was told that it was a Lower East Side New York accent. It had no negative connotation to me at the time, but it was hardly pleasing to the ear. She would always say to Maman that they were so alike—trying to claim my mother's Frenchness as their heart-and-soul connection. "Oh, yes, my husband's family," she had told us. "Well, certainly you have guessed from the name— originally from France, as well." If my mother were here again, she would have been mumbling "Busybody" to Blanche's every word. Thinking of that kind of made me want to laugh, understanding that Mrs. Deloitte's tone lacked any sincerity and that her sole purpose for the visit was to report her findings back to the others, probably inferring that she had a special link to me—the French thing, you know.

A couple of other neighbors came in pairs, apologizing for waiting a few days and actually saying to me that they were concerned about bringing their children with them: "You know, honey, this hospital is not in a good neighborhood—so close to the tragedy." Even then, I didn't think it was an appropriate thought to share with me.

Our across-the-street neighbor, Mrs. Annette Earlman, wanted me to be aware that two squad cars, one the Chicago Police and the other the Winnetka Police, had gone into our home and were going through my parents' papers. "Honey, they've been asking if we knew of your next of kin—well, closest relative, that is. They say they have numerous albums and coffee-table books by Maxwell Noble. Could he be a relative? He's that famous photographer. I can't imagine they never shared that." Of course, I knew this was going on; the police themselves had already assured me that they were trying to locate Uncle Maxwell.

But I let her think she was the first to ask this because she was among those nice enough to risk her life with the visit. "Oh, yes—Uncle Maxwell. Well, he is my uncle. But I haven't seen him in a while—maybe not in a couple of years. But I used to see him a lot more."

The look on her face was as if I said we were related to the Queen of England. And I am sure she was happy to be the first to spread that confirmation.

The hospital staff felt so sorry for me that they bent the strict rules of the era and never complained about my stream of visitors increasing over the next days. My friends, probably on instructions from their parents, tried best to cheer me up and brought decks of cards so I could play gin rummy when they were there and solitaire when they left. One group even came with a Monopoly board, which balanced precariously on my bed, the tiny hotels shifting neighborhoods with each movement of their fidgeting bodies. Sherry Beckman entered my room with an explosion of pastel-colored helium balloons and the scrumptious pillow from her bedroom that I loved to hug when I spent the night there.

Mostly, I knew, the kids were mesmerized by the event, not accepting the fact that I had no memory of the crime. Karen Deider's brother, Jeff, who was the heartthrob of the grade ahead of me, had designated himself the gruesome spokesman and interrogator for the group.

"Do you have the bullet? Can we see it?" Jeff asked. But Steve Miller first shot him a look and then jabbed him in the side with his elbow, filling his role as the sensitive older statesman, having been my brother's best friend. "Don't listen to him—you don't have to think about stuff like that."

All of these distractions did work to give me a brief return to normalcy, a slight escape from my new reality. But then, without warning, I would scan the people in the room, the kids close to me, the parents talking discreetly in the corner, and realize just how alone I was. I would begin to tear up, although I would try to hide behind a pathetic half smile. And then I would catch

Gladys's eye, and she would be the one to say that maybe it was time I get some rest.

On Thursday, I opened my eyes from an afternoon nap, and there was Sally—our cleaning lady—hovering over me as if it were another Friday morning at my own home. At first, when I caught sight of the black arm extending a Styrofoam water cup with a bent straw, I thought it was Gladys. But when I looked up, I knew I was smiling broadly. The cup was quickly set back down, and I was lovingly embraced by the familiar floral dress and jasmine scent that was distinctly Sally. And finally I felt at home in the generous folds of her large arms and the soft cushion of her full breasts. Neither of us could speak, though we each tried to start.

"Oh, my darling, Paige. I didn't know. I just—" Sally said, but she was so choked up seeing me with a bandaged head and little eyes tearing up that she started to sob.

We clutched each other for a long time, our tears intermingling on our pressed cheeks, and I was the first to regain composure. "I was looking for you, Sally." She was whimpering a bit still, but trying to hold it back. "I told them you would come. But then when you didn't, I had a nightmare that maybe you were with us in the car and that you were dead, too."

"Don't talk, sweetheart. I can't have you be upsetting yourself like that."

"I just can't seem to remember what exactly happened. But do you know? They are all gone. Did they tell you that when you came? Don't tell them. But I still hope it wasn't real—I think I know it was. I will believe what you say."

"Sweetie, sweetie. You ain't gonna believe that I did not know about nothing. You know we have no TV, and I be so busy with my kids when I come home from my jobs each night. Maybe I hear about some bad thing, but I don't pay it so much attention. I got my own problems." Her guilt was palpable, and she was ready to begin to cry again, grabbing tissues from the box by my bed, but she struggled to continue.

"It's okay, Sally. Don't cry. I don't mind. I've been sleeping mainly, I think."

"No, I need you to know this, honey. This morning, when I go to my Thursday family, the missus, she say to me, 'Sorry about the Noble family. That is the same Nobles you go to on Fridays, right?' And then I say I don't know nothin' 'bout what you saying and she say, 'Oh, Sally, they all been murdered. All dead 'cept the little girl.' She show me the newspaper stories, and then I know what hospital you be at. Well, I run out of that house so fast to get to the train, and I say to her that I gotta go see you and if she don't mind, I be 'vailable to come back to her on Friday, it seem, but I need to go to my little Paige now."

Although he seemed only barely familiar to me, a man came into my room very early on Friday morning, telling me it was nice to see me again, although he regretted the circumstances.

"Paige Noble. You certainly have grown since I last saw you. You remember me, right?"

"Um…"

"Your parents' lawyer, Henry Rosenthal. I was out at the house maybe once or twice. Well, I don't blame you. I am picturing you—you might have been just eight or nine years old at the time. Do you know why I am here?"

I shook my head.

"I can't even imagine how scary and confusing this is to you. But I am going to help you sort this all out. We want you taken care of just as you always were by your parents." He was flipping through pages in a legal binder as he spoke, although I longed for him to make the sincerity of eye contact.

"Well, I am here because it is my business to convey your parents' wishes to the authorities. You know when people die—pass away—good people, like your parents, they would have made provisions for what would happen."

"So do you know what will happen to me?" I asked sheepishly. This very question had certainly crossed my mind, but the constant attention from so many eager people in the hospital setting had kind of cocooned me in a temporarily secure environment. I cried over the past, but I had not really looked to the future.

"Yes, Paige," he answered. "As a matter of fact, I do. Your parents made out a will—set their wishes down, very specifically, in my office not too long after you were born. And over the years, when I helped your father with his patent filings, we addressed other areas of your parents' estate holdings."

"Uh-huh." That was the strongest response I could offer at that point. It's funny. I tried to digest what he was saying, but it was not the answer I was looking for. In fact, I thought he was skirting the issue, delaying the news. This much I knew; there was no one to take care of me. Who was going to watch me? Who could I live with? Who would be Maman? I was pretty sure that all of my friends had grandmothers, had aunts; they were always visiting cousins. What was going to happen to me?

"And the police have finally located your uncle, Maxwell Noble. He is your guardian, as named in the will. He has been making arrangements to return from Europe as soon as possible."

I finally summoned the courage to talk to him. "Mr. Rosenthal, I'd better tell you this now because I didn't really tell the police when they were asking me about Uncle Max. But I think that he is not going to want me." I was very hesitant to say this because I was afraid the hospital would eventually need to just kick me out. But someone had to understand the truth. "I mean, he always liked me, but then there was some kind of family problem, and we stopped seeing him. I mean, he'll come here to me. But it's not like he has a wife or kids or a family with a house."

"Well, Paige," he said. He took off his glasses, pushed all his papers aside, really looked at me, and smiled in the most grandfatherly way (not that I had a grandfather to judge by). But it made me believe he really cared. "You just work on getting well. No one would ever desert you. I promise you this—I will personally make sure that you will not be alone—even if it comes to you living with me and my wife, Claire."

No one could have said anything that would have allayed my fears more.

Chapter 3
Two Different Worlds

Exactly one week from the day of the tragedy, I had just returned from an escorted walk around the entire hospital floor, following an appointment at physical therapy. They had been trying to ease a pain in my neck that I, personally, felt resulted more from the intersection of the angle of my bed and the television screen than the effects of a gunshot wound. When the nurse and I entered my room, however, there was a disturbing commotion. We came upon a group of three uniformed Chicago policemen I had not seen before. But they were not waiting for me; they were surrounding and seemingly interrogating a very distraught Gladys.

Although I had seen her emotional and upset more than once, now she was moaning and exhibiting an almost catatonic rocking motion. Clutching a newspaper to her chest, her face was as blanched as her skin color would allow. The whole scene was very scary and confusing to me. I wanted to go over to her, but I was held back, not just by the nurse, but by the hand signal of one of the policemen, as if he were directing traffic with the palm-up "Stop" gesture. His name tag read "Sergeant Fergusson," and he must have been the one in charge.

He was talking to Gladys in a more than firm voice. "Ma'am. We are sorry for your loss, but your son is implicated in this crime—in the shooting of the Noble family—as you well know. We're here now to tell Miss Noble what's just happened, the killing, the arrests. But I know I recognize you from speaking to you at your night job. Why don't you just tell me what's going on here?"

The nurse who was with me covered her mouth, crying out, "Oh my God! This woman has been in the room all week." Still holding on to my arm, she leaned out the door and called down the corridor for someone to bring a doctor in now.

Another policeman moved to take handcuffs from his belt as the sergeant spoke. "How do you come to be here? Have you been intimidating this child?" He turned to me and added, "This witness."

Finally, Gladys stopped rocking and looked up. She did speak, but not with a forceful defense—more with a quiet tone of sadness or resignation. "No—you don't understand. It's nothing like that." Another moan escaped her, and she just shook her head. "It's all I could think to do when I found out what happened. Darren, my son, was always such a good boy. He left me a note, and I knew he would not be coming back. I felt alone and helpless." She paused and shook her head. "So, I'm sorry. I just thought I could comfort and protect this child, after what she went through, to make up to her in the smallest way for what was done."

"Mrs. Barker, let's get this straight. Your son has been a suspect for a week in the murders of the Noble family, and you have been hovering at the bedside of one of the victims." Sergeant Fergusson's tone ran between hostility and pity. It was hard not to have at least some empathy for Gladys. And then he shook his head in exasperation. He looked at his men. "Just take her to the station. We'll figure out later how to deal with this. Obstruction of justice, at the least. I don't know, but don't cuff her—just take her."

Again, I was being held back. I don't know why, but I still felt a strong bond to Gladys, no matter what they were talking about. She had been the closest thing I'd had to a mother for the past week, and there was no way she was anything but caring and sincere. But just as two of the officers lifted her from the chair, each grabbing an elbow, the newspaper she had been clinging to began a slow descent to the ground, and when I saw it, it was like a bolt ran through me. There was a large picture of a Negro boy on the front page under the bold headline, "Noble Family Suspect Murdered." I was drawn to the face and bent down to pick it up and examine it closer. Then I read the caption: "Fifteen-year-old Darren Barker is found shot to death under Dan Ryan Expressway overpass."

I was stunned. I stared at the picture for about ten seconds, and in the background I could hear the nurse whispering, "She should not have seen that—we've been keeping all that from her."

"Oh no...oh God!" I cried and then looked back up at Gladys. No one in the room had moved after my next words. "Oh my God. That's him."

Gladys began squirming, but they wouldn't let her free from their grasp. "Paige, I am so sorry. I know they say he's done this. But that's my boy, that's my baby. I couldn't tell you. I wanted to tell you, but I couldn't. I just wanted to help you. I'm sorry...I'm so sorry."

The nurse could tell I was feeling dizzy, so she quickly moved me close to the bed, pulling the sheets aside so that I could scoot to the edge. She really wanted me to lie down, but I pushed her slightly away. I needed to continue.

"It says...the headline says, "Suspect Murdered." I couldn't take my eyes off the picture, but then I looked up and directly at Gladys. "Gladys—this boy is your son?"

The look on Gladys's face reflected a further acute level of pain that came from her soul. She tried to reach out to me but was held back. "I know, Paige. My being here, this seems like the worst thing. But you need to understand; you need to let me explain."

"Don't worry, miss," the sergeant said to me. "We'll get her out of here immediately. She's had no business being by you."

I couldn't even speak. I was horrified, confused, and nervous again. "But how is he dead? Who killed him?"

I knew they wanted to shield me from all this "police business," but they could tell I was desperate for answers.

"Miss Noble," the officer said. "We came here to tell you. Your family's murderers have all been found. That one was shot by his own accomplices—his own gang.

We've been trying to track them for a week. With reward money, there were enough leads from the neighborhood. There were five boys and men total. We've got all the others in custody now. We have them all. You don't need to be afraid anymore."

"But you need to know—h…h…he's the one." I have never been a stutterer, but I couldn't get the words out. They were so eager to remove Gladys from the room that they didn't want to listen to me. I struggled to block out anything anyone was saying or doing so I could tell them. "Wait—you have to listen. He's the one. He's the one…who *saved* me."

It was like time stood still for five full seconds. The bent head of the very despondent Gladys lifted, and the men holding her visibly loosened their grip. The sergeant hushed the others so that my soft voice could be the focus.

The doctor who had entered the room at the beginning of this episode now felt he should be the one in charge. "Paige, are you remembering something?" One of the two officers reached to take out his pad and pencil.

All of a sudden, things became clearer to me. "I think it's true that I must have been sleeping from the beginning, but I was upright, leaning on the door frame on my side of the backseat. My brother, as usual, had his face in a book, and my mother had told him he'd get a headache reading in the car."

And then there was a picture of my sweet and smart brother in my head, and I realized I hadn't even begun to deal with losing him. I really wanted to cry again, but

I tried hard to push past those thoughts so that I could tell them exactly what I remembered. "But that was early in the ride, and then I just fell asleep," I continued. "I think I slept a long time, until I remember hearing a loud noise. That's what woke me. I hadn't even opened my eyes to the sound, and then there was a scream—it was my mother's voice. And then another earsplitting bang—shot, I guess, and then two or three others, a horrible cry from my brother, and then another shot—that's the one that hit me. I fell to my side, and my head was on the seat. I was out for a few seconds, I'll bet. Then I heard men talking. I slightly opened my eyes and was looking right at one boy. In a way, he reminded me of my brother. He had glasses like him. He shook his head at me, like he was trying to tell me something with his eyes. He waved the others away. I remember what he said: 'They're all dead. It's done. Let's get out of here.'"

I looked at Gladys. And this time when I reached out for her, they let her walk to me. I grabbed each of her hands as she came close. "Your son, Darren—I don't know why he was there. I can't speak to that. But he wasn't even holding a gun. This I know. They would have shot me again, if not for him."

Gladys's legs seemed to buckle, and she fell to her knees. There were no words to describe the intensity of her sobs, even though they were muffled with her head in the folds of my hospital gown. "I hate those people who shot us. And I don't understand why they did. But I'm so sorry for you, Gladys," I said, and this time I was comforting her, smoothing back the coarse rings of her hair from her forehead. Everyone in the room was respectful enough to give her a few minutes. When she rose, she reached into the pocket of her uniform, pulled out the piece of lined school paper I had seen her reading, and handed it to the sergeant. He looked as if he would start reading it aloud, but then Gladys spoke.

"I have my routine when I come home from my night shift, and that's what I did last Sunday, early morning. I peeked in Darren's room just to watch him sleeping. But he wasn't there. His bed hadn't been slept in, although it looked as if he had gone through some of his stuff. He was a very neat boy—but that morning, his room didn't look quite right. I remembered that I hadn't seen him since he went to meet friends earlier on Saturday, and then he would have gone on to his part-time job. I went to where he always hid his money from working at the grocery, but it wasn't there. My heart started racing. He was the very sweetest boy. I was worried. It was unusual. But maybe he slept at a friend's house. And maybe that worried me more. Usually on Sunday morning, he surprises me with lunch in bed after I wake up. I was pacing around the apartment for a bit, and then I didn't know what to do with myself. I went in my bedroom, and that's when I found this note on my pillow."

She simply nodded to the sergeant, and he began reading:

Mom, whatever goes down, please don't believe anything bad about me, except that I didn't have the courage or ability to stop what happened. But you know I never could hurt anybody. I never used a gun—I wouldn't even hold it. And I am not proud of that. In my mind, I was thinking I should have grabbed it, that I should have tried to kill the guys I was with before anything happened. Then no innocent people would be hurt, and you would be okay. But I was a coward—that was nothing I was capable of doing. And this is why I am trying to run—not from the police. I wish I could go to them. The Guardians are looking for me now. They know I will never join them. They know I would rather turn them in. Please never think anything bad about yourself. All you have ever done for me was to be the best mother. All I ever cared about was not letting you down. You always protected me, and now I have to find a way to protect you. They've threatened me. I just tried to keep out of their way. They don't like boys who like school—who respect any authority but the gangs. I could take that. But now they threatened to hurt you, if I didn't go with them yesterday. I wasn't brave enough to say no—and it was daytime. I didn't think much could happen. We were just walking down the street when this older guy sees this nice car pulled over with the white family inside. He just goes crazy telling the others to take out their guns and then trying to hand me one. I wouldn't even touch it—and then everything happened in a flash. It is bad, Mom. It is real bad. There was even a little girl in the car. I can't get her face out of my head. I have to go—they are looking for me. Maybe everyone will be looking for me. And if there is any possibility for a good ending to this day—I will find a way to get us both out of the housing project. There is a better world out there—it is just out of reach for us here. Know that I will always love you.

Darren

If the city had previously found our story interesting, now it was compelling. The best headline came from the *Chicago Tribune* the next day: "A Tale of Two Boys." My one sentence, "He's the one who saved me," had turned Darren Barker from a murderer to a martyr. There were interesting twists to the story that no one could have anticipated. Two boys with the same birthday—one a victim of a crime, the other, allegedly a perpetrator, became its collateral damage. Both smart young men, but living in two different worlds. They were profiled in the story, with quotes from their teachers:

"We are all grieving the loss. What a fine, exceptionally bright young man. Next week, he would have traveled to the state science fair for the second year in a row. I know he was thinking of a future in engineering."

—Mrs. Arlene Bellman, New Trier High School, Winnetka, Illinois, referring to Roger Noble

"It is hard to deal with such a tragedy. He was a wonderful boy, an exceptional student. He was quiet and shy, but in my math class he was eager to help his peers who were struggling. I had just recommended him as our school representative in an upcoming math contest. I remember he told me that he hoped to be a doctor."

—Miss Dolores Brown, Kenwood High School, Chicago, Illinois, referring to Darren Barker

Although they had tried initially to shield me from any news, at that point they asked my permission to allow some representatives of the press into my room to interview me. As I watched the reporters flipping their stenographer's notebook pages, I knew that I craved their working instruments, the pencils and the lined sheets with the spiral rings on top. They were determined and busy and useful and distracted from the worries of their own lives in so tenaciously documenting mine. All this I knew; all this I could see in their faces. And so I wanted one thing—I wanted to take back my story, to own it, as desperately as Peter Pan climbed through the window so that Wendy might sew his shadow back on to him.

Chapter 4
Somebody Important

When Maxwell Noble receives the call, he is drinking. With a stiff scotch in his right hand, the glass raised part of the way to his lips, he grabs the receiver with his left. He is enjoying the view from his favorite Roman hotel at the top of the Spanish Steps. He knows it must be his current girlfriend, Adrienne, calling. She can be relentless. He has ignored the phone for the past half hour. What would be the purpose of answering and starting the argument again? She just presumed that they were becoming a permanent couple, and she was to have accompanied him to this prized assignment in the eternal city.

"Darling," she would say. "I will not pressure you again. I promise."

But she would still pressure him. She would still think in her heart that she could plan and scheme to get him to commit to her. She would not understand—none of them could understand—this could not happen for him. Even Celine, his sister-in-law, would beg him to find someone to love, someone to share his life with. They said he needed more than professional fulfillment. But she, above all, should know that was impossible.

But it is a man's voice.

"Is this Maxwell Noble?"

"Speaking."

"Sir," he says, and then there is a long pause and Maxwell hears only heavy breathing.

Already with that word "Sir," Maxwell is becoming paralyzed. He knows that no good news will follow.

"Sir." Again, an unbearable pause. "Are you the brother of Mitchell Noble of Winnetka, Illinois?"

"I am..." There is a tentativeness, a vulnerability, even in this phrase.

"Sir, this is Detective Andrew O'Brien of the Chicago Police Department." Again, too long a pause for comfort. "I have some bad news to share with you, and I am sorry."

Officer O'Brien is a young man in the year 1962, with a full head of wavy brown hair and an unassuming intellect that reveals itself immediately. In another family, it would have opened doors in different directions. But he is from a third-generation Chicago Police Department legacy, reserved and timid, unlike the rest of the O'Brien men. His tremendous capacity for empathy has led to his job as a liaison for social services and subsequently this call to Maxwell Noble.

With the initial news of the death of his beloved brother, Max brings the glass of whiskey to his lips and takes a strong, long gulp, although the policeman on the other end of the line will hear only the spasms of a choking cough that will follow. Even in his immediate anguish, Maxwell's mind is racing. There will be time ahead to deal with the grief. Celine—he will be there for her—he will rush to be there for her. He will comfort her, and she will comfort him.

He asks if Celine knows and if Celine is there with him, not even knowing himself if "with him" means with his deceased brother or with the police officer. His first thought is not of the brother's life—over— and not of the tremendous loss of the man who had for so long been an extension of his own being—but of Celine, of helping her, supporting her in their shared grief.

Then comes the second news the policeman puts forward—the news of the death of the wife as well. Celine is also dead. She has also been shot. The whiskey glass falls to the shag carpet below, the ice cubes spilling out with the remaining liquid.

With the next news, that even his nephew has died, the brilliant, awkward, spectacled high-schooler, Roger—the clone of his brother at that age—Max begins to sob. He grabs on to the bar counter and then falls into the nearest chair, a modern half-circle design that spins slightly with the rotating base.

He pleads now with the officer, as if they have bonded and they are standing side by side, as if he is grabbing on to the policeman's own arm for strength— "Not Paige, please not precocious, precious Paige." And then he holds his breath, waiting for the final blow. But he is spared.

"We have called to inform you of the tragedy because you are the next of kin, as far as we can ascertain, and we need someone to come for Paige."

When he arrives at the hospital, it is already past 9:00 p.m. Despite the late hour, the reception-desk clerk, a heavyset woman more intent on eating her chocolate frosted doughnut than attending to any visitor, understands from the sign-in name that this is the relative they have been expecting for the Noble girl. She begins to fill out his pass. When she looks up, she is momentarily taken aback but says nothing. She writes the room number on the card and points to the appropriate elevator. Maxwell is happy to have come at this hour, when the hallways are mainly deserted and he can maneuver without drawing any unnecessary attention to himself. At a news scene, dressed in his iconic photographer's khaki camouflage vest, his camera in hand, he can blend well into a crowd, emergency crews never releasing their proper focus. But often when Maxwell Noble arrives at a social destination, attention is diverted from the event, and he owns the room. One by one, in a wave of conversation groups, people will turn toward him, as if they have just spotted Burt Lancaster. They know he must be somebody important, a movie star or a politician, and there is an immediate buzz as everyone tries to identify him. He is always embarrassed by the attention, and he will keep his focus above their heads, although people interpret his reaction as arrogance, and it elevates him even further in their eyes. He is a slightly taller version of Clark Gable, with the same thin mustache, but without the physical bravado. That is replaced with the Cary Grant charmingly sophisticated manner. His dark suit, whether black or blue or gray, is an impeccable fit. He wears a crisp white shirt with an open collar and no tie, unless he is in formal attire. He is ahead of his time in wardrobe, and he is a magnet to both men and women.

When he enters Paige's room, he sees her curled in the bed, facing away from him, the tiniest slip of an object, barely making an impression on the sterile white sheets. And then the reality strikes him. How can he be charged with taking care of her, with protecting Paige? With his history, he should be the last one considered. His own personal life is a shambles. Of course, he runs to Paige, a sense of duty, loyalty, family, and the adrenaline of circumstance pushing him on. But now—in the room with this wounded body, this wounded soul, like his—does he really have something to offer her?

He lets a slightly audible "Oh God" escape from his lips. He doesn't mean to. He meant to approach her with strength. He intended that the first words she would hear would be, "Never worry—I will always be here for you." But those words were not there now, just as they were not there before, years ago, in another life—when he could have been the navigator of his own destiny, when he could have chosen to write his own story instead of spending his life chasing other people's dramas. This was a mistake, his ever thinking he could take care of this fragile child. How could he?

But when she turns and he sees her face, the captivating neediness in her eyes, the hopeful upturn of her very slight smile, when he sees her hand reaching from under the thin coverlet—reaching out toward his—he knows he will man up. He will be there for her always. And it's not just because her eyes reflect the Noble lineage or because there are traces in her young, plain face that he knows will resemble the beautiful Celine in the not-too-distant future, but because she is now the *come to life* image from so many of his published photographs. She is his family, but she is also hundreds of innocent victims whom he could document but not help. She is a bleeding and rubble-covered London girl, emerging from a bomb shelter in WWII, an Oklahoma child wandering the devastated streets of her neighborhood after a horrific tornado, a crying burn victim of the Our Lady of Angels school fire in Chicago….

And finally he can have his wish (although few would have identified how impacted he was with each assignment): to know how the story will continue for the hundreds, thousands of his subjects, the pictures that have haunted him most, while hanging to dry in his darkroom. This one he can save.

Chapter 5
No Temporary Home

Once her uncle entered the scene, Paige's recuperation progressed at a rapid pace. Her frequent headaches eased, and her periods of anxiety abated. Over the next few days, Maxwell Noble tried to remain at her bedside as much as possible, planning to be the one to personally escort her on rehabilitative walks around the hospital corridor. But he was continually being called away. Her physicians wanted to make sure that he was clear on the extent of her injury, while assuring him that the prognosis was good. The police wanted him fully apprised of the events of the tragedy. The psychologist, who was called for consultation on the team, recognized a "transference" process occurring, although this term, he explained, did not have the inappropriate implications of the Freudian model, in which the feelings were transferred to the psychoanalyst. This transference targeted her complicated connection with Gladys Barker. Paige was dealing with her tremendous losses, most especially the loss of her mother, with her bond to Gladys. They felt that Maxwell should try to accommodate the situation temporarily, while positioning himself to be the next logical step in the "transference" stream. Even in the first few days, Maxwell had witnessed Paige's strong attachment to the woman, and he, also, had recognized that his acceptance of Gladys was paramount to Paige's emotional stability.

It was hard not to be captured by Gladys. She had a welcoming softness about her that belied the hard ridges of life she had climbed. It was unclear whether Gladys was a young-looking forty-year-old or an old-looking thirty-year-old. She was taller than most of the other attendants. Her uniforms were always a bit too large, but too short, as if they were hand-me-downs. So it was hard to tell if she was chubby or stocky, or if her clothes were hiding a leaner physique. She was quick to show a sweet smile and sparkling eyes when she wanted to encourage Paige, but when alone and undisturbed, she was expressionless. When she moved in a rush to help out, her body reshaped her matronly outfit, and she looked like a young woman who might like to dance but has never been asked to a dance. She looked like somebody who could be pretty.

Gladys's availability during the afternoon hours made it easier for Maxwell to deal with other matters without fearing he had abandoned his niece. The lawyer had reams of papers to review and sign. The school district had its own share of documents. Their administrative staff and counselors were convincing Maxwell to return with Paige to the Winnetka residence to finish out the year, to integrate himself into her world just initially, and then in the summer he could determine a fresh path if he wished. And then there was the funeral home, eager for instructions.

While all of this was going on, he tried to project an image to the professionals that he was a capable and responsible person who was up to this task. Most especially, he wanted to convey that image to Paige. Although he hadn't been with her in almost two years, he knew she was a smart and perceptive little girl. He knew she had to be feeling scared and vulnerable and that he needed to be a strong father figure for her. But more than once, her mother, Celine, his sister-in-law, had likened him to "an irresponsible child," and it was likely that Paige had overheard those kitchen conversations on his visits. These past days, he could sense that she was monitoring his moves with her eyes, as if preparing herself for him to bolt from this responsibility at any time. Yes, he was very sure that his small family had always been aware of the self-centered limitations of their famous relative.

So Maxwell listened to all of the instructions and advice, initially nodding acquiescence—not just playing a role to appease the professionals, but truly thinking he was too overwhelmed to deviate from their suggested course. When he returned to Paige's room, he sat on her bed and watched a show on television with her. It was Perry Mason, with a young and thin Raymond Burr. Before it was revealed, Paige identified the murderer and articulated the complicated motive and hidden relationships of the players.

He was in awe of her. "Did you see this before, you cheater?" he asked.

"Uncle Max, that's not nice. Maybe I'm just smart. You know I come from a very accomplished family."

What strength this little girl had, he was thinking. She was going to be okay. She was a survivor. If she could be strong, he would be strong, as well. And he returned to a plan he had been formulating on the long trip from Europe. He would not try to reconstruct her damaged world, but he would bring her into his world. In the weeks to come, he would go through the Noble family residence in Winnetka and collect what needed to be collected and sell or donate what needed to be discarded, but her memories of a wonderful childhood there would remain intact. She could easily finish the school year with tutors; barely six weeks were left in the term. No, there would be no temporary home for the two of them in the suburbs, where he always felt out of place. The casserole- and pity-bearing neighborhood mothers would not be disturbing their privacy during this crucial time for bonding. When he was in the Midwest, which he still considered his home base, he felt most comfortable in only two locations: his elegant Lake Shore Drive co-op apartment in the Drake Tower on Chicago's Gold Coast and the summer estate in Lake Geneva, Wisconsin, which had been in the family since the early nineteen hundreds. This was what he would do now—he felt certain. He and Paige would move to his apartment, and they would store items to save from Winnetka up north once he sold that home. When he revealed his plan to her, she was relieved about not facing the memories and excited about living in the city.

And when Maxwell said she could have anything she wanted to make the transition easier, her request did not surprise him. There was no lengthy time for consideration, no list of clothes or toys, or even books or objects of memorabilia that she set forth. "I want Gladys to come with us—to live with us. You know that she is alone, too. Is that okay, Uncle Max?" And when, with no hesitation, he smiled and nodded eagerly, she turned to Gladys, with the deference one would offer to a friend or a relative or the most respected employee, and asked, "Is that okay with you, Gladys?"

Gladys didn't need to answer directly. She quickly sat back down in her chair, as if the wind were knocked out of her. She was again overcome with emotion, with heaving cries they knew were for both the anguish of the past and the hope for the future. They were all thinking the same thing: in a shocking way, both bad and good, her son's words had come to fruition. Slowly, Gladys once more removed the note from her pocket. With Maxwell and Paige each balancing themselves on a wide leather arm of her chair, the three of them focused on the prophetic lines: "And if there is any possibility for a good ending to this day, I will find a way to get us both out of the housing project. There is a better world out there— it is just out of reach for us here."

Without being asked, Maxwell escorted Gladys to the nearby Brooks Memorial Parlor and underwrote all of the funeral expenses for her son. The crowds that came to pay their respects overwhelmed the small chapel; the outpouring headlined the local evening news. Gladys resigned from her job at the nursing home and terminated her lease, grateful for a most sympathetic on-site manager's help in loading her personal belongings in a taxi that would take her to 179 East Lake Shore Drive. Tearfully, she had packed up just one box of her son's belongings and keepsakes that would soon be stacked with the Nobles' items in storage. She sealed it with a label that said, "Darren—Forever 15."

On the day that Paige was allowed to leave the hospital, it was decided that there would be no fanfare, no press releases. The plan was that she would depart as anonymously as she had arrived, through the emergency-room doors. As was hospital protocol, she remained in a wheelchair until she was outside. There was a slight drizzle, and she raised her face to meet the raindrops. She wanted to breathe in the air of the spring day and searched for the crescent of sun that was just emerging from behind the clouds in the distance. In the cement field of the hospital campus, there were no enticing floral beds, but she took in a deep breath as if it would contain the most pleasant scents. It made her feel alive. When she reached out to her uncle, he gently pulled her from the chair. The two of them walked hand in hand to the limousine he had waiting. Maxwell understood that life, once measured only by events on the world's theater, would now also be made up of precious personal moments.

To the outside world, Maxwell Noble knew that people might be envious of the incredible life he lived, filled with the most interesting people, set against a backdrop of the most fascinating places, timed to coincide with the most pivotal events of the eras. But it was also a life with vacuous spaces. There was no real home in either a physical or emotional sense; there was no real anchor. Between assignments, between trysts and the selective whirlwind of party invitations he would accept, there were times of loneliness, of a despair that could be alleviated only with prescriptions of sleeping pills or antidepressants, and, of course, liquor.

If Paige had no one in the family, if she would have been relegated to the foster-care system, he would never have passed muster as a guardian. And now this horrific episode had occurred, and he reaped the rewards of the fallout. Something wonderful happened for him in the most tragic of times for his unfortunate family. He would play the role he was assigned to fill. The lawyers had called him her custodian, and he swore he would dedicate his life to protecting Paige. But within months, he predicted, it would be obvious: she would be *his* guardian. He may have appeared to be a man of strength on the outside, but he was a dark, empty shell on the inside. And this wisp of a girl named Paige would be his protector, not the converse; she would be sunshine to light the depths of his soul. All this he could foresee. Physically and emotionally, she would cling to him; he would be her new home. But just as she clung to him, he would lean on her. He had distanced himself from family for so long, searched for something to fill those spaces, and now he had Paige.

Chapter 6
Taken Too Soon

As the car pulled out of the hospital complex, Maxwell started to hum. Paige had forgotten that he was a hummer. But now she could picture him at their kitchen table, unselfconsciously creating the tune to "The Tennessee Waltz," her mother unable to hide a smile and a slight swaying movement as she wiped the dishes. Paige remembered this specifically because it was unusual for her mother to be so casual and relaxed when her uncle was around. Paige never really understood this; she always thought her uncle brought such laughter and entertainment into the house when he was there. Who wouldn't be captivated by tales of his latest adventures? Yet she knew that was it. That was what unnerved her mother—knowing that he would always be off on another adventure. He couldn't be counted on. And that was counterintuitive to her sensibilities. This was what her mother had valued most—reliability, stability, and constancy.

That is what most women want, Paige would come to understand. She did not know this, but that was how Adrienne Saxon had felt less than a month before when she had danced with Maxwell on the terrace of an elegant New York hotel, swept off her feet by his smooth Fred Astaire moves. When he turned her body, he stopped her midway to have her back lean against his chest, and they rocked to the last verses of the song he was humming. Nothing could interrupt this magical moment for her, not even the cacophony of horns and sirens climbing toward them from the street far below. She decided not to think about the cars and traffic. If she was to focus on lights, it would be the lights of the stars sparkling overhead, as she dreamed of a future with the dashing Maxwell Noble.

So she was not prepared for his reaction when the telephone rang in the suite, her less attuned ear not even hearing it initially. His embrace was immediately withdrawn, and he ran inside as if he were a heart surgeon on call. He was used to disruptions like this—the Associated Press or United Press International tracking him at any location. This time he would be off to Rome. And this relationship, like so many throughout the year, would end abruptly. And one more hopeful woman would learn that the camera was his mistress and the event, his passion.

But now things were beginning to change in Maxwell's world. For the first time in his life, he became a planner. Until this month, he was always at the receiving end of the telephone, not initiating the call, but accepting the assignment. Wherever he was located, he would often complete his work as expeditiously as possible and then explore the locale on his own if it was an interesting, exotic, and safe place. If it wasn't, he would fly back to a favorite hotel in a nearby country until the phone would ring again. He was an itinerant globetrotter, living the life of a bachelor vagabond, but one of means who could easily sustain his lifestyle between jobs. And before he would get bored with a location or companion, he would be off again.

However proud he was of these first planning efforts, this was his second painful mission since he had returned to Chicago. First, he had helped Gladys with her son's funeral arrangements, and now he had to complete the same task for his own family. He had not told Paige where they were headed, and she entered the vehicle thinking it would be the short trip to his apartment, where Gladys was already settling in and preparing the rooms for their arrival. So Paige was not really paying attention to the longer-than-anticipated drive to Waldheim Cemetery in the western suburb of Forest Park. She was leaning on Maxwell's chest, the top of her head resting gently in the crook of his underarm. This was a closeness he had never experienced with a child. When he had popped in for visits over the years, many times when they were babies or toddlers, he had airplaned Paige or her brother, Roger, holding their torsos high and flying them around the room to all of his favorite cities. And he had swung them too rambunctiously at the park when they were young children. His interactions with them were action filled and brief, and if the children needed comfort after a fall, they ran immediately to the arms of their parents. When they were in grade school, he had guided them on art projects, but he knew he judged them too critically, often grabbing away a crayon or a colored pencil and completing the design himself. When Paige or Roger would run to their mother's embrace and whine that "he did it again," she would merely shake her head in frustration and glance at her brother-in-law, sitting innocently at the table with his signature smirk.

Dozens of women in his past had wedged themselves like Paige was now, as close as possible to him in the backseats of limousines headed to dinner or the theater, especially when he was in Manhattan. But then he often felt ill at ease, smoothing the wrinkles of his clothes, not even enjoying the delicious fruit scents of their hair. If he had his way, he would have asked them to "please inch over a bit," especially on the way to an event. But to have Paige snuggle so closely was a gift—a gift that, if he could, he would wrap up and tie with a bow, enduring and even cherishing every rumple and ill-gotten crease along the way. He was even thinking of the ride home, how he would undoubtedly be gently blotting her tears of grief, not even caring if they stained his silk tie.

Finally, just as Paige perked up and looked out the window, just as she questioned the distance they had traveled and the route that did not have the lake view she had anticipated, they were pulling into the cemetery. It was, undoubtedly, the road that had turned from the smoothness of streets to the uneven gravel of the cemetery grounds that had alerted her. When the limo driver opened her door, she scooted back over to the passenger door and stepped out to the messy crunch of fallen branches, small stones, and uneven patches of grass. When she looked around, she had no idea where she was. She could see only a wall of three long, black, slightly domed vehicles, like oversized station wagons.

Maxwell rushed around his side of the car to take her hand. This had started all wrong, he realized. He should have been the first to emerge from the backseat, but the driver had inadvertently opened Paige's door. "Are you okay, honey? I wanted to explain this to you before we came, but you were resting so comfortably, I just let you be," he said apologetically.

She didn't say anything. She led him toward the first vehicle and read aloud the small funeral-home sign on the side window. She peered in through a partially opened drape. "They're in there, right?" She turned to him, and he nodded. "What are those cars called? Something like *hershes?*"

"They're called hearses. It's something that young people like you shouldn't have to know. I am sorry, honey."

"No. I know. I get it. I know about it from my friends—when their grandparents have died. And I've seen pictures, you know."

"It's okay to be sad. You're going to see them take out what is inside. And they will be very careful, very gentle."

"You mean the caskets, don't you? You mean my parents and my brother." She pointed with her finger at each hearse, counting slowly, "One...two...three." She said nothing as the attendants lifted and then wheeled the coffins. She counted again, "One...two... three." She joined in the very slow, private procession along the dirt path, holding her uncle's hand again, the other attendees only the paid workers. And then she counted the deep dirt wells of the gravesites, perfectly carved rectangles, matching side by side. "One... two...three." She pulled on his sleeve, as if she didn't already have his attention. "Will you make sure that Roger is in the middle?" All the while, she had maintained an unemotional cadence and kept a blank-faced composure, until suddenly she raised her hands to her mouth to muffle a gasp. And then her fingers moved to cover her eyes. She couldn't look up, so Maxwell stooped down to her level and gathered her into his arms. He knew what she was thinking even before she spoke again. "What about me? Will there be a place for me?" She said it in a whisper, directly into his ear. "And what about you?"

That was it for Maxwell. He could hold it in no longer. From his hunched position, he lowered himself to balance on his knees, his head resting on Paige's bony chest, and he started to cry. Except for her, everyone he truly cared for, truly ever loved, was now gone. Like all the others, these three had died too soon. They had died before the right words were said to patch up the sores of the past. That would have happened in time; he knew that. He counted on that—that time would finally bring them all together again. But time had run out, unexpectedly. And he would never have the chance to say how much he loved them. He would never have the chance to be forgiven.

Paige had never heard this—a man's cry, a man's moan. This she thought at first, until she remembered hearing her father's final cry, final moan. And then she fell to her knees as well, and she and Maxwell sobbed in a mutual embrace, until he could pull himself away to answer her. "It's you and me, girl. You and me, together, from now till eternity, until we join them at a hundred and twenty years—please, God." He surprised himself at the use of that phrase, as if he had said it many times before. It had come to him from his mother's treasure of Jewish phrases. It was always "God willing you should live to be a hundred and twenty years old." Of course, he had questioned it at the time, always the challenging son: "Why only a hundred and twenty years, mother?" he had asked. She was content to answer, "It is just what you say." But eventually his inquisitive nature had led him to their rabbi, who explained that Moses and Hillel and Rabbi Akivah and many of the other beloved and revered leaders of Jewish history were said to have lived to that age, living full, impressive, perfect lives.

So it was appropriate that a third person should join their circle and slowly raise them together. It was the rabbi whom Maxwell had called to officiate at this funeral. He shook Maxwell's hand and turned to Paige. "Paige, my name is Rabbi Arthur Weiner. I am sorry for your loss. This is an unbearable tragedy. I hope I will be able to bring you some peace today." Immediately, Paige was taken aback. She had never seen him before but understood who he was, what his role was. He was wearing a small cap on his head, and she did know the word for it. She whispered *kepa* to herself. He handed one to Maxwell, who secured it with its small accompanying clip. Once more, Paige pulled on Maxwell's sleeve, and he bent to her voice. "Will my mother be mad?"

Maxwell smiled. "It's okay, sweetie. It is what's right. Don't worry. I am in charge now."

The rabbi pinned a black ribbon on each of their outfits. And then he tore the ribbon slightly. Maxwell did not mind the pinholes in his suit jacket. This was the modern symbolic rendering of anguish that in earlier times, or for the most religious today, would have meant the actual tearing of the clothing of the mourners. He understood how cathartic that would have been, if his finest suit lapel was torn. If he had torn it himself, he almost felt that it would have been a relief, a comfort. He understood that in the tradition of his religion, you are officially a mourner only for the immediate family, so for him, this ribbon was only for the loss of his brother. But the holes pricked his heart as deeply for his sister-in-law and his nephew. Paige's ribbon was for all three—mother, father, brother.

They were directed to take seats at the front of two rows of empty folding chairs, and then the rabbi walked to take his place at a wooden lectern. As the rabbi began to speak, Paige scrutinized his face. He did not appear to be very old. Even though she was only twelve and only the year before she had first heard the word "puberty," Paige understood that someone with his position, an adult man, should not have cheeks devoid of even a modicum of razor stubble. His face was pink and baby-tushy soft. Where was the black-and-gray-bearded, top-hatted, long-coated rabbi she had seen in pictures? She was not sure she could believe in the words of someone who looked as juvenile and innocent as she, herself, did. Could he have enough experience in life to talk about death? When he spoke, he said the word "bereaved," and she wondered if that came from the concept *to grieve*. She was grateful for this distraction and was thinking that she would look up "bereaved" and its synonyms when she would have a chance.

Although Paige had always known that her family was Jewish, that she was Jewish, her experience with her religion was not just minimal, but nonexistent. It was her mother, she knew, who wanted nothing to do with any observance. She had overheard this word "observance" in her parents' few arguments. "This you promised. There would be no observance. This you promised when you married me."

Yet Paige knew her father did not keep that promise. This was the one big secret her brother had shared with her years ago: that he was being privately tutored for a bar mitzvah, that her father had not blindly followed all of their mother's directives. It was doubtful that her mother had been unaware of what was going on, but perhaps she chose to look the other way for Roger. And when Paige had asked her father if she might be tutored for a bat mitzvah, he said he could not do that to her mother; that would be too much. And when she pleaded with her mother, "Could we go to the synagogue one time?" her mother had her standard reply, and it was curt: "Paige, you don't know what you are saying. You don't know."

"But I want to know, so why can't you tell me? I don't understand."

"Then you don't need to understand."

And the subject would be closed. Her mother, who was only sweetness and softness and nurturing almost all of the time, closed her open arms and heart and mind whenever the subject of their being Jewish came up. And her father, who was a scientific scholar, who had a mind that questioned the slightest alignment of a molecule or an atom, who engaged them to challenge the world—on this, he would say only, "Respect your mother's wishes. No more questions, Paige."

Paige emerged from her reverie but was having trouble following the rabbi's words.

"Is he making a speech?" she whispered to Uncle Maxwell.

"It's called a 'eulogy,' darling. The rabbi wants us to understand the significance of our loss." Maxwell knew he must spell the word for her—*e-u-l-o-g-y*. Even as a very little girl, that was always her demand. She wanted to visualize each new word.

The rabbi continued, "Mitchell Noble was a very bright and respected member of the scientific community in Chicago and had a national reputation. Because he served in the armed forces in Europe during World War Two, the family of Mitchell Noble will receive a flag honoring his service to our country. It is my pleasure to introduce—" He paused and looked down to read from an index card, and then he cleared his throat. "I am pleased to introduce Aaron Mayworth of the local Veterans of Foreign Wars unit, who will make the presentation."

An older man in an ill-fitting army suit stepped forward from his unseen position behind the chairs, walking slowly in a rhythmic, straight-arm-and-leg marching style, and handed the triangular red, white, and blue folded package to Paige. She was surprised by its weight and immediately transferred it to her uncle, who accepted it easily and kept it close to his chest. Paige was glad she had given it to him because she could tell it held a special significance that her uncle could best understand.

"I know my dad was in a war because that's where he met my mom—at the end of the war. But why was she in the war?"

"Shh, shh, sweetie. One day I will explain more to you."

"They never did, you know…"

"Never did what?"

"Explain anything to me. They just changed the subject whenever I asked about their pasts. Especially my mother."

The rabbi began listing various awards Mitchell Noble had won, along with the names of the patented devices he had registered. "And if he were not robbed of a lengthy life, perhaps one day he would have his own namesake award. It would not have been a stretch to see him as a winner of the Nobel Prize one day."

"He's talking like there are lots of people here, not just us," Paige whispered again, pulling on Maxwell's sleeve for his attention.

"Shh, shh. I know, darling. He prepared very nicely. He wants to make a good impression. He didn't really know that it would only be us. He just wants to do a good job from his little podium."

The rabbi did not realize that if there were an audience of close friends and colleagues, if Maxwell Noble had allowed the funeral to have been a public affair, that those in attendance would have heard that line at more than one of Dr. Mitchell Noble's recognition events. And so without the eye rolls of an audience, the young rabbi was extremely proud of his twist.

There were more words about her mother and brother, but Paige tried hard to shut them all out. She did not like this whole eulogy. Instead of listening to what he was saying, she said the word *eulogy*, spelling it over and over in her mind, and then repeating the word very softly, letting the letters roll off her tongue.

She took in sentences here and there and tried to digest them. "She was a wonderful mother, devoting herself to seeing to all of the needs and desires of her husband and children. She was a beautiful woman." Now, this was what disturbed Paige most—that word "was." And then when the rabbi spoke of Roger, it was the same. "He was an inquisitive boy with a great intelligence. He was an avid reader." She covered her ears. She did not want to hear that again—*was*—past tense of the infinitive *to be*—present tense *is*. "My mother *is* my beautiful Maman. Roger *is* my really nice older brother. Roger *is* going to the science fair," she whispered to herself. She mumbled aloud the word "is," but the rabbi did not hear or understand her pain. Maxwell took her hand and squeezed it. He did understand. He was thinking the same thing. To himself, he mumbled, "Out of the mouths of babes." She did not totally hear or comprehend him and asked what he said. He smiled and repeated only what he said earlier: "It's you and me, honey. You and me from now on."

Finally, Rabbi Weiner stopped speaking and approached them. He did not yet ask them to stand. It was easier to hold his hands flat with the palms down, trying to cover both of their heads, when they were seated. He was blessing them, asking God to give each of them strength. When he did ask them to stand, he pointed to the prayer pamphlets they had each been holding. Together, he and Maxwell recited in Hebrew: "*Yisgadal v'yiskadash shmai rabah...*"

Paige's mind wandered again. She did not attempt the words, even though there was an English alliterative translation. She pointed instead to the words of the title, "Mourner's Kaddish," and she rolled that around in her mouth.

When the final prayer was completed, the rabbi approached each of them, individually. One at a time, he reached for their right hand, initiating a handshake that melded into the covering of their hand in a comforting gesture. Then he motioned them forward until they were within feet of the graves. He led them to the two piles of dirt that were in front of the two adult graves. A large shovel was embedded in each pile. He instructed them that three portions of earth were to be emptied on top of each of the three caskets.

"It is symbolic only. As Jews, it is our responsibility to bury our own. We will start only; the men here will complete the job."

Luckily, Paige focused on the mechanics of the act. The shovel was heavy; the dirt was matted. She bit her lip and concentrated on doing as instructed. After her first try with the large shovel, the rabbi realized that he did not direct them to simply use the ten-inch trowel, which she should be able to handle easily. But even this assignment was surprisingly exhausting for Paige, who had certainly had limited activity in the past weeks. Maxwell, seeing her struggle with the scoop, moved to help her. Three times, she dug into a pile of dirt, emptied it into each grave, and moved on. Maxwell, though, took his turn with the large shovel and attacked the pile with all of his power.

The funeral was over. Rabbi Weiner assured Maxwell that he would remain by the gravesides to oversee that the cemetery staff completed the burial quickly and respectfully.

And now finally, Paige, with one more egregious event behind her, stepped back and surveyed the landscape of the area. Maxwell was waiting for it to catch her eye. Seated before the podium, it had previously been blocked from her view. It was a huge and impressive concrete edifice, engraved with the words "Weiss-Noble Family." When Paige read it, she had a surprised look on her face, almost a look of awe. There was something about the stone that even a young girl knew reflected a certain status and prestige. Of course, the name Noble was her own name, but she also had a familiarity with the name Weiss. That was the name of their Lake Geneva property—the summer home that her family had always shared with Uncle Maxwell, Weiss House. This much she had always known: her father's mother—her grandmother and the mother of Uncle Maxwell—had lived in the Lake Geneva home for most of the summers of her youth. Her name had been Amanda Weiss before she married and became a Noble.

Paige was used to a family that did not speak about the past, so she knew only that the large old mansion was left vacant and partially boarded up for decades, until right after she was born, when the Noble brothers decided to revive it. She had seen a few pictures of her great-grandparents and her beautiful grandmother placed on walls of fading brocade wallpaper, but she had been told nothing of their story. But on her own, she had discovered a cache of fantastic items living in bedroom closets and bureau drawers, just waiting for an inquisitive little girl to give them life again.

There was an entire wardrobe of dresses that looked like they were from the turn of the century, right out of the pages of her treasured romance novels—long and frilly skirts with wide sashes at the waist, and high-neck, collared blouses, one with thirty-seven buttons sewn down the back. There were hats with wide brims, flopping from the weight of thick ornaments. There was an entire drawer full of gloves—some too small for even her hand at seven or eight years old. She would dress up in the costumes and prepare tea parties for her dolls.

So now at the cemetery, she was glued to the ground, standing before this impressive headstone shaped like

the pages of an open book, and she read what was
engraved:

Weiss-Noble Family
In Blessed Memory—Taken Too Soon
Meyer Weiss—1867–1915
Margaret Weiss—1871–1915
Morris Noble—1865–1915
Hannah Noble—1866–1915
Isadore Noble—1903–1915

And in another patch of the little private courtyard
that she had not previously realized they were enclosed
within were two more prominent tombstones:

Lawrence Noble—1891–1934
Amanda Noble—1897–1937

Finally, after reading and rereading all that she had
discovered on these markers, she turned to her uncle.
"Is this our family? Did you know these people?" She
had a bewildered look on her face. "I mean, did you
know who they were? Did you know how those five people all died in the same year? Was it on the same date?
Did they have cars then? I don't even really know. Were
they in a car accident together? Or were there planes?
Was it a plane crash? Or a train crash?"

Maxwell bent down to her once more, balancing on
one knee. "Sweetie, I promise I will tell you all I know.
But today has been too much, even for me. We are going
to go home now. We are going to be our own new little

family now. And we are going to find a way to heal. And as we heal, I will tell you what you want to know." He placed his hand under her chin and raised it slightly. "Your mother, I know this, always wanted to protect you from the sad realities of life. One day you will understand that she only wanted to do what she thought was best. But, sometimes, maybe, that isn't best. And I promise this—I will be the one to tell you the stories of our family that need to be kept as living memories."

He said no more and slowly stood, brushing off the dirt embedded in his pants. He began to gather stray stones from around the vicinity of all of the graves. Uncle Maxwell placed one stone at each of the markers. He didn't have to encourage Paige to do the same. She gathered up some of the little stones and bits of broken rocks that proliferated the lawn on the paths and imitated his act.

Then she reached for his hand. "Thank you, Uncle Maxwell," she said, looking up at him and meeting his eyes. "I'm really lucky that you came for me."

Chapter 7
A Good Team

Maxwell Noble's apartment home was originally purchased by Amanda and Lawrence Noble, the parents of Maxwell and Mitchell, in the year 1927, when construction was reaching its peak for the decade and there was no anticipation of the stock-market crash just a few years away. The impressive thirty-story co-op building was designed by Benjamin Marshall in the Beaux Arts style for sixty-eight apartments. The Drake Tower was connected not only by name to the prestigious and beautiful Drake Hotel just west of it, but by an actual interior access passage so that the affluent occupants could most easily enjoy high tea in the Palm Court or dinner in the Cape Cod Room.

It was a grand place by apartment standards, occupying one-half of the fourteenth floor. The breathtaking view was multilayered, encompassing the bustling traffic that negotiated the curve of the busy Outer Drive, the wide stretch of sand of Oak Street Beach, and then the whiteheads of the waves of Lake Michigan. The interior of the Noble unit was decorated in the same Beaux Art style as the exterior, and, like the building itself, was both inviting and intimidating. The black-marble entry hall was so highly polished that a visitor would stop to make sure he was not stepping into a dark pool of water. The exquisite chandelier threw its own light down to reproduce a mirror image on the floor, which further baffled and impressed.

The living space in the unit was designed just as if it were waiting for this exact new combination of people. There was one master suite that had originally been his parents' and then the big bedroom Maxwell had shared with his brother when they were little. Across from that was a small guest suite. And to the far right was a smaller bedroom with its own bathroom, just off the kitchen, perfect for a live-in housekeeper or nanny. Just to the left of the foyer was the most inviting library/study. In the living room, there were enough couch and conversation seating areas for a dozen or more people, and a shiny ebony baby-grand piano sat at an angle in the far corner.

The walls of the residence were lined with works of art from prestigious modern artists working in every medium. There was an oil by Roy Lichtenstein that Maxwell was quick to point out to any visitor was the gift of the artist, a close friend. Two paintings by Edward Hopper, whose name people recognize from his mesmerizing *Nighthawks* at the Art Institute of Chicago, hung side by side in the corridor. They were reminiscent of his *Rooms by the Sea* series, from his Cape

Cod, as opposed to Manhattan settings, and were an incredibly impressive addition to a private collection. And then there were rows and rows of Maxwell's own photographs. There was a striking black-and-white image from the 1953 coronation of Queen Elizabeth II after the death of her father, King George VI. The young queen and her husband, Prince Philip, were waving from the balcony, the stars and medals and decorations on his uniform almost outshining her regal crown and jeweled necklace. Next to it was the wedding picture of Prince Rainier of Monaco and the American movie star, Grace Kelly. The new princess, Maxwell would relate, recognized him from the press corps and extended him an invitation to attend the reception. While those two pictures were a compatible pair, farther down the hall, Elvis Presley was caught amid a hip shake, his Gibson J-200 acoustic guitar gleaming across his body, and next to that hung the heartrending sight of East Berliners crying at the newly constructed Berlin Wall.

Paige was drawn immediately to the room closest to the foyer, a dark-paneled library, richly detailed with boards of the most exquisitely marbled oak from Vermont. This would become her favorite retreat; it would be her home within the residence. She would not love the pink, tufted window-seat cushions that would be in her own feminine bedroom once the decorator stepped in as much as she would the itchy, black-and-brown tweed hexagon of fabric over a compressed stuffing that would soften the hard wood of the study vestibule. This is where Gladys would find her when it was time for dinner or to go to bed, or when it was time for a walk along the beach that was just across the street from their front door.

When Paige first saw what would be her bedroom, she asked for something very specific. Instead of the twin beds that flanked either side of the room, where Maxwell and his brother, Mitchell, her father, had their first pillow fights, terrorized each other with their stories of ghosts and mutilated bodies, and hid their first girlie magazines between the springs and mattresses, she could envision one big bed with four posts, and, if he would not mind, a canopy. The tall, sculptured ceilings of the apartment could easily accommodate the height. She thought of asking for twin canopies, for sleepovers, but was feeling it unlikely that she would be making friends in the community of this very adult, old-world building.

Of course, Gladys was awestruck by her new environment. The gold and black hues in the draperies, bedspread, and pillows of her lovely bedroom, the fabrics of satin and plush velour, seemed much too elegant a décor for the "help," and though she loved the look and texture of it all, it made her feel a bit like a trespasser. She wavered between trying her best to stay inconspicuous, spending most of her free time in her room, and leaving herself accessible for Paige by sitting at the kitchen table. She did not know yet where any grocery stores might be in the area, but the pantry and refrigerator seemed stocked already for a month. Twice during the first week, just as she was beginning to change the sheets on a bed, she was startled by the sound of a key in the lock, and someone in a maid's uniform appeared and shooed her away from her chores.

But the apartment was often empty at mealtimes; Paige and her uncle took lunch or dinner at a nearby restaurant. Although Maxwell enjoyed his meals at the Drake Hotel, his favorite location required a brisk walk or cab ride to the Pump Room in the Ambassador East. There, he would often hold court in Booth One, an honor shared with mayors, movie stars, and especially his good friend, the much-beloved syndicated newspaper columnist and talk-show host, Irv Kupcinet.

After one week, Gladys awoke to an envelope under her door, and, though no specifics had ever been discussed, there was a generous amount of cash inside, far exceeding her previous weekly salary. She wondered if it was to be a severance pay because she was barely needed. But nothing more was said.

When Gladys was alone, at first she didn't know what to do with herself. So she began selecting books from the library shelves, initially delving into the decadent Roaring Twenties world of F. Scott Fitzgerald's *The Great Gatsby.* Paige had spent much of the first weeks simply lounging and recovering when she was not being tutored, and when she was awake and searching for something to do, Gladys helped wash her hair carefully under the kitchen spigot, avoiding stitches as best she could, or they would play the card game "war" or tackle a crossword puzzle. Or they would sit together on the couch to watch a show on television, quickly becoming hooked on the soap opera "Guiding Light." Often, they passed the time paging through the fashion magazines and weeklies that had been hospital presents and were piled up in the den.

After a month of Saturdays in the residence, Maxwell called both Paige and Gladys into his study, where he was buried behind a stack of photographs that he was cataloguing. He handed Gladys a yellow envelope. When she opened it, she saw that it was filled with cash. He instructed her to tuck it into her undergarments and then to take Paige in a taxicab to the Marshall Field's flagship store on State Street for a lunch outing, an updated hairdo for Gladys, and new outfits for each of them. He insisted that Gladys choose at least five dresses to wear instead of her old uniforms. They each hugged him and laughed. "And Gladys, something that fits," he called after them. "Start with size six, not size twelve." When they finished their shopping, they ate in the beautiful, multistoried Walnut Room of the department store, their bags occupying the remaining pair of seats at a table for four.

The next week, when Paige was occupied in her room with a book, Maxwell asked just Gladys to join him in the study. "Gladys, I am going to ask you something—something somewhat personal—and I hope you will answer me honestly."

"Mr. Noble. I hope I haven't displeased you so far. You just tell me, and I will do my best to do whatever you ask for—for Paige or for you."

"No, really, you may misunderstand me—misunderstand my intent in this. I know when you agreed to come with us that I never made your role clear. And I apologize for that. It is just that these first weeks, while

I am still home before I start some assignments I had already committed to, I just wanted to be with Paige as much as I could so we could really get to know each other. Like I said, I never made your role clear, so let's address that first."

"Yes, sir," she answered with the cadence of a military cadet. "Would you excuse me for one minute, please?" She didn't wait for an answer, popped right out of her chair, and hurried from the library to her bedroom at the opposite end of the long hall. She returned quickly with a pad of paper and a pencil and sat back down. "Mr. Noble, sir. I hope it is okay with you if I take some notes. I've always felt best writing down instructions. Leaves less room for error. I did that in the nursing home. Helps you remember that Mr. Burton likes his bread buttered, and don't go giving Miss Cauterman coffee instead of her Lipton tea or you'll have it flung from her tray, right on your uniform."

He stared at Gladys for a minute before he continued. "Gladys, I have to say this."

"Yes, sir."

"You are one impressive individual. You are a hard worker, but besides that, I can't tell you how much I enjoy your nice disposition. You have a good heart."

"I cry sometimes. I know that. Maybe too often—that I apologize for, sir. Time will heal, they say."

"Gladys, you wouldn't be you if you didn't cry after your tremendous loss. We all cry some now. That's why we're a good team—a trio." He looked at her with his most endearing grin. "I mean it. We've got to help each other heal. But that is not what I wanted to speak to you about. Two things, really. First, your role here. Like I said, it's never been defined, and I don't want you to get the wrong idea."

"No, sir. I understand. It has been a privilege to accompany you here to your beautiful home. But I understand—my helping you—that's to be temporary. You already seem to have a maid. Please, I still appreciate all you have done, and I won't overstay. Maybe you don't think my cleaning or cooking is up to your standards, but I've still got more special dishes."

She was beginning to speak nervously with an increasing pace. He reached over a stack of papers cluttering his desk and took both her hands in his to slow her down and grab her attention.

"Gladys—you don't get it," he said, shaking his head. "You don't get just how special you are. And I would never have taken you from your obviously nurturing job at the nursing home for you to come here as our maid or cook. A little cooking, yes, please, especially after I've had such a lovely introduction to your skills. But what I wanted, what I knew we needed, was a companion for Paige when I'm gone—so she won't be alone, so she can have someone to escort her where she needs to go when I'm on a job, to see her to school, to take her shopping or to friends' houses, to care about her like you have in the short time we've known you." He stopped, and then put his head down. "You know what I am saying without my saying it. She needs a substitute mother—and someone who I know was wonderful in that role."

Gladys was touched by his words. But she was still confused and hesitatingly generated the nerve to ask him what he meant. "When you called me in to talk, you said you had something personal to ask."

"Gladys. I am only asking you this—well, not because you do not seem educated—quite the contrary—but because I am wondering if you may have had your child when you were only a teenager yourself."

She kept her head down and waited for him to continue. "This all is none of my business," Maxwell conceded. "I can only imagine that things have not been easy for you. But I wondered if you did finish high school or not—there is a reason I am asking."

She shook her head, embarrassed to even say the word "no."

"Okay. That's what I thought might be the story. What I mean is, you have nothing to be ashamed of. I am sure you did what you needed to do for your situation. But you know what our story has been since we have been together in this place. We are not dwelling on the past. We are dealing with it. We are talking together about good memories. Paige has had her recommended sessions with the psychologist to help her deal with our tragedy, but what we are focusing on is the future. And I brought you here not just to help us, but to help you. I want to offer you some opportunities that might have been out of your reach before. I don't know if this was in your vision or not, but I could see you as more than a nurse's aide. I apologize for being blunt here, and I do not mean to imply that it was a job to be ashamed of. In fact, I really do feel a bit guilty about removing you from those you helped. But honestly, I'd like to see you as a real nurse. Paige mentioned that had been a dream of yours."

Finally, Gladys looked up at Maxwell cautiously, afraid to have overinterpreted his intentions, so keeping the smile rising from her chest still unexposed. Maxwell pushed back his desk chair on its rollers and stood up. He looked out the window for a bit and then turned back toward her and began speaking again. "You know, it won't be that long before our Paige will be off on her own at college and beyond. And I want you to be prepared for a life ahead, as well," he continued. "If you would agree—and believe me, you don't have to answer me this second—but I would like to have you tutored for something call the GED. I researched this—the General Equivalency Degree. It would mean a high-school diploma for you and will give you entry to the city junior college system for that nursing certification." He walked back to his desk and lifted a blue folder that was lying there. He moved right next to Gladys's chair and opened it to reveal the collection of pamphlets he had accumulated about his proposed plan for her. She leafed through them for a minute, and when she looked back up at him, her hidden smile had broadly emerged.

Chapter 8
Frozen in Time

The next months flew by. Paige completed her sixth-grade curriculum with a private tutor, who worked with her for three hours each weekday, incredibly impressed by her abilities. And after each of those sessions, the tutor moved on to spend two additional hours with Gladys, who easily passed the GED test. Much of the summer was spent in Wisconsin, enjoying the boat trips, bike rides, food, and amusements of the Lake Geneva area. But Maxwell missed the vibrancy of the city of Chicago and returned with them often for weekends of theater, museums, or gourmet restaurants. Paige's favorite evening out was downtown at Fritzel's. In a "fancy" dress, entering the room hand in hand with her distinguished uncle, Paige knew that the single women ran to fawn over her, but only to be in the proximity of Maxwell. She would have done the same.

Throughout that summer, when Paige curled up on the alcove seat in the library, she felt happiest. Despite the fact that if she leaned too hard on the window, there was always the chance that it could give way and she would fall to the sidewalk many stories below, she loved to watch the people at the beach. Pressing her forehead against the glass, she strained to see the families together, wondering if any of them would match up to the family that was stolen from her. So she always, no matter her age at the time, would look only for the age match of her family as they were frozen in time in the car, in the year 1962. First, she would see a mom and a dad and a girl about twelve, but the brother would be younger, smaller, maybe nine. Next, she would spot parents, a fifteen-year-old son, and a twelve-year-old girl, and she would think her game had been won. But then, all of the sudden, a third child, a son about seven, would run into the scene from the water. And she knew she would have to return another day to continue her search.

One day when she caught Maxwell briefly peering into the room, she called him to her. "Uncle Maxwell, do you want to know this crazy thing I have been thinking about?"

He took this opportunity to join her at the window seat. Maxwell, who years ago would have thought he'd be suffocated by the attention and responsibility, had come to treasure it, to revel in it. He was finding sentiments that he never knew existed within him. *Is she hungry? Is she entertained?* These thoughts would replace *I am hungry; I am bored.* This was new for him. Even he wondered if it was a fleeting new dimension of his character, a positive but unsustainable quality—to care about someone more than he cared about himself.

"It's like I know my life will always be defined by *before and after*. So when I am twenty-four, from then on I will have more *after*," Paige said.

He knew what she meant. It was the same for him, although the *before and after* began much earlier.

Even if she was alone in the room, she felt secure in her special spot and felt that way nowhere else. She experienced a clarity of thought at that command post. Sometimes, she felt like she was just under the clouds, that she was close to the spiritual being that was manipulating the events of her life, that maybe he could see her there, and maybe he was ready to recognize her need and protect her.

❧

In September, Paige was not only enrolled in the prestigious, private school called Francis Parker, but she was proudly learning about her heritage, attending confirmation classes at the nearby Anshe Emet Synagogue. Gladys, meanwhile, began her classes, working around Paige's schedule. At her pace, she would have a valid associate degree and be a qualified nurse in three years. During all of these months, Maxwell completed a whirlwind of assignments, mainly from *Life* magazine. He promised to return every week or so but more than once was hijacked from a planned event to witness and immortalize the more spontaneous, pinnacle moments of the year.

He traveled to the University of Mississippi on October 1, 1962. On that historic day in the civil rights movement, federal marshals, against the wishes of the state's own governor, and skirting the racist, angry mobs, escorted James H. Meredith so he could be the first Negro to register at the segregated school. While Maxwell shot his prize-winning photograph of the milestone, Paige and Gladys, mesmerized at home in front of the television coverage of the event, were certain that they had spotted him working at his camera stand.

Paige was happy to have some religion in her life. And sometimes when she spoke to God, she remained relentless in questioning his design. She didn't understand how she could have no grandparents—everyone had at least two—how could she have none? No brothers, no sisters, no aunts. Just one uncle. One uncle who knew nothing about being a dad and who her own mother had referred to as a child. And what if something happened to Uncle Maxwell? Or what if he found her too tedious, too boring? What if his attention span would not be enough to maintain a guardianship? She hovered over him when he was not on an assignment, and when he went out in the evening, she would sit on her bedroom window seat, awaiting his return like a worried mother looking for her teenage daughter after a date. When he was away on a job, even from her favorite spot, her anxiety increased. He was forever flying halfway around the world. There could be a plane crash, or the cab he took to his photography assignment could crash, or he could be too adventurous and fall off a cliff. Oh, she had immediately bonded with Uncle Max, and she would die if he was lost to her as well, but sometimes she saw almost the inevitability in that. She

needed a backup plan. Could there be no other relatives who were alive? Finally, at least, she knew that her
parents didn't just pop up on the face of the earth. But
now, she needed to know their history. If Uncle Maxwell
asked her again what she wanted most, she would make
him tell the story.

And not long after that, she had her wish. Almost a
year after the shootings, the reporters were still hound-
ing the family for follow-up features on the tragic
event. Maxwell had just slammed the phone back on
its receiver. After politely repeating his mantra, "Thank
you for your interest, but we are asking now for privacy," it went unheeded, and the caller rambled on with
questions.

Paige was reading at her spot nearby, and when he
looked at her, apologetic for the rude encounter she
had witnessed, she smiled at him with a "good for you"
that lifted his spirits. "This is the thing I don't get. The
thing that makes it harder," she said. "I mean, I understand that bad things happen, that people die. But why
did our family have to be front-page news?"

He stopped what he was doing and tilted back in
his chair. He tapped the top of his pen against his forehead, and then he leaned forward again, his elbows
on the desk, his hands clasped at his chin. "Okay, my
dear, let's do it. It's almost funny how you hit on it. I
am going to tell you the story of the Weiss-Noble family in 1915. You won't believe this, but you will see that
your family, our family, unfortunately, actually has a
legacy on the front page. Let me show you something,
Paige."

He walked over to a lower cabinet under the bookshelves, opened the door, and searched through it. He seemed surprised, even delighted, by what he pulled out first. It was a beautiful, vintage Leica camera. "I was wondering where I put that," he said thoughtfully, blowing dust from the crevices of the black instrument. He could tell that Paige was intrigued with it and anxious to take her turn, and he placed it gently in her hands. She examined every part of it, fiddling with the lens cap, bringing the viewfinder to her eye, maneuvering the strap around her neck.

"Uncle Maxwell, what made you decide to become a photographer?" she asked.

"Well, you know," he paused and thought for a minute how best to phrase it. "I was called to it. Because of what happened—how I became obsessed with documenting events because of our own family history." He shook his head because he couldn't believe how easy and natural this next segue would be. He reached back under the cabinet and pulled out a large box that seemed to come from the bottom of a pile. From inside the box, he carefully withdrew a stored album with cellophane-covered pages. He gently placed it on the coffee table in front of the study sofa that was wedged into the wood-framed wall unit. He patted the cushion next to him for Paige to sit down. There were sheets of photographs and newspaper clippings. The pictures were both intriguing and disturbing. They featured some vessels on the Chicago River. There was a front-page series that chronicled the boarding of a ship by multitudes of families, with women in white dresses and with hats and gloves on a summer morning, and men in suits and ties. It was picnic attire for the conservative year of 1915.

Paige took some time to survey the memorabilia. "Uncle Maxwell, did you capture these pictures?" she asked.

He was taken aback, as always, by her intuitive choice of words. Another child might have used the word "take" these pictures. But not Paige. He could only repeat what she said. "Did I capture these pictures?" A slight chuckle escaped involuntarily. "No, my darling. I was not even born when they were taken. But the truth is that when I first saw them, they captured me. One day, when I was maybe your age, I found this album just where I pulled it from today. And just like you, I asked my mother to explain what I was seeing and why she had cut out these pictures and articles and saved them."

"Really. You asked like me?" she interrupted.

"Yes, I did. And it wasn't until after she told Mitchell and me this important part of our family history that she finally took us to the grave sites that you have seen." He stood and walked over to his desk, leaning against its front edge as if he were ready to sit on it. Then he went back to the couch and put the album across his lap. He leafed quickly through some of the pages, as if to remind himself of their contents, and then he put Paige right in front of him so they could go through it together.

Chapter 9
"The Millionaires' Special"

Maxwell tried to share with Paige the parts of the story that he could remember. But he could only call upon the recollections of his mother, embellishing his narrative with the pictures before him. There was no way he could have understood the historical significance of the event of July 24, 1915, and the convergence of time and place and happenstance that set his family in the wrong place at the wrong time, just as it would generations later. The detailed history leading up to the event, the real-time stories of the principal characters, these are things beyond the simple pages of a scrapbook, stories he could not have told Paige himself:

Lake Geneva, Wisconsin, in the year 1915, was already such a beautiful resort community that it was often called "The Newport of the West." Like its Rhode Island counterpart, it boasted the summer "cottages" that were actually impressive mansions of many of the wealthiest families in America. While Newport was home to the Vanderbilts and their crowd on the East Coast, Lake Geneva, close to Chicago, attracted the scions of business and industry of the Midwest. The city of Lake Geneva encompassed much of the land around the glacier-formed Geneva Lake, a body of water seven and a half miles long. Because the lake featured more than twenty miles of shoreline, with a surrounding terrain amenable to home and pier development, it became an attractive summer retreat destination.

Ironically, the Great Chicago Fire of 1871, with all of the devastation it wrought on the older wooden structures, happened at a time that was ripe for progress and development of that "prairie town." And the mounting wealth of the great entrepreneurs of Chicago positively impacted the growth of the Lake Geneva community. The Solomon Sturges family, early merchants in the grain-storage business and founders of banks, including the Northwestern National Bank of Chicago, had already constructed a small vacation home along Geneva Lake more than ten years earlier. They settled there permanently when some of their holdings in the big city succumbed to the flames. Their fortune still intact, they built a family estate on the lake, along with a legacy of giving through the generations. Donating the original residence, Snug Harbor, and its surrounding acreage to the town, it was with the edict that it remain preserved as a public park and library. Eventually, the newer Sturgeses' estate, Maple Lawn, was purchased by Henry Porter, a principal in such entities as US Steel and the Chicago and North Western Railroad.

In 1879, Levi Leiter, a Mormon who was an astute businessman, built one of the most prestigious estates on the shore of Geneva Lake, Linden Lodge. Years before, he had used his financial acumen and partnered with a retail mastermind to create the department store Field, Leiter, and Company, which would eventually be known as Marshall Field and Company. The history of that store was also associated with such prominent names as Potter Palmer, Harry Gordon Selfridge, and John G. Shedd. Leiter's wealth continued to increase long after he sold his interest in the department store. He had seen the opportunities in Chicago real estate after the fire and had bought up prime properties in what would become the central "Loop" area of the city.

Construction on the most prominent mansion on the lake began in 1901 with a $150,000 budget that soared to an almost $2 million expenditure by the time it was completed. The owner of Younglands, Otto Young, was a German immigrant, originally working in New York with a peddler's pushcart of costume jewelry. He was another entrepreneur drawn to Chicago after the fire, and his real-estate speculations made him an incredibly rich man. Just five years after his 1906 death, however, his wife and family no longer were interested in the huge stone manor, and it remained vacant, a symbolic white elephant, for years.

Frank Lloyd Wright's architectural influence was reflected in many of the homes of the area, and in 1912, he designed the Imperial Hotel. It was a building reminiscent of his previous hotel of the same name in Tokyo, Japan.

Martin Ryerson Jr. bought and expanded a Lake Geneva home named Bonnie Brae, with proceeds from his successful lumber and sawmill company, which escaped damage from the fire and saw only future profits from the extensive need to rebuild Chicago. Along the lake path in 1915, there were so many other homes of prominent Chicagoans. William K. Wrigley Jr., founder of the chewing-gum company bearing his name, was updating the home he had purchased four years earlier, Green Gables. Another mansion, Villa Hortensia, was named for Hortense Newcomer Swift, the wife of Edward F. Swift, one of the sons of the Swift Meat Packing dynasty. The famous architect, Howard Van Doren Shaw, designed that estate in 1906. In the same year, the Olmstead Brothers, who were sought-after landscape architects in municipalities across the country, crafted the grounds for Wadsworth Hall, which was owned by Norman Harris, the founder of Harris Trust and Savings Bank in Chicago.

These and so many other captains of industry not only consummated business deals with bourbons and iced tea while lounging on wooden porches, but they encouraged each other and teamed together to make Lake Geneva one of the biggest enclaves of philanthropists. Corporate presidents and managers and chairmen of the boards of businesses became builders of museums, trustees of libraries, patrons of homes for the underprivileged, and pioneers in landscape preservation. They supported everything from local garden clubs to national parks. Their endowments in their hometown went to such establishments as the

Art Institute of Chicago, The Field Museum of Natural History, and the University of Chicago.

Perhaps most important to the development of the area was the Chicago and North Western railroad line to Williams Bay, a small town along Geneva Lake. The train, which boasted "The Millionaires' Special" club car, was filled each evening with the most affluent businessmen traveling easily and in style after their workday in Chicago. From that point on the lake, a steamboat, the public ferry, or often a resident's private yacht would complete the trip to their summer home.

Meyer Weiss, a manager and board member of the huge Western Electric company anchored outside of Chicago, had returned a few hours earlier on that very club car on a summer evening in 1915. He had greeted his wife and then settled comfortably in his favorite chair in the expansive drawing room of his home, his *Chicago Daily News* spread wide in his fingertips. Not that long after he sat down, however, he thought he heard voices on the front veranda but tried his best to ignore them. Then his daughter opened the door fully and came bounding into the room, as she always did, with her explosion of energy that was impossible to disregard.

"Isn't he wonderful, Father? I mean absolutely dreamy. I mean his eyes. Did you see how aqua they were—how they were like pools of the bluest lakes? And the way he looked at me with them, as if they were pulling me in to float away with him."

"Well, perhaps I could have seen that had you actually brought him into the house just now," was her father's mumbled answer as Amanda allowed the impressive wooden entry to swing shut with a reverberating *thwack*. Her father cringed slightly behind the shelter of his newspaper. His head momentarily seemed to rise in further response, but then he buried his face closer to the printed page, either drawn to the reality of a news article or escaping the harsher reality of his daughter's burgeoning womanhood. Amanda came up behind him, placing both hands on his shoulders, and she leaned forward to kiss the top of his only slightly receding hairline.

"It's okay, Father. I will always be your little girl. You will always be my number one man." And then she walked in front of his chair to try to catch his expression. "But still, I may be in love. I mean really this time." She knew what the response would be, and she was not surprised. He moved the oversized pages slightly aside and called for his wife, who was sitting with tea in the adjacent parlor.

"Margaret, Amanda wants you. Could you please come in here to talk to her?" It was not a dismissive move on his part. It was actually endearing. Although he had no interest in approving his daughter's attentions to any young man, and perhaps especially this one, he never wished to play the role of the spoiler. Strong and opinionated in his position at work, he left the running of the home to his very capable and insightful wife, who would handle any situation swiftly. This was a job for the much more pragmatic Margaret.

In the other room, Margaret had heard the exchange and was already pulling back her chair and formulating her response. She rose with her tea cup and saucer in hand and approached the pair. "Amanda, dear. I have one question first. How did you leave the house with our permission for a picnic today with your friend, Charlotte, and return unescorted with the Taylor boy? May we start there, please?" She shook her head at her daughter's innocent grin. "Amanda, let's just think this through. So you believe there is a future with this Peter boy—"

She was interrupted immediately. "Peter is his brother. This is Paul, Paul Taylor."

"Oh, thank you for that clarification. Perhaps the whole clan has names of the Christian apostles."

"The *what*, Mother?"

"Yes, case in point, Amanda." Margaret stretched her neck upward, closed her eyes, and shook her head. She let out her trademark elongated puff of air that would clear away any tactful niceties that may have been floating in the space and replace them with her signature sarcastic and dismissive tones. "This is something you do not understand—the apostles of Christ, as in his friends, the ones to whom he chose to spread his gospel."

"But, Mother, you don't even know Paul. You would love him. You do know his parents, of course; you've been with them, I know. Dad is often meeting with Mr. Taylor regarding the lake path, and you've done charities with Mrs. Taylor."

"Yes, dear. But let's just follow this through. So you are in love. So you decide to marry. And the wedding is

where? At their club? But unfortunately we cannot go…
no Jews are allowed, you know."

And while Paul Taylor had won the heart of Amanda
Weiss, Lawrence Noble had continually humiliated himself in his pursuit of that same beautiful young lady. She
ignored all of his advances initially, until he pursued
a new tactic that he remembered his friend, Joe, had
often employed in his rise as the heartbreaker of their
Chicago high school. "I'm telling you, you have to play
hard to get," Joe had admonished him. Lawrence had
never before employed the tactic, and it seemed now an
especially schoolboyish move.

It would be torture, pretending not to watch her
walking past him or to react to her sweet and lyrical
voice, hoping that finally she would say hello to him
and give him the chance to snub her. So he tried just
one time to give her a taste of her own medicine and
to ignore her and, surprisingly, it worked. He was certain that with her bevy of suitors, she wouldn't fall prey
to that silliness—but she did. He actually sensed her
glancing back over her shoulder when she passed him
by, unacknowledged, in the corridor of her home.

The weeks he had spent at her family's Lake Geneva
compound had been the most wonderful weeks of his
life. He worked with her father and the other company
managers on long-range plans during the day. And in
the lasting light of the summer evenings, he spent social
time with the other novices and the families of the owners. One magical night, she was in his arms at a dinner-
party dance her mother had hosted in the family parlor,
but she seemed distracted, watching the front door, as

if she were waiting for a more suitable partner. But he was undaunted. Every time she turned her head away from him, he sniffed in the sweet, perfumed-soap scent of her deep brown curls, until eventually she asked him if he had a cold.

He could only think how lucky he was in so many ways to have qualified for the Western Electric summer program for young executives. Western Electric was the huge communications equipment manufacturing arm of the many Bell systems, and one of its largest facilities was its Hawthorne Works Plant, employing more than seven thousand workers. It was located just to the west of Chicago. In recent years, the board members and high-ranking officials of the company had one by one been purchasing, building, or renovating estate properties in the Lake Geneva, Wisconsin, circle of homes. Their wives and children would spend the summer months enjoying the activities the area could offer, and the men would meet them on weekends after the train ride from Chicago. During the previous winter months, one of the men came up with the idea of adding a three-week retreat to the company business plan during which they could educate, nurture, and analyze young executive prospects—a working vacation. So in 1915, Lawrence Noble was in the first group to be billeted at one of the mansions along the lakefront. Their group included eight young associates—four in the engineering field and four in management positions.

Originally, he was assigned to a grand suite that he shared with Andrew Garland in the family home of Western Electric's First Vice President Merritt DeWitt. The accommodations surpassed anything Lawrence could ever have imagined, and he only wished that his mother could spend a night in this luxury. The elegance and softness of every linen, bedspread, hand towel, and bath sheet would not be wasted on her. The ratio of maids, butlers, and cooks to the occupants was astounding. The furniture was so stunningly polished to a rich deep shine that his first evening there, he continually used his own handkerchief to wipe surfaces where he might have left a fingerprint when reaching for an object or closing a drawer. The array of toiletries in the bathroom reminded him of the shelves of an apothecary. As he eagerly dressed for dinner, he found little notes in the room that encouraged him to choose a dinner jacket or tie from the full closet. The hosting families knew that at least a few of the young gentleman they were sponsoring might not have been from similar backgrounds, so there was a social grooming curriculum that would subtly emerge. Only college graduates were accepted for this program, so many of those participating had been the children of long-time acquaintances from their Oak Park primary residences, the upscale western Chicago suburb with which the famous architect Frank Lloyd Wright would long be associated. But at least three of the eight young men who had earned their places in the program had been the first generation of their families to rise this high professionally, and they were said to be the brightest of the group.

On the first evening, hungry and eager to have a full view of the rooms of the main floor, Lawrence's mouth watered imagining what fabulous feast might be awaiting him. But as he descended the grand staircase, a smell was emanating from the kitchen that quickly turned his stomach. As he entered the dining room for this opening-night dinner, he was astonished at the crystal and silver display before him on a table that seated twenty-four people. Then he was introduced to the wives of the men he had been working with, so he tried his best to hide his queasiness and any sour expression on his face. But when a first course of some sort of green soup held large chunky elements of some unidentifiable meat, he could not pretend to do anything other than stare at the broth, after choosing the correct spoon from an array of three. And when someone chimed to the hostess (as if she had been the cook), "Adele, I was hoping for your famous split-pea-and-ham soup," this prompted Lawrence to excuse himself from the table and move too quickly to scout out a nearby washroom.

When he returned to his seat, by chance, the woman seated to his right, Mrs. Margaret Weiss, her soup dish untouched as well, introduced herself and then whispered to him discreetly, "No *barucha* over this food, I guess," indicating that she had identified him as a fellow Jew and that no premeal Jewish blessings would be appropriate for a pork feast.

The following morning, the very determined Mrs. Weiss, quite surprising her neighbor, Adele DeWitt, with the early visit, interrupted a bacon-and-egg breakfast to rescue Lawrence, negotiating an intern swap, because the young man assigned to them seemed to be allergic to their cat. With this, she quickly and discretely succeeded in extracting him from this gentile wonderland.

He appeared genuinely grateful, not even aware yet that although his new residence would not be quite as large and lavish as the DeWitts', it did house a most treasured prize: the adorable, though sometimes incorrigible, Amanda Weiss.

∽

Amanda was trying not to be impatient, but less than two weeks were left at this point before the summer ball at the Geneva Gables Country Club. For days, she had been wondering how Paul would finally ask her to be his date. Every evening, she expected the invitation before they escaped to their private spot for their good-night kiss. A few times, he said he wanted to ask her something, and she could barely breathe. She tilted her head to the side in a most flirtatious manner and girlishly played with the twists of her hair that had escaped her bracing combs. But the question was of no consequence. One time, he inquired if she thought he might be able to borrow her father's tennis racquet because he had misplaced his and had an upcoming match against his brother. He seemed surprised by her answer, that she had never seen her father with a racquet in his hand and that his only sport was croquet, if that even counts as an activity, since he barely moved a muscle in its execution, except possibly when he initially set the ball down. Another time, the question was as inconsequential as wondering if her mother had an extra piece of that great apple pie, and then Amanda could only answer him rudely that it was apple *strudel*, and no—nothing was left. She had all but given up expecting a personal, verbal invitation and began to understand that it would possibly come by post or by messenger, and she was even more excited about the prospect of this much more sophisticated milieu. But the day was fast approaching, and her daily stops at the town post office, her running to the door at the slightest knock of a neighbor, had produced nothing of consequence except a Sears catalog in the first case and a housemaid searching for a runaway pet dog in the second.

Didn't Paul understand all the preparations a young woman would need to attend a dance? There were dresses to purchase, probably two—one very formal ball gown for the evening itself and then a more casual, flirty choice for the Sunday brunch. These required shopping outings, perhaps even to Chicago, and fittings, of course, plus shoes, gloves, and one, or perhaps two, summer shawls. She wanted to experiment with hairstyles as well. So, in anticipation of the weekend, a month earlier she had convinced her mother that a preemptive shopping spree was in order. Her mother had reluctantly agreed, not because that wise woman had signed on to this possible fiasco, but because she had her own ideas of how these items might eventually be used.

Amanda had half a mind to turn Paul down flatly when eventually he would ask. How happy that would make her parents. They were in the midst of a series of confrontations regarding the date, anyway. It seemed that her father's company was having its annual employee picnic on that day, and the entire event would require them all to take the train back to Chicago for the same weekend.

"Amanda, sweetie," her father had said earlier in the week. "Please remember that I want you to accompany us to the outing this year." He saw her wrinkle her nose and purse her lips, like a seven-year-old rejecting a plate of vegetables. "It is a great spirit raiser when our workers see that we have shared our own families with them. It makes them feel important."

She knew his real motive, however. He was always shoving that inscrutable protégé of his in her path, Lawrence something. Really, he was like an old man, she thought—maybe twenty-two or twenty-three. This whole situation had become untenable. Her parents had arranged, in fact, for him to board at their house for the previous two weeks; her mother had literally moved him with his belongings from the home of one of the other Western Electric board members, the DeWitts, and she was rattled by his constant surveillance. Then suddenly, he started all but ignoring her. She wasn't used to such treatment by a young man, and she had made a mental note to speak to her father about it. He, who was always so cognizant of the interactions of people, who judged her various suitors on the strength of their handshake, the firmly established eye contact, the self-assured patterns in a person's speech, was nevertheless enamored with Mr. Noble. But his newest sidekick had suddenly become rude and dismissive to her. He offered no polite gesture of recognition with a look, smile, or nod when their paths subsequently crossed. It was as if she were the most ordinary thing in the room—a chair, a table, a lamp, an inanimate object not worthy of any type of acknowledgment. And now there was this most recent confusing and unsettling interaction.

Lawrence had found her walking in the garden in the late afternoon, and she envisioned that it was no coincidence that he appeared by her side. She imagined him on his way to the study before he spotted her through the sunroom windows, and thus diverted his route to meet hers. He did not even wait to be acknowledged with a simple salutation; he just approached her from behind, tapping her shoulder for her attention, startling her half out of her wits.

"Miss Weiss, would it be possible that I could be bold enough to ask—when and where exactly do you go shopping, and why you are always shopping? Perhaps I am naïve, but I do believe in the short time I have been here that you have had several deliveries of dresses and gowns and hats and—"

She was taken aback by his forwardness in addressing her like this. "I wonder, Mr. Noble, how it is you have had such idle time during your work day to be spying on me. I hardly think that my father would be impressed by that or find it appropriate."

"It is not so much spying as seeking a very accessible distraction when we are at our drawing boards in the study. I think you know it…"

"Whatever do you mean—you think I know *it*— what is *it?*" Undertones in her voice ranged somewhere between angry, insulted, and embarrassed.

"It would be that I have watched you parading down the halls. But you need to understand. I make no criticism. Certainly, quite the contrary," he said with a slight chuckle. "I have thoroughly enjoyed the fashion shows."

"Well, you are mistaken. I had no idea I was on a stage. It is just that the largest mirror in the house is in the hall adjacent to the study, and..." She paused and stuttered to collect herself, "and this entire conversation is very unpleasant, I have to say."

He looked at her and shook his head. He didn't believe her. Somehow he felt he had finally gotten to her; he felt that perhaps she was starting to value any conversation with him, no matter what the topic. Any answer to her at this point, he said only with his eyes focused on hers.

But she was the first to break away from the stare.

"Well, sir, undoubtedly you understand that this is my season. I have waited many years for this."

"Your season—summer, then? Doesn't that—well, even if you say that season is yours, perhaps you mean it delights you. Then I would still ask, doesn't that come every year? That is the general scheme of things. Every year the same rotation—winter, spring, summer, fall. You needn't wait years for a season..."

"Lawrence Noble. You must know that in the fall I will have my presentation parties. I cannot tell if you are making fun of me, which would be poor manners, or if you are truly ignorant of the traditions of our set."

He loved that she was the first to offer the intimacy of using first names. And he wondered if her use of "our set" had been incredibly inclusive of him or if she meant "our set" as opposed to "his set," which would have been a dismissive, conceited, condescending phrase—but certainly quite closer to the truth.

With eight days left before the country-club dance, Amanda was just descending the main staircase when she heard a knock at the door. She opened it to find two of her summer friends standing before her, the plump and perky Beatrice Brown and her cousin, the exquisitely beautiful Katherine Giles.

They seemed almost surprised to find her answering the door so quickly and exchanged urging glances, as if each was prodding the other to be the one to speak first. Finally Katherine smiled and played with a long curl in her hair. "Amanda, come stroll with us. It is so beautiful out today," she said.

But there was something about her too-casual composure, her side looks to Beatrice, that made Amanda slightly circumspect. "You mean now? I was...well, just about to sit down with a book. It is a bit hot out right now for a walk, don't you think?" She could tell that her tone was unwelcoming, especially saying this to people who had just ventured a good distance to ask her to join them. She didn't even know why herself, but her guard was certainly up, and she had rudely extended them no invitation to enter the slightly cooler comfort of her home.

"Oh, it's not so bad out. But if you just want to stay on the porch, certainly there is enough shade under this eave." Katherine seemed insistent in coaxing Amanda from the house.

And then Beatrice, who had more acutely felt the effects of the heat, added, "Maybe if you had some iced tea or lemonade..."

Amanda was weighing her options. Certainly if she invited them in, the most courteous thing to do, she could find herself having to entertain them for a longer period. Yes, offering them a drink and sending them on their way seemed reasonable.

"Of course. Just make yourselves comfortable on the swing chair or the chaise, and I will be right out. I'll just check the icebox to see what we have."

Within a short time, Amanda had returned with their maid, Elise, carrying a tray of three glasses of lemonade. Although Elise had suggested it to her, Amanda had refused adding an accompanying plate of cookies.

When the three young women were seated on the front veranda with drinks in their hands, Elise took her leave, and Katherine began speaking.

"Well, maybe you have guessed. We really wanted to talk to you about something. And we know that you will understand, but we—well, I just wanted to make sure that you already were aware so that you—"

Amanda broke in at this point. "If there is something you want to say or ask, please just come out with it." There was a staccato pace to her last words.

"Okay. You know, of course, that a week from Saturday is the Geneva Gables Country Club dance."

"I am aware."

"And we know that you have been seen kind of a lot lately with Paul Taylor." Katherine waited for an answer, but Amanda didn't react, so she continued. "And maybe if circumstances were different, you would expect to go to the dance with him. But, of course, that is not the case, and so he did ask me to go with him to the dance." She was speaking very quickly, keeping her eyes focused on her own drink. "Well, really, to all of the events of the weekend, and, well, because I like you and I wouldn't want it to come between us, I just wanted to make sure you understood and that you were good with it." Finally, Katherine raised her head and faced the one she was addressing.

Amanda just looked at them with a blank stare, and so the fidgety (but no longer parched) Beatrice took her turn. "Well, you know, obviously, he wouldn't be asking you. So we were thinking you wouldn't mind since you couldn't have gone anyway." So unalike in looks, Amanda was thinking, their ridiculously juvenile speech patterns were becoming a glaringly reprehensible genetic link.

And now Katherine cut in. "But I said—because, of course, that is the type of person I am—'I just want to make sure Amanda is okay with it.' I mean, I wouldn't want it to be a problem between us, as we've become such good friends."

When Amanda still said nothing, Katherine continued, undeterred. "Well, I am here for only a short stay this summer, and he was so nice to make me feel welcome. I know you have a close relationship, but my cousin said you couldn't go to the dance anyway because…" She turned to Beatrice to continue.

"Well, because I know that there are not, you know—well, your religion, I mean. I know the club has these—what they call 'standards,' but they don't mean anything to me, personally."

Amanda's emotions were running from annoyance to sadness to humiliation to anger, all within the brief span of this bumbling conversation. So her mother was right—a Jewish girl would not be welcome there. And she now had the added disappointment of a boyfriend who had no spine to even tell her himself. It took these two nitwits to actually address the offensive topic.

"I mean, I just felt that we had such a great friendship. The Jewish thing does not bother me at all," Beatrice said, finishing her speech.

Friends, Amanda mouthed silently and then let out a slight nervous chuckle. *Do they think I am a fool?* Finally, she just stood, looking at the two of them. She tried thinking of a suitable response, started more than once to formulate words, but she was speechless. And then she countered with the most appropriate retort she could muster. She simply collected their unfinished lemonades, placed them neatly back on the tray, pushed open the slightly askew front door, walked back into the house, and, as they rose to follow her inside, closed the door on the pair. And in the second-most-mature move of her young life, a move that her mother would find Amanda's most endearing, generous interaction to date, she waited until she heard the retreating footsteps of her "friends" and yelled up the stairs, at the top of her lungs, "Mother—you were right." There would be no Gables Country Club dance for her.

Chapter 10
The Unthinkable

The story of the Western Electric Company just before and after the turn of the twentieth century was the story of America. It was a great melting pot of the immigrant experience, a place of innovation and opportunity, and a relatively new entity that would lead the world into the future.

The end of the eighteen hundreds was an exciting time of progress in all areas of technology and communications. Elisha Gray and Enos Barton, who had formed the Chicago company of Gray and Barton, were poised to be at the forefront of the successes. Barton was a business visionary, and Gray was an ingenious man who was engaged in a patent fight with Alexander Graham Bell over who had first invented the telephonic device. Eventually, Gray and Barton formed the Western Electric Manufacturing Company, and Gray soon sold his shares to Western Union, for whom they were a major supplier.

By 1881, the business had become a subsidiary of the Bell Telephone Company. Inventions were beginning to surface that would revolutionize life in industries and in homes. And Western Electric, with Barton as president, was positioned to be a key player for the coming century. They would be the exclusive designer and manufacturer of the electrical instruments and networks for Bell and A T & T communications systems—in other words, for the nation. So many of the technological advances of the decades would be given life through Bell Labs in Western Electric facilities, from improved telecommunications equipment to advances in radios to typewriters and radar to sound for motion pictures. Not that long before the day of the 1915 picnic, they were responsible for the implementation of the trailblazing transcontinental telephone service lines, when Alexander Graham Bell and Thomas Watson had reenacted their famous first telephone conversation, but now in rooms across the country. There was a great feeling of pride among all of the Western Electric workers, whether they were making the smallest component parts or the largest cables.

The Hawthorn Works in Cicero, Illinois, just outside the city of Chicago, was in a setting of more than two hundred acres and was the largest and most impressive plant of the company. Working at this Western Electric facility was a sought-after position, a great entry into the country's workforce for thousands of people, mainly those of Eastern European descent, either new immigrants or first-generation Americans. The campus could offer almost every amenity of a small city. There were places to gather to eat, a library, a hospital, and a fire station. There were social and cultural clubs for the potpourri of nationalities. There were sports teams and even beauty contests. And this would be the fifth year of a company-sponsored employee outing across Lake Michigan. The owners had a paternalistic sense to create a cohesive and friendly work environment.

When Lawrence Noble arrived early at the Chicago River embarkation site that July 24, 1915, he was hardly one of the first. The day was not beginning as a perfect, sunny, summer morning by any means. The sky was overcast, and constant precipitation, ranging between a mist and a drizzle, was present. But it did not seem to be dampening the spirits of the growing crowds. Music from an orchestra on the promenade deck of the largest ship was already giving the early-morning gathering a festive mood.

Employees of the Western Electric facilities were invited, along with their families, to enjoy a day's excursion on one of five large passenger touring vessels, heading to Michigan City, Indiana, for food and festivities before returning home that evening. Although they had to purchase tickets for this outing, they knew it would be a fantastic day and well worth it. The married men were eager to take their spouses and children. So the line to board each ship was anything but an orderly queue. Young girls with ribbons in their hair were skipping around the dock, their satin bows waving like giant pastel butterflies. Little boys in suspenders and knickers were playing tag rambunctiously, weaving through the lines of their embarrassed and scolding parents, tut-tutting matriarchs annoyed by the slightest deviation from proper etiquette, and a few elderly gentlemen, happy to further stir the fracas with their laughter and an occasional swipe and toss of some of the runners' hats. It was to be a glorious day, no matter the weather, a wonderful respite from the tedium of factory life.

Lawrence watched the coworkers closest to his age and gave a wave or tilt of the hat to those he knew who were too far packed into the throng for him to extend a handshake. He saw Joseph Marwick from a distance and offered him a hearty "Hi there, Joe," and to Mr. and Mrs. Marwick by their son's side, he shouted, "Enjoy the day!" as if he were the host of the events. He had grown up only houses away from the Marwicks, and he and Joe had started together at the plant the summer after highschool graduation. But for Lawrence, that was what it was—just a summer job to be returned to annually to help pay for his college education. And now, six years later, while Joe had proudly moved to the position of crew leader, Lawrence had an electrical engineering degree from the University of Illinois to his credit and was a suit-wearing young executive in the main offices.

He felt a pang of guilt witnessing how much Joe's parents were close by his side, enjoying just the first organizational bits of this special day. His own parents deserved this same treat, and he had almost denied them this luxury, this day to enter their son's world. The truth was that he did it mainly for his young brother, Isadore, who was ten years his junior and just preparing for his bar mitzvah. The previous year, he had come down with a case of scarlet fever that began with a temperature the previous day. By the morning of the excursion, he had exhibited its characteristic bumpy red rash, beginning behind his ears and mapping itself out along his throat and chest.

So Izzy had focused on little else than the anticipation of this voyage during the ensuing year. Until his illness, Izzy had been the strongest athlete in his age group. An extremely well-liked boy whose body had been maturing quickly, he was already five foot nine at the age of twelve. There had been little doubt he would sprout quickly enough to overtake his older brother in short fashion. But the scarlet fever had ravaged his body beyond any expectations. Although only time could be the healer, within this time period, his strength and endurance were still severely diminished.

Never before had Lawrence even thought to exclude his parents from his life. Never before had he thought of being embarrassed by them. But somehow in the previous year, with his newest position, he felt distanced from his old summer-job coworkers. Now, two years after his college graduation, he had been promoted many times through the ranks of a desk engineer and was spending an increasing amount of time with officers of the company.

He had always expressed such pride in his parents' story. He admired their determination to escape the hardships and Jewish discrimination of "the old country," which was how they referred to their Russian birthplace. Morris Noble had actually stowed away on a boat to England before arranging for his wife, Hannah, to join him in London, and then he worked until he could earn enough for a more traditional steerage passage to America for both of them. Lawrence had always credited his father's tenacity as the impetus for his own achievements. This amazing man deserved respect, and Lawrence now was ashamed—not of them, but of himself for even considering denying them this day. And although he did take his family, he quickly escorted them aboard, settling them comfortably in prime seats on the best ship before scurrying back outside to wait for his boss. He hoped that they took his actions as polite, even gallant, and were unaware of his true motives.

As he rose in the company, things were different for him. Among the highest-level managers, his parents seemed so Old World, with their thick accents, their outdated clothing, and their humble demeanor. He was less anxious to introduce them around as he had done in the past.

And when he looked around at all of the happy faces, happy families, he wondered just where he fit in. There was barely a man without parents or a wife or a sweetheart by his side. That was his intent. He had targeted this date to share with the woman of his dreams, but the woman—the girl, really—could barely give him the time of day.

Amanda Weiss had made it very clear: she did not want to go on the outing. He had overheard the fight she had with her father weeks earlier. All she could think about was going to the country-club party with that Paul Taylor on the same date. There would be no way would she leave Lake Geneva to go back to Chicago. This he had heard most clearly, as she stormed out of the room, saying, "Really, Father. I am not a little child to accompany her parents and miss such an evening."

Meyer Weiss's explanation, that it was more for the goodwill of the employees if the families of the bosses do go, had fallen on deaf ears, and at that point, even he was reluctant to take a pouty-faced young adult along, so he retreated. Even her mother, who cringed at the thought of such an exhausting excursion, had lost interest in convincing the obstinate Amanda to do the right thing. They had both hoped it would be Lawrence Noble, that young engineer, who could be the draw, that somehow Amanda would eventually see him as the handsome, bright, young man they knew he was.

Lawrence stood stalwartly in front of the *SS Eastland*, taking his time to return to the vessel after having settled his family in their seats. Suddenly, a scream and then what looked from afar as a slight ruckus drew his attention to the ship anchored just to the east, receiving its own share of the Western Electric group. As he walked briskly toward the commotion, he saw that an elderly woman must have lost her footing on the slippery ramp, and the activity was no more than the group of men around her, each vying to be more gentlemanly and helpful than the other. When they lifted her upright, there was a slight applause from the surrounding crowd, and normalcy had been restored well before Lawrence could make his way to be of assistance.

As he turned back toward his own ship, he could see from the familiar hat of Mrs. Weiss and the notable taller physique of Mr. Weiss that they had begun boarding just as he had turned his attention away. He really had planned to greet them as they entered and then escort them to the seats he had saved for them. He was annoyed at himself for allowing this momentary and manageable distraction to impact his strategy. But then, suddenly, he couldn't comprehend what he was seeing. Could it be Amanda? It was Amanda! He couldn't see her face, but the beautiful flow of her hair beneath the midnight-blue hat he had seen her modeling in the hallway, her exquisite figure that hourglassed to the tiniest waist, were unmistakable. He couldn't believe it. He was sure that she had refused to come, even though he was well aware that her country-club dance plans had not come to fruition.

Before he could even think to be more formal in front of her parents, as he made hand movements to part the line in front of him, he called out, "Amanda. I can't believe you are here." And when her parents turned around at the announcement, he cleared his throat and said, "Mr. and Mrs. Weiss, I have chosen some seats for you. The crew will know where," and then, "Miss Weiss, what a pleasant surprise."

Margaret and Meyer Weiss gave each other knowing looks of satisfaction and decided to carry on with their own boarding, leaving Lawrence Noble to address their daughter. Amanda, however, had not taken the cue and continued following them.

"Wait," Lawrence said. "Amanda, wait. I was just standing by that very stair the whole time, and I was only called away a minute ago." He was finally next to her, and instead of helping her onto the ship, he took her gloved hand and led her down the ramp a bit, positioning her to stand out of the way of the others. "I can't believe it. I thought you wouldn't come. 'No matter what.'" He imitated her now, his hand on his hip. "Yes, I did overhear your conversation with your parents. 'No matter what.' That's what you said." She looked a bit annoyed, so he thought he would just come out with it. "And no matter what—I really wanted to spend this day with you."

As they stood, they were being constantly butted by the throng of passengers eager to find a place on the *Eastland.* People had known to come early to try to claim a spot on this recognized luxury steamship of the fleet, nicknamed "The Greyhound of the Lakes." The ship was the length of a football field and more than four stories tall. Lawrence took Amanda's hand once more and led her farther back down the dock. He wanted some time to be alone with her.

She actually smiled at him, and the softening of her guard made him feel that perhaps he was now one of the men with a sweetheart on board. It was still very early in the morning, and he knew from the weeks at her parents' residence that Amanda was not used to dressing before 9:00 a.m. in the summer. He had just checked his pocket watch to see how much time they had before the scheduled 7:30 a.m. departure of their boat, and he saw that it was not yet 6:40 a.m. Undoubtedly, the Weiss family had come up to their Chicago-area residence the night before, but even then, they would have had to begin preparations for the day hours ago. She must have been out of bed by 5:00 a.m., just

like him. Lawrence loved the innocent, sleepy-eyed look
she had on this day. It made him feel protective toward
her. Together, they stood for a minute, just looking at
each other. He knew what she must be thinking: that
she had never seen him so relaxed. She had never really
entered his world to know that the loss of nervousness
and anxiety will give a certain lift to the posture, a hand-
someness to a face. This is what can happen when a
man feels more in control, in his element. Perhaps at
Lake Geneva, he was always well out of his realm, maybe
trying too hard to prove himself. But here, he felt very
comfortable around all of the workers.

"Shouldn't we go on board? We don't want to be the
last," she finally said.

"I'd love just a minute out here with you. It is a nice
ship, but a little claustrophobic. Just give us a minute.
Here, let me hold your parasol." He was so tempted to
put his arm around her thin waist as he did that, but he
would need to take small steps if he was going to make
something happen. Together they stood for a minute,
content to watch the people boarding. All the while, he
was considering what would be his next move. And then
he did it. He gave her a slight kiss on the cheek and then
turned away, as if searching for the scoundrel who had
done the act. As he made that move, he looked back
once more in the direction of the *Eastland*. Suddenly, he
had a new perspective of the tall and sleek ship, and from
an engineer's point of view, he did not like what he saw.
"Wait. We're not going anywhere. There is something
about that ship I don't like…Something is not right."

And then they felt the first vibrations. There was a startling movement of the dock they were on, a shaking, as if a wave was lifting it and then setting it back down. The ship had first listed toward its starboard side, perhaps because of the hundreds of passengers waving to friends on the wharf. It righted itself, but then listed again, this time to the opposite side. There were some screams, along with the nervous laughter of people distressed but trying not to overreact. But soon the celebratory tenor of the day returned, the band starting up again with a lively tune. Amanda moved toward the boat when the rocking was over, but Lawrence held her back again. When Amanda heard the engines revving up, she became more anxious. "Oh, no!" Amanda shouted. "Our ship is leaving. Maybe we can run to it."

"Wait. Wait, Amanda," Lawrence said, first to her privately. And when Amanda turned to him with a fearful look, he had a determination in his eyes. "You stay put." He actually pushed her two steps back, and then he made a turn toward the vessel. "I want our families off."

And then he ran ahead, weaving forcefully back through the lines to one of the crew members helping people on board, and he shouted to him and the crowd, putting up his hands. "Wait a minute! Something is happening. Don't let more people board." He looked over the heads of the others, searching for Amanda. "Amanda, no closer. Everyone back. This ship is not stable!" he yelled. But his voice had no power over the actions of the busy and boisterous crowd. There was no

way that the passengers or even the crew could identify
him as anything more than an excitable traveler.

By 7:10 a.m., two thousand five hundred passengers
and crew were on the *Eastland* alone, and the ship had
reached its capacity. The remainder of the five thousand
men, women, and children arriving for the day's excursion were directed toward the other vessels. Lawrence
had retreated from his public admonitions because the
crew on the *Eastland* were all but ignoring him, and he
understood then that it would be almost impossible to
reach their families and coax them off. He returned to
Amanda, who still had a look of desperation and confusion on her face, but he still wouldn't let her board. "I
can't do it; I can't let you go on."

The ship swayed again and again, and he ran back
to the ramp, waving his hands, but still he was ignored.
Even the shouts from the crew to reposition the passengers to the starboard side went unheeded. The listing
continued to increase by degrees. And then there was
the unmistakable sound of the engines starting up once
more.

Lawrence was incredulous when all of a sudden, the
ramp to board was being raised and the ropes were being
unwound from their posts and flung back on the ship's
deck. Now there was no opportunity for him to get their
families off, even if he tried. Men on the steel balconies
of commercial buildings lining the Chicago River at the
dock site, having witnessed daily the launching of excursion ships, were also becoming gravely concerned at the
stability of this one and began waving and shouting. And
then there was an uproar from the crowd. "Look at it.

It's gonna tip!" many frightened observers screamed in unison. And individual prayers rose above the sound of the motors. "Oh my God." "Oh, please God, my cousin is on board." "Oh God, Marie." "Ethel." "Albert..." The unthinkable was happening. Although there had been orders to open valves to fill ballast tanks, that strategy was slow and unsuccessful. And even then, Captain Harry Patterson, the commander of the *Eastland*, issued no order to abandon ship, gave no distress signal until it was too late. He was most concerned that his ship leave the dock on time, having been criticized for delays the year before. After a few more seconds of rocking, right before the eyes of all of the spectators, the entire ship slowly rolled completely onto its port side, the side away from the dock. Men, women, and children slipped off the open decks as if they were on a park slide. And thousands of others on board were fighting for their lives, although they were no more than twenty feet from the safety of the river walk. Suddenly, the Chicago River, never an inviting venue for swimming, was filled with hundreds of passengers—flailing, crying, grabbing for anything to float on. And many were simply, quickly, and effortlessly drowning, sinking into the dark waters, weighed down by suits and shoes and restricted by tightened corsets. It was an instant morgue for bodies of all ages. Newspaper accounts for months would interview those who were there—the surviving passengers of the *Eastland*, the passengers and crew of the other ships, those riding streetcars on the Clark Street Bridge, and the rescuers from nearby. None could rid their dreams of the floating babies...

The crews of the *Theodore Roosevelt* and the *Petoskey*, loading their own groups of picnickers, were quick to respond with rescue efforts. And the captain of the *Kenosha*, a tugboat on the scene, maneuvered alongside the downed ship so that passengers could follow a walking path from her capsized hull to the *Kenosha*'s deck and then the safety of the pier. One eyewitness account in the *Herald & Examiner* described the ship on its side as "a whale going to take a nap."

On a lower level, inside the vessel, there was a desperation that few could imagine. With the strongest swaying motions, items on shelves and eventually large pieces of furniture began to tip and to pin unknowing, innocent victims beneath. The first of the Weiss and Noble families to be injured was Lawrence's mother. She was knocked unconscious when a bottle soared from a bar shelf and smacked her between the eyes, breaking itself with the blow and cutting a ragged-edged line across her forehead. When her husband went to help, he was met with the first gush of river water, and it propelled him half the length of the ship away from her. Izzy, luckily, had not witnessed his parents' fate. He had been walking the hall with his new friends, Mr. and Mrs. Weiss. They had been so engaged by his personality that they asked him to join them as they ventured a level above. They were already woozy and a bit nervous from the rocking. When the huge cabinet by the kitchen could not maintain its footing with the final roll, it resettled itself with a large thump right on top of the Weisses. And the once solid, strong, and athletic Izzy Noble, now in his weakened state, stayed with them, straining to lift the bureau up and off the pair, until the water eclipsed even his head and he had no strength left to attempt to swim to safety.

Eight hundred and forty-four of the more than two thousand five hundred passengers on the *Eastland* lost their lives that day. Twenty-two entire families would be buried. Eighty-four men survived as widowers. One hundred seventy-five women, including three who were pregnant, were now widows. And most of those lost, people with their whole futures ahead of them, were under twenty-three years old. Fifty-eight of the victims were babies and young children.

Newspaper articles and photographs revealed the ghastly aftermath of the event, which has remained as the worst maritime disaster of the Great Lakes. It became clear that other dramas played out beneath the surface of the water, as so many of the mortalities had not occurred from drowning. Many were crushed to death by debris or suffocated by the mass of bodies piling on one another, especially near the stairwell. In the following days, horrified family members, bent over and racked by their sobs, would search the Second Regiment Armory on Sangamon Street, where a majority of the bodies were laid out for processing and identification.

As with so many disasters, there is often not just one cause, but a host of contributing factors. For years before this outing, the *Eastland* already had a reputation as a poorly constructed vessel, with numerous design flaws, yet it was a draw for the company to offer this luxurious excursion ride. There was little doubt that the ship was overloaded with passengers. It was a ship built to be sleek and fast, but it was always a top-heavy, unstable cruiser. Despite this already having led to problems in the past, in an effort to fix some of the rotting wood on the deck floors, additional concrete had been added recently. And perhaps the worst move that sealed its fate as a ship of doom was the mandate that it be fitted with additional lifeboats and rafts. The country had been reeling from the *Titanic* sinking only three years earlier. There had been a groundswell to encourage Congress to pass legislation increasing the emergency escape boat capacity to 75 percent of a ship's passengers, regardless of its weight or construction. It was felt that the additional rescue crafts may have added up to fourteen tons to the top deck, contributing further to the boat's instability. Headlines of the day were calling for investigations and criminal charges; someone had to accept responsibility. The families of the victims and the entire city of Chicago, at the time, were shaken and heartbroken. The focus of a first trial was on holding the shipbuilding company and the captain and crew accountable. Clarence Darrow, ten years before he entered the national spotlight with the historic "Scopes Monkey Trials," represented Chief Engineer Joseph Erickson at Chicago's federal court. It was a long and complicated trial, with each of the ten defendants having his own lawyer, presenting a deluge of theories to absolve their clients of blame. Darrow's assertion that there was an underwater obstruction of pilings at the launch site served to aggravate the city because it implied fault on their part, and it was eventually discounted. Others blamed the passengers themselves for their shift to port or the movements of a tugboat, or perhaps a passing fire boat caused another distraction. On the stand, the shipbuilding company's owner, Sidney Jenks, testified that the ship he was commissioned to build was to be a speedy fruit-hauling vessel, designed for only about five hundred passengers. He claimed no knowledge of or responsibility for modifications after it left his shipyard. It was noted, however, that even on the ship's initial launching, there was a 45-degree listing before it righted itself and began its maiden voyage.

The charges began as criminal negligence and manslaughter, but ultimately Judge Clarence Sessions amended them to "criminal conspiracy to operate an unsafe ship." In the end, this charge could not hold up, and the February 18, 1916, verdict was "not guilty on all counts." There was no evidence of a conspiracy of people, many of whom, such as the owners, were not even present at the time the ship capsized. The court ruled that the crew on board acted "in the ordinary course of business" and were innocent of any criminal responsibility.

It would take another twenty years to complete proceedings in civil litigation. Although Chief Engineer Erickson had stayed with the ship until the end, unlike many of the other crew, risking his life to attend to the boilers, he was eventually the only one found guilty of negligence. Perhaps an easy scapegoat, Erickson, after serving in World War I when a heart condition was detected, had died in 1919. It was a posthumous decision against him.

As for payments to victims and surviving family members, there were none. The monetary award from the civil suit was set at the $50,000 valuation of the *East-land*'s hull. But then the first of the payments had to go to the salvage company that raised the ship from the Chicago River. That totaled $35,000. Next in line were vendors and creditors, until there was nothing left for the families of the victims. After the *Eastland* was righted from the water, it was repaired and renamed the USS *Wilmette* and was put back into service, until 1947, as a training ship for the navy.

The only relief that had come to some was initially through the benevolence of the Western Electric Company, as well as contributions from Chicago charities and the Red Cross. There were additional efforts by the company, already an innovator in methods of industrial psychology, to help the survivors deal emotionally with the losses. Some months after the tragedy, even Alexander Graham Bell and his wife, Mabel, toured the production lines, speaking to the workers, writing down notes about their stories, and then sending little gifts. But eventually new employees were hired to fill the hundreds of positions that were available. The company, though devastated, was able to move forward. It was not as easy for families who lost mothers, fathers, and children.

Chapter 11
Wealthy People

That full and detailed accounting of the history of the Western Electric Company and the personal interactions of the day of the tragedy would have been beyond the scope of Maxwell's knowledge. But elements of the story that Maxwell could explain from Amanda Weiss's oral history and the articles and images of the press painted a bleak enough picture of the public and personal *Eastland* disaster. When they reached the last clippings of the scrapbook, Paige saw a final article featuring her grandparents in a formal portrait, headlined "Margaret and Meyer Weiss among the Dead."

For a long time, Paige studied the picture. She wanted to find something of her father or her uncle within their eyes, or outlined by a chin or a cheek. But the time-faded portraits yielded a familiarity only because they were similar to ones in their summer home. The straight-faced, almost frowning poses of the

era could never express the warm smiles of the grand-
sons they would never know.

Paige rose and walked slowly to the window, uncharacteristically biting on her nails. She curled up in her
favorite window seat. "Oh God, that is such a horrible
story," she said, shaking her head and turning her view
to escape to the more serene world of the placid lake.
"And it's like it happened maybe a couple of miles from
here. It can hardly be possible that this happened to our
own family."

At first, Maxwell was annoyed with himself for his mis-
calculation, for opening up this wound for her. Maybe his
judgment had been faulty. He went to her side and took
her hands in his. And then he thought of the spin of the
story that could move them forward once more. "Do you
get it? Do you get how smart your grandfather was—how
smart my father was? Lawrence Noble recognized the
imminent disaster and held back my mother, Amanda—
your grandmother—from joining the family. Because of
this, they survived. Although she was distraught by what
happened, she was so proud of our father when she told
us the story. This tragedy bonded Amanda and Lawrence
more than anyone could imagine, and so they married,
and the next generations of a family could exist."

Maxwell told Paige how so few people, even lifetime
Chicagoans, had even heard of the *Eastland* disaster.
The only historic tragedy most could detail was the lore
of Mrs. O'Leary's cow kicking over a lantern to start the
Great Chicago Fire in 1871.

"I know. That's what I was thinking," Paige agreed.
"We just read something in the scrapbook about the

connection with the *Titanic*, and I think I was in fourth grade when I read a book about that ship sinking."

"I can give you one main reason for that." Maxwell stopped speaking for a moment and had her stand up with him. "I want you to turn around in this room." She did as she was asked, not understanding his motive. "Now I want you to walk to the front entry and walk back to me." Again, she did as asked. "Now I want you to tell me what kind of people you think live in a place like this."

She wasn't sure what he wanted her to say. "I don't know. Maybe people who like art and like books."

"Go on."

"Maybe people who like nice things."

"Doesn't everyone like nice things?" Maxwell posed. "Go on."

"Maybe people who can afford nice things."

"You are getting closer."

"Maybe rich people?" she said, tentatively.

Maxwell knew that she had not been raised to draw attention to the family wealth. Where they lived, in beautiful locations, they were surrounded by homes that dwarfed theirs. Their car, her mother's jewelry, and her own possessions certainly did not stand out in her environment. If anything, she was raised to value knowledge and education, to project modesty. She had identified other friends as rich; she was not senseless. But it had not occurred to her that they were "rich" as well. She was not raised to be a snob. For this, Maxwell applauded her parents, and he made a mental note to try to keep her grounded.

"Yes, my dear. Four steps, and I got you there." He took a deep breath as if he needed power to reveal something to her. "When the *Titanic* went down, although many of those who lost their lives were crew members and people from the lower-class decks, it was the grandest luxury ocean liner of the times. So it was filled with passengers in first class from some of the wealthiest families from our country and abroad. There were Astors and there were Guggenheims; there were business magnates and multimillionaires from America, and there were European aristocrats." He took her hand again and sat with her on the couch. "The *Titanic* disaster captured the nation and is remembered well decades later, at least partially because so many important people were among its survivors and its victims. You have to understand, I am not making this judgment, but as a part of the newspaper community, I understand what sells papers and holds the readers' interest." She looked up at him, nodding that she understood. "I never really told you in the story that some of the only people on the ship who were not ordinary workers were your great-grandparents, Margaret and Meyer Weiss. That is why their picture is one of those that you saw featured in the newspaper clippings. You see, attending the picnic was not a requirement for the company managers and board members; it was really an employee outing. But my grandfather felt it was important that he represent the owners. That was the kind of man he was." He stopped and laughed at himself for a second. "Of course, I didn't know him, obviously. But my mother…she liked talking about him, about her parents. She missed them. Now I ask you one more thing. I want you to envision our large property in Lake Geneva during its heyday in 1915. And then I need to tell you that the Weisses also owned a Frank Lloyd Wright-designed home in Oak Park, Illinois. Weiss House was just the summer home. Our mother's parents were extremely wealthy people for the day. For any day. Meyer Weiss was not only an officer of Western Electric, but he made many smart investments in businesses that became some of the most successful ones in Chicago. When her parents died on the *Eastland*, their daughter, my mother, was not left impoverished like so many of the other children of victims. She was an heiress.

"There are more things, historical things, things that you will learn about, maybe in high school. Like the Great Depression that affected even the wealthy. But my father—your grandfather, Lawrence—had made some incredibly prudent decisions about what they sold and what they held on to before and after those years, and from that we benefited greatly. Margaret and Meyer Weiss were not wrong in their early assessment that Lawrence was the perfect one for their daughter when they first met him. After the tragedy, he stayed on with the company, and his position rose with the years." Suddenly, Maxwell stood up as a perfect illustration came to him. "You see that telephone over there?" Maxwell continued, pointing to the one at his desk. "Well, my dad was one of the designers of that when he worked for Western Electric. Before that phone with a base and handset was introduced—well, you've seen it in old movies—it was called a candlestick model. Kind of one long pole and then an earpiece you'd have to hold up." He paused, pride in his voice. "He actually helped design the modern phone. But eventually, as an electrical engineer, he wanted to concentrate on his own inventions. So he left the company and began his own business. Another smart move. Even today, the proceeds of his patents have increased our trusts. I'm sure you understand that your dad—my brother, Mitchell—well, he's the one who inherited the brains. He continued on to be just like our father."

"I get it," Paige said with a laugh. "You're the one with the looks."

He smiled back at her, enjoying the half compliment.

"Just kidding," she said. "You are the most well known of the whole family. You must know that. And that takes brains and talent."

He gave her a big squeeze. He stretched out his arms, but his hands were still holding her at the shoulders. He looked as if he had something to add, but then he just smiled and let go of her. Paige wanted to hear what he still had tucked away for her; she had a feeling that more stories needed to be told. But they both knew there would be time enough ahead for that. Paige kissed him with an exaggerated sound on the cheek and rather meekly asked if she could take the album back to her room. "Just for a few days, if that's okay. I will be *sooo* careful with it," she promised.

She placed the scrapbook back in its box, lifting it gingerly from the table, and left the room. Maxwell was proud of himself. Another parental task fulfilled. He sat down again, threw his head back, and rested his outstretched arms on the lowest shelf of the bookcase that acted as a second table behind the sofa, his fingers nudging an unexpected object. When he turned to see what he was touching, he was drawn once more to the rediscovered Leica camera.

The Leica—how she was so much another appendage on his body for so many years. Not just for the war years, but it was his favorite camera choice many times when he was no longer an enlisted man but a professional photographer. It was a gift from the army for his service. He actually thought he had left it at their Lake Geneva home a few years earlier, the last time he was there. There had been no way he could return to retrieve it. He closed his eyes and rubbed them hard. If he were to go back in time, he wanted to go to the beginning. He wanted to remember the path the camera had paved for him.

Chapter 12

"It's about the Camera"

The Japanese bombing of Pearl Harbor had devastated a nation complacent to distance itself from a world at war. Immediately, President Franklin D. Roosevelt labeled December 7, 1941, as "a date which will live in infamy." And Admiral Yamamoto was attributed with the prophetic words, "I fear we have awakened a sleeping giant and filled him with a terrible resolve." Neither had overstated the impact of that event. Within a month, an overwhelming number of men and women had found within them a patriotic spirit they had never anticipated.

The army had not yet identified the potential horror of so many traumatized families that would eventually lead to eliminating the placement of siblings in the same unit. Maxwell and Mitchell were prepared to plead the Noble cause that they could not be separated. The brothers were orphans, technically since the ages of eighteen and seventeen, when their mother finally succeeded in escaping the world with a prescription drug overdose. But in their minds, they were alone since two years before that, when she had become emotionally paralyzed after the death of their father in an industrial accident. Amanda Noble had always admitted to her sons that she could never be a strong person. She was so thankful that she had found a husband who would always take care of her, a man like her father. So many nights, she cried to her husband, Lawrence, and apologized to him for her neediness. She wished she could have had her mother's strong constitution and not her own sensitivities, her inability to cope that exhibited itself after the death of her parents on the *Eastland*.

With both their parents gone, Maxwell, the elder brother by only fourteen months, felt more than a brotherly bond toward the younger Mitchell and easily stepped into a paternal role. Maxwell wanted to protect Mitchell and nurture his obvious genius, just as his parents, in their short-lived prime, had been supportive, even indulgent of Maxwell's artistic, creative leanings. And, although they had each completed their college degrees in separate locations, Maxwell at Syracuse University and Mitchell at MIT, they were both back in Chicago beginning their careers.

Together, they had gone to the army registration board, along with all of the other eager volunteers within the month after the Pearl Harbor attack. They each woke early that morning, buoyed with energy by their mutual decision to enlist, not having a more cautious, teary-eyed mother who would try to hold them back. The downtown Chicago recruitment office was an assembly line of half-dressed young men who were completing physicals and waiting to be processed. Everyone was standing bare chested, holding their shirts in their hands. Maxwell, as always, had one more item hanging from his wrist by a simple black cord. It was his last gift from his mother, on his high-school graduation, and he had rarely been without it the past six years: an Argus C camera. Although it was worn-looking and hosted its share of dents from careless handling, it was his constant companion. His own brother was jealous of his attachment to it.

"Son, I received a series of specialized requests from headquarters, and one of those was for a photographer," a recruiting officer said to Maxwell, having targeted him in the line of young men. He had a strong Southern accent rarely heard in the Midwest. "Mr.—" He took the papers Maxwell was holding in his hand and looked at his name. "Mr. Maxwell Noble. You any good with that thing?" He pointed to the Argus camera Maxwell was carrying.

"Uh-huh" he answered.

"Just a heads-up on life for you from now on, young man," the sergeant said, looking directly into Maxwell's eyes. 'Uh-huh' is for the reject boys. I'm gonna need from you a strong 'Yes, sir.'"

"Yes, sir," Maxwell repeated loudly and emphatically. His brother, Mitchell, farther back in the line, hoped Maxwell wasn't already in some sort of trouble. He knew that in an ordinary setting, Maxwell ingratiated himself with new acquaintances within minutes of meeting them, but he feared that his brother may have misjudged his charisma in a rigid army setting. He caught

Maxwell's eye and received a "Don't worry, brother… all's good here" type of look.

The recruiter asked Maxwell to step out of line and go with him to an office in the back area. Once more, Maxwell caught Mitchell's concerned face and shrugged his shoulders, indicating that he had no idea where he was going. He mouthed, "It's about the camera" while pointing to the device. When they entered the other room, the man in uniform went to his desk chair and motioned for Maxwell to take a seat on the other side.

"I want to show you something." He reached for a small box stamped on the side with *Quartermaster Corps.* The box had been opened previously. He moved aside some of the packing paper and set a camera on the table. Maxwell saw right away that it was a beauty.

"Go ahead. You can pick it up. You're the photographer, not me. Oh, I got a Brownie at home, but it's mainly for the kids' birthday parties. You. What's your experience with a camera? Do you mind if I take a look at yours?"

Maxwell handed the camera to him. He turned it over and said aloud, "Angus…looks nice enough."

"Argus," Maxwell said too quickly, upset with his need to correct such a minor mistake. He tried to ameliorate the *faux pas* by adding, "Argus, sir."

"Well, here's the story. You got any experience besides…well, like mine…family photos?"

"Yes, sir, I have." There was a certain pride in his voice. "I am what's called a stringer. That's a photographer various papers might use. They pay me if they buy my shot."

"Any pictures I might have seen?" he asked.

Maxwell pondered which feature to mention until it struck him as obvious. "Front page a few weeks ago, as a matter of fact," he said. *The Chicago Daily News*, right after the bombings in Hawaii. It was a picture right outside this office, the men lining up to enlist."

"Hey, you're good. I saw that. We all saw it. Passed it around a bit. Hey, thank you, by the way. Think it encouraged even greater numbers."

"Well, you give me too much credit on that. Everyone wants to be able-bodied enough to serve now."

"No, no. People follow a crowd."

"It's called 'bandwagon,'" Maxwell said.

"Excuse me?" The Southern drawl became quite pronounced.

"Smart that you knew that. I needed a degree in journalism to learn that. It's a marketing technique called 'bandwagon.' If people think everyone is doing it, they want to jump on the bandwagon and be a part as well."

"Son, we've been given a couple of these cameras," the army man said. "And I think you just earned yourself this new Leica." He pronounced it as if it were spelled Leeka, with the long *e* sound, not Lika, with a long *i*. But this time, Maxwell, familiar with its fantastic reputation and not wanting to sabotage the opportunity, chose not to correct the mispronunciation and simply thanked the man.

"Crazy, I know, German cameras bought and used by the Americans. Not sure Hitler knows they're going right to us. Oh, don't you worry; we checked them out for exploding devices. No, they are top-notch. Maybe best in the world. Would you mind keeping your camera back home and using this one over there, wherever they send you?"

It would be many years before the story of the Leica Company's efforts would be unveiled as one of the greatest examples of gentile benevolence during the Holocaust. The Leitz family of Germany established the camera brand, its name, Leica, a melding of the first three letters of their surname and the first two letters of the word "camera." Ernst Leitz II, who took over the company in 1920, loathed the rise of Adolf Hitler following his 1933 election. Although Leitz was not Jewish, he was an astute businessman who greatly valued his workers, recognizing that many of his most skilled employees were Jews. And he was a good, compassionate man. Reacting to Hitler's edicts against that population, he devised a way to help them escape the country under the pretense of reassignments to Leica sales offices elsewhere in Europe and even in America. At first, Leitz had few problems in executing his plan. There was great respect for the Leica brand worldwide in all areas of the optical field, including equipment for the military. Hitler understood that expanding the Leica reputation would reflect well on his vision of German superiority. Further, the Third Reich recognized that these increasing sales served to bring sought-after currencies into their country as it was poised for war. Initially, this "Leica Freedom Train," an "underground railroad," was not questioned. The bulk of its "passengers" were relocated in the year following Kristallnacht in November 1938. Leitz helped many hundreds of people escape, stretching his acts to include not only his own workers, but also his German suppliers and store owners, their families, and their friends. These "employees" would report to a sales office in their assigned country and would actually receive Leica cameras. Arrangements were then made for the refugees to have some support while they found their own jobs, although many of the immigrants who landed in New York remained to become the company's own valued employees in design, sales, technology, and marketing. Sales and distribution of the Leica cameras extended to the US military during World War II, and even Army Commander General George S. Patton, an amateur photographer, used his Leica to document his marches.

Chapter 13
Children of Privilege

For the first months of their service, both Mitchell and Maxwell remained in the United States. Just as Maxwell, holding his camera, was easily selected from the recruitment line for his special assignment, Mitchell had taken a copy of *Scientific American* with him for leisure reading in case there was a wait and was chosen for the intelligence corps.

When the Nobles were entering military service in early 1942, the War Department was forming and expanding the Army Counter Intelligence Corps, the CIC. Initially, Mitchell was assigned to a unit in Washington, DC, one of many spread throughout the nation, investigating domestic subversive activity. Maxwell was also on the East Coast, charged with taking military publicity pictures to sustain the patriotic tenor of the nation. At West Point Military Academy in the Hudson River Valley, he took a series of photos of the cadets perfecting their marching maneuvers. Those photos were distributed to the media, and from that group, his first credited print appeared in *Life* magazine. By chance, on his second day on the West Point campus, President Roosevelt participated in an impromptu inspection of troops. He had been visiting from his nearby Hyde Park home. The commander-in-chief was so pleased with Maxwell's picture of him that he invited Maxwell to the White House for more photo shoots. Because of this, Mitchell and Maxwell saw each other more often than either of them could ever have anticipated.

But eventually, Maxwell's assignment came through, and he left from the New York Harbor on May 11, 1942. He was aboard the *RMS Queen Mary* with almost ten thousand other soldiers, the fourth increment of troops to arrive in Great Britain as part of an advance command post. This was the first military sailing for both the *Queen Mary* and her sister ship, the *Queen Elizabeth*, the premier luxury liners of the Cunard Line. They had each been refitted to move masses of military personnel for the war effort. On May 16, Maxwell's ship pulled into the port at the Firth of Clyde, a Scottish inlet that was a vast area with deep coastal waters. As it was sheltered from the Atlantic, it continuously hosted convoys of Allied ships entering with merchant and military supplies and soldiers.

When twenty-four-year-old Maxwell Noble, proudly accompanied by his still-shiny, new Leica camera, arrived at the Scottish destination, he was one of a smaller group of men who would not be stationed nearby in Northern Ireland but would be moving on to England. He was thrilled that when the final deployment papers were distributed, his assignment was London. Actually, he had assumed it, just another step in a series of lucky moves—chance opportunities, really—more than the maneuvers he would learn later in life to make his way.

From the time the ship left the American harbor, Maxwell had been thinking that his army gig could be an actual opportunity. As long as he could stay out of harm's way, he could use the time as an invitation to see the sites that previously he could only dream about. In this way, he was no different than the other thousands of young men who had traveled overseas from farm communities and small towns which would never even be identified as more than a map dot, young men who had visions of life in big cities, who longed to dance with beautiful women in foreign countries. But the Noble brothers were different. They were children of privilege, and tours of the capital cities of the world could have been within their reach. Their mother, in fact, had spoken to them often about taking them all on a European trip, but she, understandably, could never muster the courage for the sea voyage.

His initial wish list of destinations to experience and to photograph was as elementary as the most unseasoned tourist—the Eiffel Tower and the Arc d'Triomphe in Paris and Buckingham Palace and Westminster Abbey in London. But, of course now, his first target city had also been targeted by the Nazis. There was no vision of the famous photojournalist he would become. He would not even include his subsequent pictures of those landmarks in any museum showing or retrospective book. He had not yet learned that the photographs that would move people, including himself, would be ones documenting the unexpected, not the anticipated.

Maxwell's ship had docked following what might only have been remembered as a nightmare trip of sea sickness and overcrowded conditions, if not for the bolstering camaraderie of his fellow troops with card games, practical jokes, and their constant vying for a position in one of his pictures. This led him to become one of the most popular GIs on the vessel.

"Hey, Maxwell, catch this," one recruit said, and as he reached for his camera, the young man walked on his hands across the deck while the others shrieked at him, "It's not a movie camera, jerk!" And then Maxwell did get his still shot—the inevitable collapse of the acrobat in the arms of a group of laughing young men. Only at the end of the war would he see how the photo had received a great placement in army publicity, with the caption "Spirits are high aboard the *Queen Mary*." He wondered how many of those men had survived the battles. He promised himself, specifically, to look for his bunkmate, always sad and pining for his fiancée at home, and he remembered how he longed for that same emotion that had still eluded him at that point in his young life.

Chapter 14
The Clear Blue Water

In the time just before Paige was released from the hospital, the physicians had asked that Maxwell be present for her final assessment and consultations. The social worker, always in her skirt version of a man's suit, substituting a paisley scarf where a similar tie would have been, had wanted to prepare them for any physical or emotional repercussions in the months ahead. And so it came, as predicted, possibly not coincidentally, only days after the story of her relatives' fate on the *Eastland* was revealed to her. It was a night terror so strong that Paige's screams were heard at either end of the apartment, awakening both Maxwell and Gladys, and even the one neighbor who shared their elevator landing knocked on the door with an "Is everything okay?" He didn't even take the time to put a robe on over his pajamas.

Although her previous life was one that was mainly full of the normal joys and activities of a loving family, now Paige could only think of the frightening episodes that occasionally invade even the most sheltered life. She remembered the time that she thought she might drown at their summer home.

The dream is an accurate replay of the event. They are at Lake Geneva on their boat, which they all describe as a floating dining room. It is a pontoon anchored maybe two hundred feet from the shore. Uncle Maxwell has taken, as a weekend guest, a beautiful blond woman who smokes incessantly. The adults are drinking, and a transistor radio is trying its best to entertain them with the hit songs but has the same static, raspy voice as the woman. Paige's mother has on a two piece swimsuit. She has a white shirt over it, like a man's shirt, but small enough to flatter her body. She has tied the front tails into a flat bow at the waistline. Every time the blond woman nestles her mouth into Maxwell's neck, Paige's mother, Celine, makes a move to embrace her father. Eventually, she pulls him up to sway to the slow song that is playing.

Paige does not understand what she is seeing, but she knows she is uncomfortable with it. She has never seen her mother finish an alcoholic drink, and now she is seductively licking the olive on a second glass. She has never thought of or said this word before, *seductive*, but she had heard her mother say it the night before, when she was speaking to her father about Uncle Maxwell's new girlfriend. "Could he have brought a more seductive creature to our home?" her mother had asked. "I am only glad that Roger is away at camp," she continued, pacing as she spoke. "Certainly, we have seen women flirt with Maxwell, but she is acting quite inappropriately, in my opinion." And when her father laughed it off, her mother just shrugged, said "Men," and walked away.

On the pontoon now, Paige is starting to feel ignored. Rarely has she cared about things like that, always happy to escape into the world of a good book. But now she has nothing to do and no brother for a companion. She had begged to go to camp as well, but they told her that, of course, she is too young for weeks at a sleep-away. The four adults continue their talking, laughing, and drinking, so Paige begins to do her dance routines, her silly, awkward moves that have always entertained her parents. But now she cannot capture the attention of the adults, until Maxwell's date looks at her bemusedly and says, "Well, aren't you a dear little marionette."

Paige is not pleased, although the woman perhaps meant it only as some endearing phrase for a child. She had no idea of Paige's relationship with language. "What?" Paige challenges. "Is someone pulling my strings? Do you see strings attached to the canopy—or do you think they are invisible, like me? You all think I am invisible." Her voice has reached a whiny, shouting pitch.

Celine and Mitchell break from their dancing embrace and turn toward their daughter. "Paige, please apologize," her mother reprimands quickly. Looking at the woman, Celine says, "I am so sorry. She never speaks like that." Paige's parents have never seen her act so defiantly, and they are cautious to give in to this public tantrum.

The next scene the adults would all later remember as seeming to play out in slow motion. Paige is facing

them with tears in her eyes, but she keeps backing away
until she reaches the rear of the boat. She feels behind
her to unlatch the pontoon railing where the opening is
to the steel platform that swimmers use to jump into the
water. Her parents are afraid that a quick movement from
either of them will send her over the edge, as if she were
attempting suicide from a ten-story height. There should
be no concern, even if she jumps into the water; she is an
excellent swimmer. Suddenly, however, as she is backing
up, she does not see—no one sees,—an ice chest placed
precariously in her way. She smacks into it with her heels
and is propelled over the top in a backward somersault
motion, hitting her head on the edge of the stern when
she lands. She slides, semiconscious, into the clear blue
water of the lake. She senses herself being pulled down
deeper into the water, but she is too dazed to react and
cannot even discern which direction the surface is.

After a few seconds, her father and her Uncle Maxwell kick off their boat shoes and jump in after her. At
first, they each wonder if it might be a prank she staged
for attention, her fall both frightening and impressive
as an acrobatic maneuver. But it is no prank, they can
see when they disentangle her from a clump of algae
and bring her, groggy, to the surface.

The distraught women reach to help lift her back
on board, but her tiny body is still too much weight for
them above the water line. The men realize that one of
them must maneuver himself back onto the platform
to help. Maxwell is in the best shape to pull himself up.
Mitchell raises her to his brother, who quickly moves
her back through the open railing and sets her on the

floor of the boat. He is ready to do his best to perform the mouth-to-mouth resuscitation he had learned in his army years, but when he turns her on her side, she starts to cough and spew out water, take in labored breaths, and then open her eyes.

Mitchell and Maxwell, drenched in their clothes, each hover over her little body, checking her eyes, listening to her breathing. Then they lie on their own backs inhaling and exhaling rapidly, trying to calm themselves down. They both understand how close Paige came to striking her face on the blades of the rear propeller, and it is an image they do not share with the women, though it will haunt them for some time. Celine moves to the front of the pontoon and whips off the tablecloth, sending plastic glasses and paper plates to the deck. She wraps the cloth around Paige tightly, as she did when swaddling her as a newborn. She is kissing her cheeks and crying. "I am so sorry, my darling. I didn't mean to wound you so with my words."

Paige finally says, "No, Maman. I think it was my fault," and her mother only whispers "Shh, shh" into her ear. The incident has ended and would not be brought up again, until this many years later, when the memory of drowning invades her sleep. She screams in the night at her new home because she is underwater and trapped, but this time when she wakes, the nightmare is worse. Although it is Uncle Maxwell who saves her once more from the horror, shaking her from the dream so she can escape to the surface, there is no mother to soothe her and to forgive her.

Chapter 15
Vivid Memories

In the fall of 1958, the movie *Gigi* has completed its downtown Chicago run and has moved on to local theaters. There is excitement surrounding our suburban premiere, and that first Saturday matinee, the theater is filled with families who want to watch it together, like they would *The Sound of Music* in 1965. We have all heard Maurice Chevalier singing the song, "Thank Heaven for Little Girls," and it seems like it will be a nice family movie. In reality, the plot of a young woman being prepared to be a paramour is anything but appropriate, but most of us children probably never understood the true implications.

I am excited to go because my mother, *ma mère*—"Maman," as I call her—is French, and I can't wait to see the scenery of her childhood, especially because she rarely will talk about it. Picture Leslie Caron in *Gigi* and my eight-year-old self at the theater with my parents. As Ms. Caron appears on the screen, I turn to my mother, incredulous. "Is it you, Maman?" She offers only an enigmatic smile. Is it because it is true or is she secretly pleased at the comparison, too self-conscious to admit it? "Maybe it was you when you were younger, and you never told me," I ramble on. Papa is laughing, but I am not. There are whispers around us. "Mrs. Noble," they say. They are patting her shoulder, but no one is hushing them as they all think it, as well—my mother is a twin for the movie star on the big screen. Even the adults wonder if that could be true.

But, of course not. Ms. Caron is about twenty-seven years old, and my mother must be—is certainly—well, a mother's age, whatever that would be. Even thirty-five seemed ancient to me then.

She laughs it all away, but everyone is still skeptical. And when the theater empties at the end of the show, they are scrutinizing her intently as they pretend a neighborly greeting, until Mrs. Blackman, Ellen's mother, finally says, "Celine, dear, you haven't been hiding this, have you?"

But Leslie Caron is more a boyish nymph until she becomes Cinderella. My mother has her face but a full woman's figure—not at all voluptuous, but shapely enough to have the other PTA mothers keeping their husbands well in sight when they are fraternizing.

I see now that my parents were a mismatched couple like Marilyn Monroe and Arthur Miller. In fact, I believe someone would double take my father as that famous playwright. Both were thin men, more distinguished looking than handsome, their black glasses validating their intellectual bent, although my father's led him toward scientific pursuits, whereas

Mr. Miller's talents were literary. Maman was hardly a brunette Marilyn Monroe. She was far less flirty and flashy, although she exuded that same innocence and vulnerability that made the movie star endearing to millions worldwide.

My mother was never like the moms of my friends. She most often kept to herself. In some ways, it was an embarrassment to me how she would stand to the side of any room where we went to a school function. The other mothers would greet each other with superficial air kisses, but with the most effusive emotions that seemed genuine to me then. At back-to-school open houses, they would emit squeals of delight, as if uttered from the school children themselves. "Darling, where have you been keeping yourself all summer?" or "Oh, didn't we have the most delicious time at South Haven? We must reserve for next season already." But there would be my mother, complacent in the corner, curiously eyeing the other adults as if watching the mating ritual of an exotic species of bird, the look on her face not that of the vulnerable outcast, but more of the elitist observer. While going through painful machinations of my adolescent society, I would monitor her interactions as a distraction for my own awkwardness and insecurity. I would question if I was adopted, having no evidence of this secure genetic makeup in my being.

It's funny what vivid memories I had of Uncle Maxwell's visits to our home when I was younger. On a Sunday morning, rising early and nursing a hot cup of coffee at our kitchen table, the *Chicago Daily News* spread out in front of him, with sections here and there discarded haphazardly on the shiny ceramic floor, Uncle Maxwell could resemble the most unappealing recluse. There was no hint of the sophisticated *bon vivant* who had stood in front of our hall bathroom mirror the night before, resplendent in a starched white formal shirt and black silk bow tie, as he prepared for his evening social engagement. His five o'clock shadow, which was meticulously eliminated prior to his finishing his toilette the night before, had by the next morning reappeared and doubled in volume. His smoke-imbued robe would be half open, though with luck, the fly of his pajama bottoms would this time be laying discretely closed, and my mother would not have to loudly clear her throat with that "ah-hum, ah-hum" in her irritated manner, so that there would be no embarrassing revelations of underwear.

Her posturing as the prim and virtuous housewife was accentuated whenever Uncle Maxwell was present. It was obvious to me that my mother somewhat disapproved of her own brother-in-law. Though she always seemed to perk up a bit when he called to come over, once he was at our home, she acted as though she barely tolerated his visits, her eyes squinting, her shoulders cringing at some of the stories he told us. "Please, Maxwell, not in front of the children," would ring through the air like the chirps of a cuckoo clock every quarter of an hour. Even his stories that would educate us about the latest historical event he had witnessed and documented were always spiced with swear words and what he thought were humorous behind-the-scenes details of sex, drinking, and "debauchery" (my mother's term).

But once I was introduced to Shakespeare through my private junior high-school curriculum, I could not help but think back to those years with "the lady doth protest too much methinks." Perhaps you can imagine that at times, both before and increasingly after our family tragedy, I would fantasize that she had actually been in love with my uncle, so much more intriguing and flamboyant than my own father—and that perhaps I was his true daughter. Finally, at thirteen years of age, after having lived with him for almost a year, I summoned the courage to pose this very question to Uncle Maxwell, and the raw honesty of his answer made me believe him, at first.

"I had often wondered myself if she was staging a flirtatious game, and I won't pretend that I would have been incorruptible enough to resist her. Let us just say that we never had the chance to know how that story would end...And of course you know the love and devotion I always had for my brother, your father. No, Precious Paige (his alliterative term of endearment for me), it was a story that never even had a chance to begin. I am being honest with you because I would do anything to claim you for real, my dear. You know that you are the best, most stable, down-to-earth thing that has ever happened to me. But your mother and I were not lovers, not then or ever, as it turned out. I seem to remember, and you can look this up, as I am sure it is chronicled somewhere, that I received notice of your birth in 1950, I believe, during my one-year assignment with the *Stars and Stripes* military paper in Japan."

Right when he said it, I wavered between the emotions of disappointment and relief. Although I may have fanaticized an alternative reality in which he was my real father, children are certainly comforted by reassurances of the integrity of their parents' marriage. But there was something about his answer. Too perfect, too practiced, too structured for a man whose life had no structure, no timetable.

Gladys monitored his comings and goings far better than I ever could. On a school day at breakfast, she would offer up an account along with my toast and scrambled eggs. "That man did not come home until two in the morning, oh my. And he brought with him some missy, and I will not tell you the state of affairs of their clothing strewn all over the floor from the foyer to his room." But she did want to tell me, way more than I needed to know—about bras and panties and items that were hardly any of my business. And then she would insist that she recognized the woman as some senator's wife. "Oh, she slipped out early enough, and she doesn't know that fancy man will not even remember her in two weeks' time."

Days after my conversation with Uncle Maxwell, I woke in the middle of the night thinking, *How would he even remember such a thing as where he was when he heard I was born, and, in what part of that year his stint was? No,* I told myself then, *I'm not sure I will accept his answer.* He was, after all, a master storyteller with pictures, so why not with words? If someone were to insist that his photo images were always depictions of reality, I would counter that he used his conversational narratives as an outlet for his fiction.

In one sense, Uncle Maxwell couldn't do enough for me. And in another sense, he didn't know what to do for me. On winter and spring breaks and over the summer months, he wanted to take me with on any assignment where he might be in an historical or vibrant city, obviously leaving me at home, should there be any possibility of being in harm's way. So in the summer of 1963, he steered clear of any jobs involving the race riots in the Southern cities, although with Gladys by our side, on the couch with us, we were all glued to coverage of the events. And in August, we began my first grand tour of Europe, financed by a commissioned work on the most eligible bachelors of the wealthiest aristocratic families. Gladys and I had tremendous fun preparing and shopping for our adventures abroad. I understood so well by then the symbiotic relationships in life. Gladys was without her child, and I was without a mother. Our relationship helped make us whole again. She was more than a maid/chaperone to me; she was a mentor, a confidante, a shoulder to cry on, and a stalwart gym dummy to pounce on when I was uncontrollably sad or distressed. And I was her reason to go on living. The more needy I was, the more she felt needed. But she didn't try to keep me dependent on her; she encouraged me to fly. I needed this surrogate mother because my uncle was away most of the days and half of the nights, attending to his own affairs. And never was a word, "affairs," so broadly appropriate to a circumstance. Yes, all types of affairs, business and private affairs. His incredible access to these families of royalty so that he could profile their sons also provided him with bevies of debutante daughters and their bored mothers to succumb to his charms. His final work was accompanied by great fanfare, a fantasy respite from the bleak reality of the times in the United Sates that his sponsoring prominent magazine would also need to document. The celebrity he achieved with what he felt was a most frivolous photographic essay opened doors for us to the most beautiful homes in America when we returned. Never could there be a more interesting and dashing addition to any dinner party than Maxwell Noble. "And imagine," they would all say, "he is the guardian of his poor, darling, orphaned niece." He was so highly situated on a pedestal as he moved from one society party to another that even years later, those invitations kept coming. This was despite more than a few disturbing confrontations I had overheard the next morning from my guest bedroom. More than once, a wealthy gentleman who had so openly embraced Uncle Maxwell and allowed us into his home found later that he had been cuckolded by the dashing photographer. He had found his wife in the bed of this man. But, of course, he would be too embarrassed to publicly denounce Maxwell Noble.

In November 1963, another young family experienced our tragedy, but on a broader stage—and nothing was the same. Our handsome, charismatic President John F. Kennedy was shot to death in Dallas, Texas. No one wanted dinner-table discussions to dwell on eligible bachelors of Europe. It seemed trivial. And Uncle Maxwell himself was becoming exhausted by the attention. He took time off to care for me once more, sensing that our own pain would become fresh again. And then his next assignment was given by none other than Theodore H. White, the accomplished political journalist and confidante to the Kennedy family. Maxwell was commissioned to chronicle a week in the new life of the bereaved First Lady Jacqueline Kennedy and her children. Together with official sanction, not the lens of the paparazzi that would hound her family in the future, we spent a week in a hotel by the Georgetown home that the Averell Harrimans had vacated for their use in the winter of 1964. And that beautiful, elegant, grieving widow, who had tears in her eyes when she said she now had such empathy for my own story, spoke to me in her soft, lean-in way and asked me to spend some time with her daughter, the enchanting young Caroline.

Chapter 16
Affairs, But Not Commitments

In 1965, Florence Bronstein, of the distinguished New York investment family, was courting Maxwell Noble, and he was well aware of her intentions. He knew that what he was considering as just another interlude in his life was not inconsequential to her. And although he always tried to end a relationship quickly when he sensed the intensity of his partner, he just wasn't ready to extricate himself from this one. He was enjoying the ride. And perhaps "courting" was too strong a word. What future that could truly lead to marriage could ever really be expected for a couple who were not only separated constantly by the demands of Maxwell's work, but also by the fact that they did not even live in the same state?

Florence was different from so many of the women he had dated. She was as beautiful as most, but unlike those others who relied on that attribute to make their way in life, she had a depth of character he had rarely encountered. She was a wealthy, philanthropic socialite, but she was not just a check-writing young matron. She had a need to investigate each charity she was drawn to, to see that dollars were well spent on the cause itself and not just lining the pockets of the administrators. Most likely, this was an extension of her business acumen. She had not been content to accept only the proceeds of her trust fund. She also worked at the investment firm, alongside brothers and cousins and unrelated graduates of the top Ivy League colleges. She found her niche in scrutinizing the integrity and credibility of their clients' charitable choices, demanding accountability. This skill of hers was widely recognized by her crowd and led to her becoming a sought-after member of the most prestigious charity boards.

Although Florence grew up in a life of privilege, residing in an enormous townhome in a recognizably upscale Manhattan neighborhood, and had attended the most elite schools, she developed an unrelenting social conscience through her own demoralizing circumstance. When she was twenty-one years old, she entered into a brief and unsuccessful marriage. She would have viewed it as the biggest mistake of her life had it not resulted in the birth of her precious son David, now a seventeen-year-old brown-haired Adonis. Only the inner circle of the family understood that he was named for Michelangelo's marble masterpiece in Italy, which had entranced Florence on a visit to her namesake city. Through the years, her son's attractive face had maintained the chiseled, sculpted look of his birth. He was just finishing his last year at Choate.

Many years before, as the divorced mother of a young boy, while sitting in playgrounds, parks, and zoos, she began meeting other women who were alone, raising a child. Talking with them, actually listening to them, she understood just how fortunate she was with her situation. Maybe money wasn't everything, but it certainly was a cushion in life. She could not help but be moved by stories she heard of unwed mothers suffering through absent, alcoholic, and abusive fathers; rampant unemployment; and hunger. She developed a deep empathy for their plight. But it was not a *cause celeb* in her circles. So she purposely took herself outside of her little universe and made her way to the Lower East Side to establish a learning-skills center with an attached child-care facility so these young mothers could strive for better futures for their families more easily. This would be the first of many women's foundations she would create.

Only two years before David's birth, Florence had been a freshman at a small, private college less than fifty miles from her home. For the first time in her life, she was terribly unhappy. She could no longer take the society of women that had been her world during her grammar-school and high-school years in Manhattan. She was tired of the pettiness of her female classmates, the mediocrity of her course content, and the general culture of the school as one more step in the social grooming of a future wife and mother. She wanted to join her brothers, instead, in Boston at Harvard. She wanted to be taking curriculum requirements such as World Economic Theory instead of generalized courses in the arts and humanities. Yet she did the one thing that was counterproductive to her lofty goals. While visiting her brother, Daniel, she immediately fell for his senior-class roommate. The attraction was mutual. Florence was drawn to his magnetic blue eyes and the blond waves of his chin-length hair. And the young man, a scholarship student from the area, saw immediately a golden opportunity to marry a beautiful girl and ease himself into a position at a top New York firm. Florence had been so sheltered from boys most of her life that she could not identify her own vulnerability. Their marriage lasted less than two years. The young man proved himself disloyal to both his wife and the company, extorting a large settlement from her father to disappear from both commitments and allow David to take the Bronstein name.

It was actually at the opening of the newest Bronstein Women's Center, the crown of a rehabbed area of the city that Maxwell Noble had been assigned to photograph, where Florence and Maxwell had met three years earlier. Maxwell, uncharacteristically listening to her speak as he took his shots, found her compelling. He admitted to her later that he first started paying attention because he thought she was so incredibly attractive. But then he could tell quickly—she was the whole package. He didn't even have to ask around if she was married because she was forthcoming with parts of her story in her speech. And then there was the connection that they were each raising a child alone. He already knew he wanted to share that with her. She cautiously accepted his invitation for drinks that evening. Although she also thought he was incredibly good-looking, at the time, she had not recognized him as the famous Maxwell Noble. He was just one more man in a throng of journalists she was delighted to have at the opening, not because she sought out personal publicity, on that she was camera-shy, but to promote the center, to help reach the at-risk population. She presumed he was not a man of means and he would suggest a local tavern where his friends might hang out. It was not until they sat at the Oyster Bar at the Plaza Hotel that evening that she understood she was right—his friends did hang out there. And she was further intrigued that his celebrity status far outreached hers.

This time, when Maxwell had stopped in New York to visit Florence, he was on his way back from Wales, where he had flown to cover a devastating mine accident. Lately, he had only wanted to return to Chicago and to Paige after a long assignment. But after this one, he felt he needed more time and distance between the emotional horror he had witnessed and returning to Paige. He did not want to carry the soot and ash on his body and mind to weigh on an already fragile teenager.

He had been sent to the Cambrian Colliery in Clydach Vale, Wales, for five days, chronicling the event and the rescue operations. He had spent time in the unrelenting cold wind of the landscape, his hopes raised with each positive hint at life and dashed when the thirty-one bodies were taken to the surface, as if the victims were his own friends or family. His pictures, as always, were respectful to the deceased, not glorifying the gruesome details of the corpses, but focusing instead on the anguish of the new widows, the fears of the young sons who thought they would be next for this fate, and the exhaustion of the rescue workers.

Generations of Welsh mining communities had lived through such tragedies. Only five years before, there had been an explosion at the Six Bells Colliery, and forty-five men were lost. And sixty years before, in March 1905, Clydach Vale itself had buried thirty-two of its fathers, brothers, and sons. Previously, he would have thought he had nothing in common with the people of this town, this area, so he could distance himself from the dreadfulness in his pictures. But now he felt different. Each young girl, whimpering and crying for her father or brother, was a girl just like Paige. Each loss he claimed as a personal loss, as if he had been trenching for the survivors himself.

Florence was delighted by the timing of his call the night before, inviting her to dinner. She had been thinking she had not heard from him in more than a month, but that was something she had come to expect and even accept in their on-again-off-again long-distance relationship. Surprisingly, just a week earlier, when she had turned on her television set, she caught the last part of an interview that featured her famous photographer friend:

> "It is said, Mr. Noble, if I may be direct here, that there was not one beautiful celebrity or socialite who could resist your seductive manner." Their chairs are angled slightly together, and the interviewer pauses briefly to recross her legs and pull at the length of her skirt. "Is that true?" she continues.

Maxwell looks at her incredulously. "Is it not obvious that such hyperbole, such a statement, is exaggeration by definition?"

"Perhaps; perhaps not, Mr. Noble." Now she plays with a curl of hair brushing her cheek and repositions it behind her ear. Her actions seem unprofessionally flirtatious, and even she recognizes that she is too much under his illustrious spell. She straightens up a bit and changes the intimate tone of her remarks. "There are memoires of some of those beauties that detail nights, weekends, years of affairs. Affairs, but not commitments, seem to be the pattern." The interviewer looks directly into Maxwell's eyes but sees that she will get no answer. "You are a gentleman. That is obvious in your style and demeanor. So I will ask you this. Is there anyone you have ever truly loved? Do you regret never having married?"

This question he answers quickly, before he can even bring up his usual guard. "Well, I did, once, yes. A million years ago. I was lovestruck. But time and circumstance worked against us."

The reporter is astonished to have received such an honest response and pushes him further. "And this is something you regret? Do you regret not having a family, not having had a wife, and children of your own?" She thinks her scoop will go further, but now he is closed mouthed and looks down. And then he takes a puff of his cigarette that has been smoldering in the ashtray on the small table next to him, first flicking off its growing tail. He rises and tips his head to the woman, and she realizes the interview is over.

At Sardi's in the theater district, Florence and Maxwell shared the semicircular, small banquette she called a lover's booth, and she begged him to extend his visit one extra day. She wanted him to attend a fashion show by an established designer who had just set up his own couturier house in New York. She could see that Maxwell had a sour look on his face from the suggestion.

"Maxwell, step out of your world for a second. Maybe just give yourself a break for some beauty after what you have seen." She was swirling the red wine in her oversized glass as she spoke.

"Ah, but don't you think I have taken a break for beauty by inviting you to this dinner? Or do you underestimate your appeal?"

"Okay, mister smooth talker, you have just invited yourself to my bed for the evening with that line. Now let me return the favor by bringing you to something wonderful."

"Seriously, a fashion show," he said, disinterested. "A woman's thing, I think."

"Honestly, you have no idea. Besides that men love to be in attendance, Oscar himself is so impeccably dressed, he is inspirational. You will become an instant fan, I believe."

"Oscar, really? On a first-name basis, already?"

"Listen to the beauty of his name alone: Oscar de la Renta. Don't you just love how it sounds?"

He thought then of Paige, how she would be drawn to the rhythm and roll of that name. "To be honest, I am starting to think you are not just drawn to the man's fashions, but the man himself. A previous lover, perhaps?" He said it flippantly, but she knew he was seriously asking.

"Oh, no. That is so funny. You totally have the wrong idea. I have known him for years. I followed his designs first in the Dominican Republic, where we have visited for family business, and then saw him again in Paris when he worked for another designer. But a lover—absolutely not!"

At first he was skeptical of her answer. She was admitting to seeing him in more than one country. But then Maxwell was struck with another thought. He emitted a quiet, knowing laugh. "Ah, I was not thinking this, but now I am. Is he a...you know...homosexual? I have no issue with that. Some of the most stylish of my friends—my friend Truman Capote, the writer, for instance—well, prefers the company of men."

"Maxwell, your imagination is running wild. No, you have it wrong with Oscar. No, my dear. He is not a homosexual. He is masculine, romantic, dating a friend of mine from Paris. That is how we were first introduced."

"Well, I am still not that convinced that he is not interested in you. Maybe I will just check out my competition." He took her hand in his so that their elbows rested on the table. He kissed the tips of her fingers. "Are you unhappy with my style so far, that you are encouraging my attendance?"

She knew he was kidding, but nevertheless she was quick to dispel that thought. "No, Dapper Dan. It is because you are stylish that I think you will be taken with this man and his definition of fashion."

"You know what I think?" she asked him in the morning when she awoke with him still in her bed, the smirk of his smile gazing directly at her, as he leaned his head sideways on his hand.

"I don't know what you think. I am not thinking about what you think. I am thinking about your breast lying there, peeking out at the top of your nightgown, unattended to, rising and falling slightly with each of your little sleepy breaths."

"Well, I will tell you anyway what I am thinking." She pulled up the lavender fabric and sat straighter on the bed, leaning against the tufted backboard. She loved his morning hunger for her, and she wanted to sustain it. Other men in her life had left their spot before dawn, and she had awoken to the empty well of a space that a vanishing body's deep impression will leave on a sheet for hours. "What I am thinking is that you think I am not right for you—but I am, you know. I am perfect for you."

"Wait, w...w...where is this coming from, exactly?" he stuttered. "Did we talk in my sleep? Did I miss an entire conversation? Because this segue is not making sense to me."

"Listen, Max. I need you to be honest with me. I have told others this at this point in a relationship."

He looked at her with an amused and confused expression. "Others?" he repeated. She had tossed the word "others" as if she were a paramour to the masses. If anything, he knew she had always been forthcoming with him. Since her divorce so many years earlier, she had been cautious and limited with relationships.

"I did not say others were plentiful, but for the chosen few, let's just say, I have had one steadfast rule: my bed is not big enough for a threesome. I am quick to sense when the widower has the longed-for wife sleeping between us. I know when the divorced man, spewing his venom about his ex to me over dinner, still brings her as a ghost into our bed, trying to recapture her again where the passion of the night would perhaps often overcome the poison of the day. But you—you I can't figure out. And I need to. Because I think we are really right for each other. We share many qualities. And one is that we feel happy and secure on our own. Many people I know can't bear that and dive right into the next disaster. So we avoid commitment, and we are content being alone. But the word 'alone' is still connected to the word 'loneliness.'"

His head registered a double take at what she said. He would never bring another into this bed with her, but her word analysis brought up the thought of Paige. It was something Paige would say, and it was comforting to hear it from Florence now.

"I know I could be the one to release you from the loneliness of your bachelor life," Florence continued. "Yet I would not suffocate you. We would not suffocate each other."

He began to protest. "Who said—?"

"Shh, shh." She placed two fingers on his lips. "Not now, but someday soon, maybe the next time you come back to me…maybe not in bed, but at a quiet restaurant table, over dinner, you can be ready to tell me about your ghost. You have had no one to share your real story with. I have no doubt you have loved someone deeply. That is who you are. But you have been hurt, abandoned, betrayed…Something has happened that keeps you from letting yourself love again. But you want to. You think you don't deserve to, but you need to let yourself truly love someone again. Although your route was quite different from mine, we are alike in another way. David has been the best thing in my life. And now, when I hear you speak of Paige, I know that she has filled part of that emptiness within you. But I also know it is not enough. So I keep looking, and you keep avoiding."

Later that morning, she was urging Maxwell out of bed to begin dressing for the event. She had two front-row seats reserved for her at the show. But she knew that if they were not there on time, the seats would be taken by the seat fillers, the random lucky guests offered temporary prime seats to avoid the embarrassment of vacancies. And, in the end, Maxwell admitted that not only did he love the fashion show, but he was mesmerized by both the designs and the designer. And he was already contemplating a way to maneuver himself into the fashion-photography scene without appearing that he had compromised his lofty reputation.

Chapter 17
Quick to Grow Up

The summer before my junior year of high school, my world changed once more. But this time, it was not because I had suffered a loss; it was actually because of something found—my first love. The impact of the event, the implications of it on my future, could not be overstated. After so many of my years spent feigning a self-confidence that was actually masking the standard insecurities of anyone my age, I felt safe and optimistic again. I can't even think of an approaching July Fourth holiday without that little rise of a smile, that warm feeling inside that sends shivers down my arm, prickly raises that I can actually see and feel.

Uncle Maxwell had told me that his "friend"—he did little curled-finger quote marks when he said it—would be coming to spend the long weekend with us at Lake Geneva and that her son may be with her as well. I had come to know Florence Bronstein ("Call me Florie"), and she seemed very nice and elegant;

she was a sophisticated New York woman. I knew she was raising a son by herself, kind of like Uncle Maxwell was raising me. A couple of times, we had visited with her when we went to New York, always staying at the Plaza Hotel. One time when we met her in the Palm Court for lunch, I could tell that the two adults had preplanned so that she would be the only one to accompany me on a shopping trip, making it easier to get things a girl might want or need; my uncle pretended he had an important call to make. I liked being around her because it had been so long since I'd had a mother as a role model—besides Gladys, that is. And many of Maxwell's other "friends," although beautiful, even gorgeous, lacked her sincere style. She was easy to be with and seemed very smart. She didn't talk down to me or ask what I really wanted to do when she already had a selected agenda. She was just direct.

"Okay, Paige dear. And, by the way, love, love your jeans and that top. Glad we got Maxwell out of the way. How about some shopping? Let's go to Bloomingdale's on Fifty-Ninth first. It's not that short of a walk, but we don't need to cab it. I have Maxwell's money and nothing but time. You can pick some things, and I'll choose some things to show you—but we each get veto rights. And then we are going to Serendipity for ice cream. Don't say that you think that's for babies. I'm in for the hot fudge sundae, even if you are not. Then we'll do a quick swing by the Guggenheim Art Museum. Even if you don't like what you see, it's the building that is iconic."

I wasn't that familiar with the word "iconic," but I loved it immediately. And I loved that she just assumed it was part of my vocabulary. From context, I figured it meant important or interesting, but when I looked it up later, it seemed to imply something so well known in the culture that it is recognized as the leading example...or something to that effect.

When we returned to the hotel, Maxwell was in the bar area at a booth with a boy who looked maybe three or four years older than me. They were each tossing peanuts high in the air and trying to catch them in their mouths, as if they were having a contest. When I was introduced to David, I understood that they must have been having a "get to know you" afternoon as well. My first thought, and I admit it was a creepy one in case this was leading to his becoming a "stepbrother" of sorts, was that he was gorgeous (for a guy). But a couple of years passed by, and though I saw Florie and David occasionally, it didn't seem like our "parents" had any fast-progressing relationship.

So, as I came in a bit late and a bit frenzied on that Fourth of July weekend at our Lake Geneva residence, I was more than surprised to see David Bronstein when I opened the door. He looked so imperious descending the staircase toward me, with his perfect posture and his meticulous prep-boy blazer. I was drawn immediately to the delicious flop of his dark brown hair and the charming sparkle of his deep blue eyes. But he was drawn to me in a different way. As he came down the steps, he kept looking at me more and more intently, and then finally he almost screamed at me like he was a parent.

"What in the world is wrong with you? Where have you just been?"

His indignant interrogation definitely caught me by surprise. "Well, I didn't really realize you were in charge of me, since I only really met you a few times," I said. "Anyway, I thought if you were coming, it would be with your mother tomorrow."

"I was never quite coming with her—more like meeting her here." He seemed a bit aggravated to have to continue explaining this to me, but he was, after all, almost a stranger appearing in my house. "First, I spent time at a friend's summer place in the area, a friend who goes to school out East with me, and then the plan was for me to come here tomorrow." He paused for a moment, like he wanted to choose his words carefully. "But I was ready to leave there sooner than I thought, so one of your staff here let me in." You didn't have to be a genius to translate that as "had a fight with my girlfriend." But then he continued, back to his angry tone. "Forget me—I'm still wondering where you came from in such a state."

"I can take care of myself, you know. It's not like you are even my older brother."

He held up his hands as if fending off such a statement. "No, No. No older brother. But an adult compared to you. And maybe you are lucky that I am the first adult to see you tonight. Who were you with?"

"Whoa," I said. "It was nothing serious. Well, he's just a local kid. He doesn't mean anything. He just runs the shuttle boat on Friday evenings, and he gives free rides and a little beer he keeps in his stash if you are nice to him."

"Oh my God, do you even hear yourself? This is making me sick. Who else were you with?"

"Just another town girl. I don't really have lots of friends here, but I met her last week when I was biking. She asked if I wanted to join a few kids at this local restaurant where there was some music. The kids are not like ones I know at home."

"I'll bet."

"Well, they are kind of crude. Lots of swearing. And a little wild. Maybe I don't have to be a goody-goody all the time." I thought about keeping the next part to myself, but I liked my new bad-girl image. "Okay. They were smoking, but honestly I didn't."

"Smoking what?"

"What do you mean, smoking what?"

He just shook his head, with a somewhat relieved look on his face. "Okay, never mind."

"Smoking cigarettes," I said. But I wanted to know what he meant. "What were you thinking they were smoking? What else would people smoke?"

"No, never mind," he repeated until he fell prey to my most annoyed, inquisitive look. "Well, smoking something like marijuana, weed—whatever they call it here. It's all over the campuses now." He shook his head. "Anyway, stay away from anything like that—especially, like while you're just a kid. But let's get back to the ferry-boat boy. He gives you free rides and a little beer if you are 'nice' to him—whatever that means. Seriously, this is just so bad on so many levels. First, he's driving a ferry boat and he's drunk. Are you kidding me?" he said in a disgusted fashion.

"No, calm yourself," I answered quickly. "He's just like the ticket taker—the guy who brings in the ropes. The only sailing he does is when he pushes his foot against the dock to move the boat away while the engines are revving up."

"How old are you, anyway?"

"Is that your business to ask?"

"Well, you look like you're fourteen years old."

"I'm sixteen. I could drive. I could take your fancy convertible I just saw out front and drive right back to Chicago."

"Oh, yeah—you think so? Well, I don't think you drive. I don't think you know how to drive because you are a city girl like I was a city boy until I went away to college. I didn't even become a driver until I was nineteen."

"I just don't understand why you are so upset about me," I finally said.

"As a matter of fact, I am not even sure myself. You're right. I do barely know you. But when you walked in," and then he softened a bit, "you just looked so trashed and so vulnerable. I've seen girls like you. Not like you. Probably nothing like you because maybe for you this is not a normal thing. But through my mom's work with women's shelters, I've seen plenty of girls—well, maybe girls like your townie friend. This is not who you are. First of all, you are not valuing yourself. It looks like your blouse is half unbuttoned, and—oh my God—I'm gonna puke—is your bra unhooked?" He could see the beige strap dangling through the light linen material of my shirt.

I reached behind my back to reclasp it, but it was too difficult a maneuver. "So what? Free love and all. Welcome to the sixties," I said back to him.

"As if you know the sixties, when you don't even understand there's a drug scene out there. And this to save money for a ticket when you could buy a boat if you wanted?"

He was relentless, and although I was really kind of taken by how protective he was acting, I was getting annoyed. "What's wrong with you? Are you not a normal boy? I mean, look how you're dressed. I have a school uniform myself, but it is summer now. Like, we do what we want. We wear what we want."

"You are getting the wrong idea. I was just at a country-club dance. I don't dress like this." His look became exasperated again. "Let me ask you. Does Maxwell, does your uncle know what you are up to? I'm really wondering this—"

"My uncle is busy, away, of course, as he usually is. I kind of thought your mom was flying into Chicago tonight and then they were driving up together tomorrow. Anyway, Gladys watches me, mainly."

"Well, she's not doing a good job of it, I have to say."

"Wait—now stop there. Don't say anything. You don't understand. Gladys is the best watcher. Don't you say anything to get her in trouble."

"Okay. So where is she? Where is she doing this great job of watching?"

"Okay—can you calm down and just listen for a second?"

"I can't even look at you. I'm embarrassed for you. I'm uncomfortable just thinking someone could come in now and get the wrong impression—about me."

"You're big on impressions, I see."

"I am going to count to one hundred. And when I am through counting to one hundred, you will have been to the washroom, combed your hair, brushed your teeth, reattached your bra, buttoned your shirt, and met me back outside to continue talking."

"Okay, okay. But don't say or even think anything bad about Gladys. She didn't want to go out tonight, you know. Uncle Maxwell not being here and all. You don't even understand how devoted she is to me. But I knew that this jazz player she likes was performing nearby. We saw it in the newspaper. I want her to have a life, too. So I pretended I was sick and I'd just stay in bed. We've got a whole staff here in their own wing, so it's not like I'd be home alone. I had to drag her out almost. I was putting rouge and lipstick on her when her friend came for her."

"Well, lucky you. You didn't have to lie that you were sick. It's obvious you're about ready to throw up. Go, like I said. I'm counting—one…two…three…" Then he slammed the screen door shut, leaving the heavier oak one open, and I heard the immediate squeak of the rocker. When I eventually freshened up like he said, I peeked out the door and was glad to see that he was half dozing. I walked next to him and tapped him lightly on the shoulder. I mumbled that I was sorry he had to see me like that, and he smiled at me with an inscrutable look. As I turned to walk back inside, he caught me by the hand, and I actually felt a slight electric charge. "Hey, little lady," he said. "Don't be so quick to grow up." I was too surprised by his sentiments to even respond. I didn't move for a minute, and then I slowly walked back inside, secretly bringing that touched hand to brush my cheek. And suddenly I could think of no greater wish than to be older.

Once in my room, I was restless and slow to undress. I was pacing and nervous and overtaken by a host of unfamiliar sensations. A certain giddiness was bringing an involuntary smile to my face every few minutes. I sat down on the old chair of the vanity table in my grand bedroom and looked at myself carefully in the somewhat cloudy, aging mirror. Often, Uncle Maxwell had spoken about updating the furnishings of the six suites of the estate's upper level. The main floor had already received the decorator's touch, the contractor's workmen pounding away all through one summer of the late 1950s. The exterior had a creative facelift; it was remodeled from a graying wood structure with seven gables to a white brick and limestone edifice of high, horizontal rooflines. The kitchen was fitted with every modern appliance of the decade, and a center work island had one side with counter stools, which finally gave us a spot for an informal breakfast. The once old-fashioned living room had been a showplace of vintage pieces of Queen Anne furniture that were eventually sold at auction. Their price was possibly compromised because Roger and I had bounced on and abused the biggest couches as very young children. In their place, delivery men unloaded seating arrangements with a white and gray modern design; the now sleek, tautly upholstered pieces gave the look of a movie set.

When I saw that intermittent grin of mine reflected in her old mirror, I thought about Amanda Weiss, the "never met" grandmother. I wondered if she had looked into that same glass but failed to recognize when she felt her first feelings of love. Even though she might not have acknowledged that Grandfather Lawrence was "the one" until the great tragedy, did she not feel light headed and sequin hearted, confused, and excited some of the time, when he lived under her very roof for almost a month?

And then I remembered a conversation with my friend, Marsha Tessman, after I first met David, when I described him to her and confided a slight crush. The worldly Marsha, the child of a very public and bitter divorce and custody battle, had said that I should be careful about my feelings and called them "incest." Although I nodded and indicated a complete understanding and agreement with her caution, I had to run home to my dictionary for enlightenment. The definition of "incest" was specific, something like, "sexual relations between individuals so closely related that their marriage would be prohibited by law." It really made me wonder what had gone on in Marsha's home, but I was pretty sure that it did not exactly apply to us. Still, I knew any involvement between David and me would not be warmly embraced, if for no other reason than our age difference.

When Gladys came home later and opened my door, I feigned a deep slumber. She saw me firmly ensconced in the layers of heirloom quilts that made up my bed, although I was still awake, a curious night of unexpected experiences and emotions replaying continuously in my head, not allowing the sleep of dreams to invade. I wanted to open my eyes and ask her something right then, but I kept it in me for some time. I did not want her to make a connection between the impetus for the question and our holiday guest. I finally fell asleep with these words for David on my tongue: "Wait for me."

The house remained incredibly quiet and still that next morning, and I felt no urgency to leave the shelter of my room. Normally, I was the first down to breakfast wherever we were. If I was at a hotel with Maxwell, even when I was less than thirteen years old, by seven o'clock in the morning, I would dress in the room I shared with Gladys and then take the elevator by myself to the lobby restaurant. Breakfast was always my favorite meal of the day, and I didn't mind sitting alone like a fifty-year-old businessman reading a book or the newspaper, with orange juice and scones or English muffins and jam, plus two eggs, over easy, on my plate. But that morning I was not anxious for a group breakfast where David might be telling tales of the night before.

When I was finally hungry enough that I could no longer stall, I went downstairs. Each step that day on the highly polished dark-wood staircase seemed to play a loud and squeaky concert that I had never before acknowledged, as if it were an off-key trumpeter announcing the arrival of the reprobate. But when I went into the dining room, I was relieved to see I was alone. The kitchen staff were quick to ask if I was all right. It seemed that it was already past 10:00 a.m., my first experimentation with liquor having taken its toll, and they each mentioned that they had never seen me down there so late. "I'm so sorry if you are already pre-paring for lunch, but maybe you have some toast and jam still out," I said apologetically.

Miriam, our summer cook, who I knew would never deny me a thing in her pantry, said it was no problem to extend breakfast for me. "Mr. Noble" had already called ahead and told them that the family and friends would all be eating lunch later in town. That was the first I heard that this would be one of Uncle Maxwell's "planned activity" days, and I anticipated his visitors' agenda. First, we would be driven into town and all walk together along the shore path, beginning at the library and most likely extending west for two miles or slightly more along the embankment opposite our home. So that we would not have to retrace the same route, we would reach a prearranged spot where there was another street-access easement of sorts, and the car would be waiting for us. We would possibly go to Piper's Pit for their scrumptiously seasoned hamburg-ers, hot off the charcoal barbecue grill, accompanied by crispy fries and onion rings. Sitting at a balcony table, we would catch the panoramic view of the resort area. We would all watch the water skiers on the lake jump the tails of waves of the large touring boats. Or we might have a reservation at the fancier Water's Edge Restaurant, a white-tablecloth establishment that required jackets for dinner, where the maître d'hôtel would prepare the Caesar salad on a rolling cart, and the fresh catch would make your mouth water on presentation.

As it turned out, I did not see David that morning until we each responded to the ring of the front door-bell from separate rooms flanking the entry. Because he had a book in one hand, I presumed that he had retired to the living room after he finished his meal, either purposely avoiding me or waiting at breakfast so long that he assumed that was my intention. We glanced at each other somewhat shyly, but he held back a bit so that I was the one to open the door, where we caught my uncle and his mother, arm and arm, in midkiss.

"Hi, precious," Uncle Maxwell said, scooping me into his free arm. "I don't even know if I have a key to my own place," he said with a laugh. "Although, now that I think of it, the door probably wasn't even locked."

I kissed him on the cheek. "Hi, Florie," I said, giving her a nod and smile as Maxwell proceeded inside. "You know my uncle. He just likes to make a grand entrance wherever he goes, even at his own home."

"You and I definitely have his number," she returned. Then she reached out to embrace me with one arm and drew David to her with the other. "Two of my favorite young people. A great start to a beautiful day," she said.

Within an hour, we were all gathered at the rear portico of Weiss House, Uncle Maxwell having chosen a different route than I had anticipated. We would begin our hike along the pebbled lane of our own property and walk east to our lunch destination.

I sat down on the lowest step to tie my shoe, and David joined me with, "Good idea, kid." Although I cringed at that label, I tried to get beyond it because his proximity to me was so entrancing that I was hoping I was not outwardly sparkling like the holiday display of the night to come. When we ventured down the slope of the backyard, I questioned David about the book he was reading. "Are you completing some sort of summer assignment for college?" I asked, not really knowing typical curriculum requirements for a university, but rarely seeing the boys I knew with a book in their hand outside of school.

"No, I just like reading," he answered, barely raising his eyes to me.

"Really? I like reading, too." And there was that smile on him, though he might have been trying to hide it. A new component of my previously shy personality had been emerging lately. I just couldn't keep my thoughts to myself, and I would yap away incessantly if given the chance.

"What's it called? Who wrote it?"

"It's been a best seller for a while. I think there's a movie, but I haven't seen it. *In Cold Blood* by Truman Capote."

"Wait, this is crazy. I think Uncle Max knows Truman Capote. He wrote *Breakfast at Tiffany's* a long time ago. I was obsessed with it. Now, that was a great movie. I loved Audrey Hepburn, and I loved her name in the movie: Holly Golightly. What's this one about?"

"This," he paused. "It's really good. It's every detail about a murder, the murder of a whole family in their home…shot and—" He had a sickened look on his face. "Oh God, Paige. I am so sorry…Forget it. This is not a book for you."

I was overwhelmed by his sensitivity. I actually liked the fact that my tragic past had slipped his mind. I knew that people found it hard to rid themselves of our story, as if I wore it like a red cloak over my shoulders. When I would be introduced to a new person, I was not oblivious to the fact that soon he or she would be taken aside and told, outside of my hearing, "You know, she's the girl who survived..." I wished I could just be a normal girl; I wished I could go back to the time when I was annoyed by my schoolmates saying, "You know, she's the one with the beautiful French mother." I could tell that what he said had disturbed him more than it disturbed me. He almost seemed to want to hug me, but he reached toward me and then retreated. "It's okay about the book," I said. "But thanks. Maybe I'll take a pass on that one for now."

Uncle Maxwell, a makeshift walking stick in his hand selected from an accumulation of branches scattered around from a recent windstorm, led our hiking party. He used the stick less for balance than as a pointer as he narrated the history of the homes and homeowners. It was an intriguing travelogue, but one I had heard many times before. With great foresight, the original landowners along the twenty-one-mile perimeter stretch of Geneva Lake envisioned a path that all residents and visitors of the area could enjoy. So they had reserved the first twenty feet from the shore of any property for the full circumference of the lake as land in the public domain. The width and composition of the path varied greatly between the houses. Our home was located just west of the portion of the lake known as the Narrows. It was so named because the diameter of the water at that point was less than half a mile wide, instead of its average width of about two or three times that. When Maxwell spoke of the history of the mansions, often he had to say what magnificent home had originally been there, subsequently destroyed by fire or the ravages of time. "Just use your imagination," he would say when pointing to a low-modern ranch or two-story home, where once an enormous three- or four-storied Victorian-gabled structure had stood, such as the ones like Alta Vista at Pier 86 or Folly at Pier 69. But some of our other favorite places, such as House in the Woods and Flowerside Inn, both built around 1900, received restorations over the years that maintained and enhanced their beauty.

The walking order alternated many times during the adventure, like train cars shifting and recoupling at each station, but Maxwell was always the engineer in the front car. Usually I started the walk at his side. I held his hand and could feel his pride of ownership, a floating sensation like a colorful helium balloon. At a favorite estate with a most intriguing past, he would stop and motion for Florie and David to go close by his side to hear his narration. But ever so smoothly and innocently, David would fall back to be my partner. He was quite the funny actor in front of me. Sometimes he would mimic the penguin gait of Charlie Chaplin and turn around to tip a pretend bowler hat at me. Other times, he was a marching soldier, urging me to follow in line so that he could trick me with a sudden stop, my chest crashing into him. My emotions were all over the place. My heart swelled with the annoyingly familiar brother/

sister camaraderie that I realized now I had craved to revisit. Or was it a different type of fondness that was developing?

At Snug Harbor, the site of a late-nineteenth-century French chateau built by the Sturges family and eventually becoming a Bible camp, David picked up a collection of stones and pebbles and skipped them across the lake, accomplishing up to six bounces before the eventual dive. For three times, I pretended he needed to coach me how to accomplish that feat. He shadowed the lines of my body from behind, placing in my hand a perfectly chosen pebble and then agilely guiding my fingers for the release. I was nervous that he might feel my skin react to his touch, the goose bumps as apparent to me as if they were an illuminated rash. But he seemed intent on his lesson. "Stand this way. Feet apart, maybe two feet wide. There. No, you are too straight on. I need you sideways, perpendicular to the water line. That's better…" And then his fingers intertwined with each of mine. "Okay. Thumb here, middle finger here. Now release it flat side down. There you go. Wrist back and then whip your arm. Follow through. Don't stop the motion after you let go. Send it spinning." I let him lead me as I slowly refined the technique, first two, then three, and then another three bounces, giving him the greatest satisfaction of a mentor. He was not content with any of the remaining stones in his little pile and went to another area of the path, returning with two handfuls. He selected the perfect vehicles, telling me they needed to be flat, round, and skinny to work best, and I achieved a five. "But they don't have to be perfectly smooth," he said, showing me his best example. "See this one. A couple of chips or defects can give you a better grip before the toss. They can give you the best spin." But I couldn't keep the truth in for long, and when, at the next house, I skipped a perfect seven, totally unaided, he understood that I had been playing him, and he ran back up to be Maxwell's walking partner with a flushed face, a bruised ego, but an undeniable grin. A couple of houses later, he was back by my side.

An early-morning slight drizzle had left portions of the path a bit slippery, and once, when my gym shoe skated the surface too quickly, my balance gave out; he saved me just before I was flat on the ground. He smiled broadly at me at first, obviously pleased with his quick reaction, but then, realizing that he had caught me by my underarms, his hands so close to my breasts, he shared my same embarrassed reaction and quickened his pace to walk ahead once more.

I was right about one thing: our lunch destination was Water's Edge, Maxwell's more likely choice when he really wanted to impress his visitors. Although the setting was nearly formal, we all dug into a most elaborate seafood platter, as if we had never seen or heard of knives and forks. The featured catch, Dover sole, was unlikely from the local lake we were viewing; it must have been flown in to the nearest airport and trucked to our table. One waiter filleted the fish tableside, with the most delicate movements, while another presented deep-fried hush puppies, mashed potatoes, and green beans to decorate our plates.

When we finished the meal, Maxwell had the waiter call for our houseman, Augie, who watched over and worked at the estate year-round in multiple capacities, including gardener and driver. Uncle Maxwell and Florie had intended for us all to return to the house by car. But David and I each felt seriously stuffed from the meal, pushing our chairs back from the table and patting the swells of our stomachs as if we had previously orchestrated the moves.

"Oh my God," I moaned. "I absolutely have to walk back to walk this off."

"Race you," David shot back, quickly thanking Maxwell and running out the door ahead of me. I tried not to appear too anxious to join him but left the table, kissing each of the adults, and bounded out with, "You win—I can't catch up!"

But of course, halfway down the street, where the lake-path entry met the commercial street, he was waiting for me. This time, we walked back in a rambunctious mood and style, pausing for a while to dangle our feet from an abandoned-looking private pier. At a location farther down the path, we removed our shoes to wade to our knees in the cool water, kicking and splashing each other like children, until I saw his reaction when a wave of water from an errant motor boat drenched my top in a most revealing way. I crossed my hands over my chest, and we scrambled back to the shore path. I was giddier then I had felt with my recent tastes of liquor. Within a short time, the hot sun began to dry the fabric. We did not hold hands, but the power of their pull was unmistakable. Laughing most of the way, eventually we reached our property, and we both pretended I needed him to push my backside up the incline to make the somewhat steep climb to our yard. When we hit the level land, he removed his hand abruptly. It seemed that he recognized someone on the veranda, although the person was unfamiliar to me. And then I understood. The "fought with" girl-friend had shown up, apologetic and teary eyed. As she ran into his arms, he turned back to me momentarily, meekly shrugging his shoulders.

Later that evening, his chair was pulled close to hers as we sat around the large patio table on the back veranda, a glass of lemonade in my hand while the others had Old Milwaukee beers. We watched the armada of boats circling the lake, all decorated with red, white, and blue regalia. We waved our American flags at them as they passed, until the summer sky finally was swept in darkness and the colorful combustions of the fireworks display from the largest hotel captured us with "oohs" and "ahs." At the fantastically endless finale, the girlfriend, Valerie, reached to pull David close for an equally memorable kiss, and when he emerged from it, somewhat self-conscious, he immediately glanced toward me. I wouldn't meet his gaze. But it was obvious that my personal glow had diminished as surely as the sparkler in my hand had run its course and been extinguished. Preparing for bed an hour later, I looked out my window and saw him in his car, its top still down, ready to follow Valer-ie's car. Before he pulled away, he looked up directly at my window, and when he saw me there, he smiled and waved. I did wave back, lingering at the spot until his red taillights vanished into the night.

The morning that we were packing up the estate, preparing for our drive back to Chicago at the end of the summer, I finally approached Gladys with my question: "Gladys, when did you first know you were in love?"

"Honey, what do you mean? I never said I was in love. No, darling, I had no such experience. You can't be asking me about that."

"But I don't understand. You had a baby—the baby who became the boy. I am sorry to bring him up. I don't want to make you sad."

"No, darling, thinking about him doesn't make me sad anymore. I decided to be strong. You know. I told you. How can I ask you to be strong if I am not?"

"But still, the baby. Maman explained some of the facts of life to me. Although maybe she never got all the way through the story each time, obviously by now I know the truth. But it always started like this—people in love make a baby."

She could barely look at me with her response. Her head remained down. "Paige, sometimes it doesn't start with that. Sometimes, well, we all have wanted you to remain young and innocent, but I will do you no service if we always keep you overprotected." She looked directly in my eyes and then took her hand and lifted my chin so I wouldn't skirt her gaze. "Sometimes the world can be cruel," she said.

She left the table and went to her nearby bedroom after she said it. And I think I grew up a lot in a matter of a few minutes. I was not so sheltered that I hadn't realized that she was an unwed mother, although the first year when I said those words, I might not have totally understood their meaning. But after that conversation, I started to think perhaps she had been raped, and I was so sad for the scars of her life.

Chapter 18
Be Proud of Yourself

David and I continued to share occasional dinners with our parents when arrangements put us all in the same city, and he took to calling me every couple of months, just to tell me about his life, ask about mine, and give me some guidance on my college decisions.

Once the school term started, David left his New York City home and Harvard University for his senior semester abroad in Seville, Spain, which, he was quick to point out, was pronounced "Sevilla." He promised to send me postcards of his travels, and you can imagine that I bounded into the apartment each day after school but was rewarded with his correspondence no more than five times total. With the first card, I noticed that he had addressed it to "Mr. Maxwell and Miss Paige Noble," and I was a bit wounded that he treated me as an appendage, the little girl of his mom's "friend," especially when he mocked Maxwell's use of "Precious Paige" in his salutation. But regardless, I was always searching for a hidden code interpretation in every line. "Paige, you would love to see the Leaning Tower of Pisa" or "I went to the highest level of the Eiffel Tower" was his way of secretly revealing that he thought of me up there with him. When a picture postcard came from Venice with a photo of a young couple embracing in a gondola, being serenaded by the red-striped-shirt-and-beret-sporting gondolier, I never even showed it to my uncle. So the lovers floated on the Grand Canal, hidden inside my zippered pillow protector for months, until Gladys discovered it. After that, I moved it inside the pages of the terrifying novel I had just finished, *In Cold Blood.*

In the first half of 1968, the country was already collectively distraught from a most traumatic year. I was lucky that it was my last year still at home, the second semester of my senior year of high school, and I didn't have to be alone through all of the tragedies. Like we did in 1963, Gladys and I would sit on the couch and cry together, while my uncle was often covering the aftermath of the events. On April 4 of that year, the Rev. Martin Luther King Jr. was gunned down while on the balcony of the Lorraine Hotel in Memphis. He was only thirty-nine years old when he died. And then on June 5, while campaigning for his own run for the highest office, Sen. Robert F. Kennedy, the brother of our beloved late President John F. Kennedy, met his same fate at the Ambassador Hotel in Los Angeles.

At the end of that summer, the week before Labor Day, we left Weiss House a bit early because Uncle Maxwell was called back to the heat and the beat of the Democratic National Convention, conveniently located in our hometown. From August 26 to August 29, the International Amphitheater in Chicago hosted the hotly contested political fight for the Democratic Party nomination. Just turn the corner from our apartment and head south down Michigan Avenue, cross the bridge at the Chicago River, continue on past the Art Institute, and you will see the hugely majestic Conrad Hilton Hotel, where most of the state delegates were staying. It had become a scene of demonstrations and even violence, setting the Chicago Police Department against the anti–Vietnam War protesters, the actions contrasting greatly to the hippie peace scenes of the flower children of the era. Although rarely would I have said that Uncle Maxwell kept a close watch on me, he had been in the middle of the melee to capture the most compelling shots of the conflict, and he ordered me to go nowhere near it.

Like many people my age, it was the first time I was really engaged in the election process, but for me it was mainly to share an interest with David. I knew that earlier in the year, during the primaries, he had been distributing pamphlets for Eugene McCarthy. But it was Hubert Humphrey of Minnesota who eventually won the first spot on the ticket, with Edmund Muskie of Maine as his running mate.

❦

Although Gladys had started her college path with full intentions of becoming a nurse, after her first introductory classes in psychology and sociology, she recognized her real calling. There was a long, closed-door discussion in our library with Uncle Maxwell, where I was pacing the hall outside with a fear that she was giving him notice and leaving us. I pressed my ear against the heavy walnut entry, and when they finally emerged together, it was to the cartoonish move you see in old movies, my falling into the room.

"Well, what's this about, precious?" Uncle Maxwell said, startled as I tripped into him. But Gladys shook her head, smiling with the explanation, "Little Miss Busybody."

It seemed that this time, Gladys had approached Maxwell with her own materials and was asking his blessing of sorts to pursue a career in social work, with a most distinct vision. She wanted to serve the underprivileged, the young unwed mothers and their children from her "black" neighborhood, that term increasingly in vogue.

Later that day, Gladys told me that "Mrs. Bronstein" had spent time talking with her, both in New York and at Lake Geneva, and that "She was such a smart woman, beautiful inside and out, don't you agree? Can you imagine? This busy lady—she's one of the only people who has asked for my story. And she always asks for my memories of Darren. She isn't afraid to use his name." I knew exactly what she meant. So often, I longed for people to ask me about Roger. I wanted to talk about him. I wanted to say his name aloud to someone and tell them about a life cut too short.

"Mrs. Bronstein, she's the one who first gave me the idea for a career in social work. She sees me as a spokesperson for my community. Well, I don't know about that, but I think she's right that this should be my direction. She told me that right here in Chicago was a very famous place. I was proud to tell her that I knew of it. This lady named Jane Addams was the most famous social worker, and she established Jane Addams' Hull House as a place that served people in need while training professionals to deal with their problems. This I already knew. In the past few years, she told me, the University of Illinois at the Chicago Circle campus had established the Jane Addams College of Social Work, and Mrs. Bronstein said she had often arranged for some of her staff from her New York facility to go there for seminars."

Then Gladys stopped her monologue and looked up at me. "So, Mrs. Bronstein is helping me with the application to transfer there." She could tell I was becoming a bit shaken and teary eyed. "Now, Paige, honey, don't be getting upset. The school is right here in Chicago. I'll have a similar schedule. I won't be leaving you anytime soon—I promise not until you are grown and ready."

"Oh, Gladys, what you must think of me. I'm not crying for that. It's that I am proud of you." I took her hand and raised it to my lips. "I'm really proud of you."

"No, Paige," she answered. "You be proud of yourself. Don't think even one day I have forgotten what you did for me. You were a twelve-year-old girl, devastated by your own circumstances, yet you had the foresight to see something special in me. Be proud of me, but be proud of yourself first." She turned our clasped hands around and kissed mine. "Understand how special you are."

Chapter 19
Right for Each Other

I t is the first night of winter vacation, and unlike most of her freshman classmates at Northwestern, Paige does not have to head to O'Hare airport for a flight home. She simply drives south, down Sheridan Road to the Outer Drive, and follows its path along Lake Michigan until the gateway of Chicago's Gold Coast on Michigan Avenue presents itself. She takes the first left and is already in front of the driveway of the Drake Tower. The valet opens her door, unloads her suitcase, and takes her car into the building's multilevel indoor parking lot. She loves her new car. It's her first car, a beautiful white Chevrolet Camaro. She is perhaps the only child who had to talk her "parent" out of the Corvette that he had his eye on for her.

When she hears Maxwell's voice, she goes right to the study to tell him she is home for two weeks. He bends his cheek to meet her kiss but seems preoccupied on the telephone.

"Well, here. Here's Paige," he says into the mouthpiece. And then he holds up a finger with the "wait one minute" sign and keeps her in the room. "Paige, please. Come to the phone. Florence wants to say 'hi.' She has something to tell you."

Paige is hesitant to grab the receiver. She has never seen her uncle appear so agitated, so distressed, so vulnerable. She decides to back away from whatever situation she has innocently come upon. "It's okay. I think I'm just going to leave the room. Think I'll go to the kitchen, grab a bite," she says, and then, without touching it, without taking it from him, she shouts into the receiver at the end of his outstretched arm, "Hi, Florie. Sorry—I just happened into the room."

Maxwell waits now until Paige has left the study and knows she has purposely closed the door to give him privacy. "Well, then," he says back into the phone as he paces at the window behind his desk and tries to calm himself. "That made it easy for you. You won't have to tell her good-bye. I'll say good-bye for you. Okay? I'll tell her you'll think of her from time to time."

"Maxwell, please calm down. Sit down. Take a drink." He wonders how she can possibly have eyes on him from all the way in New York, although he knows the truth. Never before has someone been so attuned to his needs and moods. "Max. Pour the drink. Pull out your desk chair. This is not you. You have never been hurtful, vindictive. This is not what you mean to be saying to me now. You mean to say the 'I love you, but' line. 'I love you, but I can't commit.' 'I love you, but I could never love you more than I loved her,' whoever she is, this ghost of yours."

"Florie, I'm sorry."

"Max, it's okay. I'm a big girl." She takes a deep breath. "Hey, you've always been honest with me. You have done nothing wrong. And it's been a good run."

"Don't marry him, Florie."

"Now, that is one thing that you cannot say." There is a pause and a strange sound. He realizes that Florie is trying to muffle cries. "That is unfair to me. You can't say, 'Don't marry him,' unless you say, 'Marry me.'"

He says nothing for a while. She hears the ice cubes fall into the glass and then the pour of the liquor. "Is he a good man?" he asks.

"Truth?"

"Truth."

"He is a great man. A real catch."

"Now you're sure he's not just after your money, like I was."

"Max. He is a Rothschild."

"Oh."

"How about the kids, our kids?" he asks, and his pitch is rising to an accusatory tone. "How are they going to handle this?"

"I have a feeling," she says cautiously, "that they will handle it extremely well." Though she has never voiced her thoughts, she is legendary for her perceptive intuition.

He is surprised at her cavalier attitude, knowing Paige's sensitivity to loss and abandonment. "You can't be sure of that," he insists. And then he realizes he is acting immaturely and unfairly. This is not a divorce from her. These are not young children who will be forced to choose a parent for custody. These "kids" are young adults. He lets it go.

After an extended silence, Maxwell tries another tactic. "What about the 'We are right for each other' you always said? What about that?" He throws it to her like a child spewing "So there!" at a playmate.

"Max. I haven't changed how I feel about you. Though God only knows why. I think you are the most wonderful, most passionate, most unnervingly multilayered soul that exists." She waits a bit, catching the beginning of another cry. "I love you, but I don't want to be alone. I don't want to be lonely. And I know now I was wrong. You are right for me, but I am not right for you. You are content with our situation because you know I can exist and function on my own. You would only need to commit to a person who needed you. You want someone or you knew someone you thought you could protect."

"Florie," he pauses and sniffles himself, "there is no one like you. You deserve Baron Rothschild, or whoever he is."

"And I hope you find this apparition that haunts you."

"You don't understand. That is impossible." He is hesitant to add what he is thinking. "Can we still be friends?"

"You know what?"

He holds his breath for her answer.

"I think yes. I think I don't want a life where I can't say that Maxwell Noble is one of my best friends. Maybe

I will need a few months. I need to distance myself from my other feelings. I love you. And I love Paige. I need 'love' to tone down to 'like.' You are a good guy. Even though you like your larger-than-life image, you are a regular, good guy. And I hope, really, I want this for you...I hope you find happiness."

Late that evening, Paige returns from a dinner with her old high-school group, home from each of their colleges for the break. She hears the princess phone in her room and runs to her bedside table to catch it on the fifth ring.

"Hello."

"Finally," the caller says.

Paige thinks she can identify who it is, but it is hard to be sure from just one word.

"Sorry?" she offers in a noncommittal attempt to cover herself.

"Paige, it's David."

She smiles. "Hey, there."

"Hey there, you," he answers.

Her heart quickens, but she silently repeats to herself, *Friends, friends, friends.* No matter what their interactions over the years, she will not be the one to cross the boundary and embarrass herself. "I don't suppose there's any chance you're coming with your mom for New Year's Eve next week," she says. She pauses to slow down her speech. "I mean, I suppose you've got your own plans with friends from school, but this guy I've been dating—"

He breaks in with "Drunk Drake?"

"Well, Drinker Drake, let's say. Well, he's going to be drinking back home in St. Louis, Missouri. I mean, that's the thing about it when you attend a school in your own hometown. From Northwestern, of course, everyone goes home for winter break, so, well, obviously you figured 'cause you called me here. I just go twenty miles from my dorm to my real bedroom."

"I know. But really, I've been calling you both places."

"Well, are you coming or not, or are you spending New Year's with this year's Natalie?" This was her tease. Any of his revolving door of girlfriends since the first one she met, she calls Natalie. Long, straight, blond hair, high cheekbones, cleavage, attending some university in or around Boston—they were all interchangeable, she insisted.

"Paige. Could you possibly stop babbling for just a minute so I can talk to you about something important?"

She is not even insulted. This is something she has heard from him many times before.

"Oh, okay. Sorry. What's up?"

"Don't you know?" he asks and then rephrases his question. "You don't know yet, do you?"

"Um, I don't think so."

"Really?" He is surprised. "You don't know what's going on with the two of them, with Maxwell and my mom?"

"Well, earlier, I did walk in on a weird phone conversation." She thinks for some time and he waits, silently. "Actually, Maxwell was upset or acting strange. Now I feel bad. Pretty insensitive of me. I never asked him about it. Actually, I'm not sure if I even saw him after that. I think he left the apartment without my seeing him. God, this is one night I didn't even look to see if or when he came back. It's different now that I'm at college, even when I come home for a weekend. We don't report to each other so much. Same with Gladys."

He cuts in. "Paige. My mom's getting married."

"They are?" She is obviously surprised. "He didn't even say. He didn't even tell me. He didn't even show me the ring—"

"Paige, please stop for a second. Stop rambling. Listen."

"Sorry."

"My mom's getting married. But not to Maxwell."

"What? You're kidding. Oh God, he must be heartbroken."

"It was his choice. She would have married him. She wanted to marry him."

And now Paige breaks in. "He couldn't do it. He wouldn't commit. Just like his interviewers say." Paige feels ready to cry. "I know he loves her. But he is Maxwell. You don't know this. My own mother begged him to find someone to marry. I'm sorry. I'm sorry for Florie. I love your mom. Tell her that, will you?"

"I will. She's excited to get married. But she really wanted to marry Maxwell, I know. She will be happy to hear what you said."

And then something dawns on Paige, and now she does let out a few sobs. Why not? What difference could it make now?

"You're crying," David says. "It's okay. They're adults. They make their choices, and they will both be okay."

"Well, you're a wise old soul," Paige says. "But I can't be that stoic." She decides to just say what she is thinking. "I don't want to lose Florie, but I couldn't bear losing you, too."

She can hear a deep breath he exhales that comes across the line as a "whew."

"I can't believe you said that," David finally responds.

"I know, rambling, but what's it matter now?"

"It matters a lot because…because I feel the same way. I can't bear the thought of losing you, because—well, here goes. Because I love you."

"What did you say?" She had been leaning back on her headboard for most of the conversation, but now she sits up and straightens her outfit, as if he can see her through the telephone.

"Paige, I love you. Okay, I said it again. I have loved you since the day I screamed at you in Lake Geneva, maybe even before that. But for so many reasons, I knew I had to fight it. Maybe we'd be siblings. You were too much younger. All that. You know…one Natalie after another. That was why. I was just biding my time. Can you imagine? My mother didn't want to tell me how she was breaking up with Maxwell, partly because she was hurt, but also because she knew how attached I was to your uncle. How much I liked him. She doesn't understand that as long as she can be happy with someone else, I greet this news with joy. With joy and relief." He stops talking, although he has so much more to add, and he waits for her to say something. "Now? Now, all of a sudden, you have nothing to say. Please say something. Can you imagine, me begging you to start talking, me asking you to—"

"I love you. I've always loved you," she whispers because she is too emotional, too choked with sobs to shout it.

Chapter 20
The Treasures Within

Paige did not discover her mother's trunk until her nineteenth birthday, when she was back at their Lake Geneva property on summer vacation, following her first year of college. She stumbled upon it in the musty, dusty basement while searching unsuccessfully for a box of antique dolls she thought she remembered from her early childhood. The trunk had been hidden behind a barricade of discarded, old Victorian furniture pieces, and it proved to be the most powerful of gifts. Oh, the secrets, the pain, and the passion of the treasures within. When she ran up the stairs to tell Uncle Maxwell of the find and ask for his help in bringing up the locked case, he, also, was anxious to know its contents. He carried it easily and placed it on the kitchen table, and then he jimmied the lock with a long, pointed skewer from a utensils drawer. The top layer held some outdated shoes and then some purses to which Paige could see herself giving renewed life. There was a set of tea cups in its original box, tied with a ribbon, as if it were an unopened present. When those items were unpacked, there was a large tablecloth with its accompanying dozen or so napkins. Nothing in the initial layers was of extreme interest, and they had no idea why these objects were not stored along with like items in the butler's pantry or the bedrooms. But then, as the fifth napkin was removed from the trunk, it felt thicker and heavier than would be expected. It was obviously enveloping a book-sized rectangular object. Slowly, Paige unwrapped it. Her eyes widened with delight. In her hands was a red leather volume with a heart motif on the inside, a commercially made diary, similar to ones she had started and discarded in her youth. But on the first page was written "Celine Noble— Private." Obviously, the other objects were simply in the container to better hide the final prize and were no more than red herrings. Maxwell had no idea what this book would reveal, but he was cautious and simply said, "Don't let this change you."

The sight of her mother's beautifully distinctive, tiny cursive, the fanciful French schoolgirl strokes that she always felt carried their own tune like notes on a musical score, unlocked in her the most comforting repressed memory. Before she began reading, she gently traced the script with her forefinger. She slowly brought the diary to her nose, as if the scent of Celine could still be lingering on the paper. She had not yet focused on the first words, although Maxwell had caught them immediately. And when Paige saw them, she couldn't express her thoughts beyond a gasp. This was not a book of

"Dear Diary" entries. This was a letter from her mother, addressed to her, Paige.

My Dearest Paige:

Precious *petit chou*, I know how you ache to hear about my past, particularly my childhood, and I am so sorry, *ma cher*, to have denied you the sweetness of a story so I could protect you from the horror of its path. Am I sparing you information, or am I sparing myself pain? This I often have struggled with… and I know it is my weakness that is so unfair to you. There are so many magical memories that I want to relive—my own mother, your grandmother, who was a beautiful ballet dancer, who taught me to dance in my dreams. If only you had known her and she had known you.

So many times, I have thought of sharing my story with you. But then I panic. I am overcome by the threads of a life that include horror, separation, loss, and grief, and I know I cannot tell you only half of a story—only the fairy-tale part. I know you cannot imagine your world changing. And truly that was me at your age, and that is what I want for you, always: the cushioning security that the embracing arms of our small family can offer you…that we will always be together.

If you had known Cherise—like you, my darling, she was a heart of my heart. Cherise, if you have been renamed, I shall always wonder, but that is who you will always be to me. Our separation was so unbearable, but so necessary for all that the war would bring. What are you doing? What do you look like? I know that I will recognize you any time, and I will pray your fate has been a good one, an easier path than if we stayed together.

That decision to separate was not a decision of the heart, but of the mind. If people knew what I have done, they would judge me, judge my choice—my abandonment. But people do not know what went on then in a world gone insane that made you feel nothing would ever be easy or normal or safe. As time goes on, in one way, it gets easier to put the past in the past and to try to close that door. But you can only try to close that door—and *close* is too strong a concept. There is no finality. The door is always open just a bit, a slight bit for the brave soul to venture through...But not for me—not yet. Maybe soon, maybe never.

I know now that you can deny the past, but you cannot erase it. To carry secrets inside all these years is a great burden on a person. There is a weight lifted when a secret is shared. And for the first half of my life, I was good at that, at sharing things, sharing secrets. And so for me, maybe more than most people, it has been harder not to have the weight of this burden half lifted. I write this now because I am in America, my new home, for some years. America to me means safety and security, and I have come to place the highest value on that. Physically and mentally, I do not want to return to the places I came from. Now I am blessed with a wonderful family to create new memories.

My darling Paige, these ramblings I apologize for because I know that if you should ever read this and I am not by your side, you will not know what to make of it. Perhaps I will be able to reveal all of this to you before you ever stumble upon this cryptic message. Maybe I write this not for you, but for me. Or maybe I write this for my first love...so he will know that I never stopped loving him.

For a long time, Paige barely moved, still trying to digest the writing before her, without understanding its details, without knowing what to think. As her mother had anticipated, she was confused by what she read. Throughout the recitation, Maxwell was uncharacteristically silent, she realized. When she finally raised her head from the pages and looked up at him, she saw that there were tears in his eyes. He looked away quickly and excused himself to the washroom.

Alone, Maxwell looked at his reflection in the mirror and saw how he had lost his composure. He ran the sink to muffle his very soft sobs and then splashed his face with cold water. He took a decorative guest towel from the rack and wiped himself thoroughly. And then he leaned on the back of the door, as if the lock would not be enough security, and he reached into his back pocket for his black leather wallet.

Maxwell carried always, hidden behind his business cards, the most recent picture he had of Celine. He had taken it in Lake Geneva three years before her death. At the time, Paige was nine years old. It was the only photograph he could justify having in his possession from a set of eight pictures that he had developed for each of them, that he thought were perfection and had remained in his very private collection. In those others, Celine is in various stage of undress. But it was not the fact that he was in possession of the sensuous images of her body that her husband, had he been privy to the photos, would have found the most disturbing. It was the look on her face as she posed for the photographer—a look of love, passion, and longing that she had never sent her husband's way in all of their years of marriage. Had Mitchell seen the pictures, he would have known immediately, and so he was spared the truth for some time. And when he found out, only a few years before he died—before they both died—when he stumbled on not the images of a lover, but the lovers themselves, he said only, "I wish I never knew." He had wondered why Celine had stayed with him—this exquisite, enigmatic, joyful, and brooding foreign beauty. How was she happy in the Midwest suburban life they maintained? He was never the fool; he knew that surely the children and the safety and security of their environment must be enough for her after her experiences during the war. Until he knew that it was *not* enough.

Alone at the table, Paige waited for a few minutes, rereading the note, and then she had another idea. She started to unfold and lay out, individually, the other remaining napkins from the set in the trunk. And when she reached the last one, again she felt something. Carefully, she opened it fully. There were at least eight hidden photographs. She leafed through them quickly and then discreetly placed them in the pocket of her pants. She refolded each of the napkins and put them back where she had found them. When Maxwell reentered the room, Paige was still standing, leaning over the chest on the table. He asked, tentatively, if anything else important was still in the box, seeing her hands in the linens once more, and she answered honestly, "no." He seemed relieved.

So much was going through her mind that she did not even know where to start. So she decided to address the most obvious, the most confusing revelation. "Uncle Maxwell, do you understand this note? So did my mother live my story as well? Did she lose all that she knew? And do you know this name, Cherise?"

He had the most serious look on his face. "Paige, honey, can you sit down for a minute?" He pulled out a kitchen stool for her and took the one beside it so they were next to each other and not talking across the table. He picked up the red book and looked directly in her eyes. "This diary—I've never seen it. I never knew it existed. And its contents are shocking to me. But, that said, I may have an idea, an explanation for this. I am trying to read between the lines as well. The most important part of what I am going to say to you, I have never known until just now. You have to believe that."

She nodded her head.

"But I have to give you some background first. And this you have to know." He raised his shoulders and drew in a deep breath, as if he were a competitive swimmer preparing to enter the water. "I knew your mother before she ever met your father." Paige jerked back with a curious look on her face. She was trying to think if this had ever been mentioned to her before, but was sure it was not. "I met your mother…knew your mother during World War Two, when I was in the army."

"Okay," Paige said tentatively, nodding for him to go on.

"I was not really a combat soldier, a fighting soldier. I was a photographer. I think that much you knew about me, that I was a photographer even in the war." He spoke slowly, pursing his lips and tapping his fingers on the table nervously between sentences. "I am not a private person, and I have lived so much of my life on a world's stage. But your mother—it was her choice never to share her story with you."

Paige gave him a validating look, as if that were the understatement of the year.

"Even I don't know her early story; I only know when her world intersected with mine. And that was in April 1943. I was stationed in London but was sent on an assignment that took me to Derbyshire in the East Midlands section of England. During this terrible chapter in history, German bombs were constantly targeting the big city, and you can imagine it was a dangerous and frightening place. Many of the small towns of the English countryside had been called on to house children sent from London. This evacuation had begun some years earlier, and I was sent to Derbyshire for a photo spread on how the evacuees and their foster families were coping. I parked my army jeep near the town square, grabbing a quick cold drink at a small store, and anxious to stretch my legs out on a park bench across the way. I looked up and saw a full sun in an almost cloudless sky and thought of the smoke and the dust and the unrelenting noise of the last London days. For the first time, I understood how important it was to remove the children from the bombardments—not just for their safety, but for their sanity. Without the noise of a city, I could hear in the distance, at the other end of the park, children laughing on swings and calling out to each other in a game of kick ball, and I thought, already, that I had my perfect first shot. But I was wrong.

"Before I even crossed the street, a group of girls, maybe sixteen years old, ran up to me with constant chatter that even I could recognize as French. They were adorable and had no intention of leaving me alone, and now I was the one laughing, trying to tell them that yes, I would take their picture if they could just stand still. And as I took my shot, I felt the slight presence of someone behind me, shadowing my moves; I smelled just a hint of a luscious perfumed scent that lingers in my senses still. And then the shadow spoke, and I turned to the lilting laughter and the lovely voice of the most beautiful girl I had ever seen.

"'*Mes jeunnes filles*—leave this man to be, *s'il vous plait.*' And that was when I met your mother. She was eighteen years old at the time." Maxwell gave a slight sniffle once more, and Paige could tell he needed a moment. She walked to the sink and returned with two glasses of cold water. After he took a sip of his, he was able to continue.

"I will admit something," he said, smiling his dapper grin, as if the story involved picking up a starlet at a Hollywood restaurant, but then he quickly refocused

on the reality. "We became very close, almost insepa-
rable, over the month that I was in the area. We rode
together in my jeep to all of the surrounding towns and
little cities. I needed to stretch a short assignment as
long as I could, creating such a detailed portfolio of that
chapter of British history that after the war, I was given
clearance to release the photographs as a small book.
And eventually, your mother told me a story that con-
tradicted the softness and innocence of her very being.
She confided in me because just as I saw the small cross
on a chain around her neck, she had read aloud my dog
tags. I loved hearing my name, Maxwell Noble, spoken
with her intriguing accent. She made me promise to
keep a secret, and then she told me that she was Jewish
also. '*Je suis juif, aussi.*' Within two days of meeting me,
she felt safe and comfortable crying this to me in my
arms. She explained that she had recently led a group
of young people from a small town outside of Pau in the
south of France. They had all been living in an area of
France where the Nazis were not yet a big presence, as
they were in the north, especially in Paris. Like her, they
were all Jewish. And you must know, the Nazis wanted to
murder all of the Jews of Europe. She told me only this:
that they had been given new identities and were living
as Catholic girls in a convent school, and for a while
they felt safe. She was acting as a teacher or escort of the
younger children. But as the war progressed, there was
increasing fear for these 'hidden children.' The unoc-
cupied zone of France was rapidly filling with Nazis as
well. Besides rumors of betrayals by the French citizens,
a group like hers, with adolescent girls, was prime prey

for the marauding appetite of the German army. Your mother, Celine, had been approached by members of what was called the French Resistance—underground freedom fighters working against the Germans. The resistance leaders had come to recruit her to help them move the children farther west and out of the country."

"Really?" Paige said with such a full exhalation, not able to disguise the implausible tone of her interjection, that it breathed life into the word itself.

"Oh, yes. Just wait—there is more," Maxwell answered slowly. "They had heard of the language skills of a beautiful French girl, and they recruited her to help relocate the children, to move them out of France, down through Spain and on to England." He paused to give her time to digest this. "So Celine, accompanied by two women from the resistance, led a group of seven to safety."

Suddenly Paige started to laugh. It began with a quiet nervous chuckle and then grew until she had to hold her breath to stop it, as if suppressing hiccups. "Uncle Maxwell, now, this isn't one of your stories, is it?" He shook his head. "Because if it is, I will be the first to say, 'You got me.'" From the look on his face, the expressionless shaking of his head, she knew it was true. "Oh my God," she said, stepping off her stool and turning a half circle away and then back. "So now I am learning that my mother, that Maman, who could not organize a PTA tea, who finally learned to drive but would never venture downtown on the expressway, had been eighteen years old—oh my God, younger than I am now—when she joined resistance fighters and led a group of children through Nazi territory. Wait—across water, even. Am I right? To safety in England."

Then Maxwell laughed a bit. "Yes, precious, really. And now this will be hard for you to hear." He gulped and looked down as he spoke. "I fell in love with her immediately. The minute I saw her, I thought she was the loveliest girl on earth. And when she told me her plight and cried in my arms, I knew I wanted to keep her protected there forever." He paused again. "And she loved me."

When he looked up, he saw that Paige was processing this revelation. She seemed more contemplative than shocked.

"Do not judge her. She was an angel. I was a young Jewish man who had come into her life when she was lonely and a great responsibility had been thrust on her. She needed love as deeply as I did. Yes, I need to tell you this, only because I think it will explain the letter. We could not help ourselves. Yes, we loved each other—intimately. We spent four weeks together. When I received my orders to return to London, I drove quickly to the house where they had been staying, and I kidnapped her right from her kitchen duties, to the snickers of all of the girls and the understanding smile of the rector's wife. We didn't drive far. I just wanted to hold her, to kiss her one more time, to tell her I would be back as soon as possible.

"But that was not for three more months. I was actually sent back up to Scotland to photograph the arrival of more troops. And when I returned, I was handed a note that she had left for me. It read that she was 'needed' again, and I knew what it meant. She must have been returning with the underground to relocate more of the French children. This is what a war will bring, I knew—separations and reunions. I never doubted that I would meet her back there again one day soon.

"Go on," Paige said, inquisitively, not accusingly.

"And now I believe from this note, something that I never knew, never imagined. But I wish so much I had known."

Paige was not sure what he would say next.

"This, I believe. This, I understand now. Weeks or months after she left, she must have realized she was pregnant. Pregnant with my baby, our baby." He made a slight crying sound and covered his mouth with his hand. He pretended he was only clearing his throat, but Paige understood the truth and reached for his hand. "I believe that Cherise, this person she refers to, this Cherise whom she abandoned, is what she must have named our baby before her name was most likely changed. This was the Cherise she thought people would not understand her motives for giving up—this was her own child. But it was a war. And Celine was a sensitive, passionate Jewish young woman hiding from the Nazis. She gave up her baby so that she could survive. Our child." He shook his head and cleared his throat again. "Somewhere, it is possible…somewhere, you and I, we each have another part of the family we both long for. This girl who she imagines would eventually look like her probably is a person who looks like you, a sister for you, a daughter for me."

Paige said nothing but rubbed her hand on her forehead. The look on her face, though, was not one of distress; it was more like a look of intrigue and hope.

"You have to believe I knew none of this," Maxwell continued, almost pleading. "I only knew that I needed to find Celine immediately after the war because I wanted to be with her forever. And I began a desperate search for her. Although the war ended, it would be a few years before I would return from overseas." He stopped, leaned back, and laughed a bit. "This I didn't even know because I was not at home to read the newspapers and see the newsreels, but my reputation as a photographer was growing. I had no idea that movie cameras had often been directed my way when I was taking still shots, and I had appeared in several short documentaries along with the others, the really talented ones, especially Robert Capa. Eventually, I did see an article about myself. I was flattered and remembered these words: 'His reputation as a photographer has become almost legend. It is known that his pictures carry such a depth of meaning that they rival printed reports.'"

"Impressive, but I'm not surprised," Paige said. "They say a picture's worth a thousand words...and you illustrated it."

"Well, maybe you're right," he said, thinking it out. "But the problem was that I was in high demand on the European continent as postwar efforts got underway, leading to one assignment after another, keeping me in uniform far beyond my promised release date. At first I was happy. I had no intention to return home until I was reunited with Celine."

"So when did you find her again?"

"You must be patient so that I can get to that answer. Okay?"

"Okay," she said softly.

"Of course, I retraced my steps immediately. And my first stop, as you can imagine, was the small town in Derbyshire, where I innocently believed my love could be waiting for me, where I truly thought she had taken more of the children. I had made a few trips over the months I was still in England, and she had not returned yet, but still I was hopeful. But eventually I was sent from England with my camera to follow the fighting men after the invasions. And when I arrived there after the war, she was still nowhere to be found. They told me that she had never returned. And the other girls had left with the refugee placement groups. It was then that I really regretted that she had never told me where she came from, originally. She said that before France, she lived in Germany and in England. She would never reveal anything about herself, except that her parents had both died and she was alone. When I had asked her full name, she said her real name was gone forever; nothing was real for her anymore.

"For some reason, though, I remained optimistic. I remembered the name of the town in France where she had been hiding. I loved hearing her describe the flowing fields of lavender, the small cafés along the roads, the beautiful shops, and how the owners would give her extra treats for the children. She described Monsieur Allend, the hefty owner of La Boulangerie, wielding his butcher's knife with a vengeance while singing operatic tunes. And in the back of Madame Marceau's clothing store, there was a secret library of beautiful, provocative love stories, she had told me. But again, in this town now, there was no evidence of Celine. This, perhaps, I could understand, and I laughed at myself for my own naïveté. Of course, with the war over, she could come out of hiding and resume her former identity. But this I could not comprehend: the townspeople pretended as if she had never existed.

"I would plead with them. I would say, 'You saw her. You were there. You helped her pack a picnic basket from items in your own stores.' Even if they couldn't understand my English words, my emotions came through, and the picture of Celine—who would forget that such a beautiful creature walked on their roads, ate at their cafés? But I had been looking through this world at war with the tunnel vision of one who is focusing only through a camera lens. I had not grasped the big picture, the fact that these people—her friends in the town who thought they were harboring an orphaned Christian girl, a girl who really only wanted, needed to escape the past—had not been friends when the Nazis came searching for the hidden Jews. Perhaps the gentle souls who had housed her and hid her were coerced or even strong-armed to betray their charge. But I felt that the others were complicitous at the least, collaborators at most, in the 'disappearance' of Celine.

"Finally, one of the storekeepers, who said he knew English because of his London suppliers, called me back after I left his shop with my picture in my hand, feeling stonewalled and defeated. He said that he would confide in me what no one else would. Yes, they did remember her, and that was why they had all hesitated so to hurt me. Very soon after she returned, a young man came by, believed to be a boyfriend from back home. Now, that was too much for me, and I held up my hand indignantly I insisted that I knew she had no boyfriend, no serious boyfriend at the very least. But he was adamant. 'It was a difficult time for all,' he said. 'Please do not judge her too harshly. She left with him as quickly and mysteriously as she had come, just gone one night, not even leaving a note for the poor Laurient family, who had offered hospitality.' I was shaken by this news. I couldn't believe what he was saying; under my breath I called them all liars. So I went to a nearby bar to drown myself in the local wines. I sat among a group of men who bought me one drink after another, and through the most limited of translation capabilities, I still came to understand one story after another of their own experiences with an abandonment by a first love. I think back often and feel that perhaps only a few of them knew the truth; they were already being cautious with revealing too much of their activities to their American liberators for fear of repercussions. The others were innocently trying to lift my spirits. But just as I was leaving, a woman quite easily matching Celine's funny description of the town busybody approached me to say *au revoir* with a double-cheeked kiss. She surreptitiously slid a folded note into my hand, and when I looked up at her with a startled expression, she met my eyes with a slight nod. I put the note in my pocket as she indicated, and when

I had it translated by an army colleague, it read, 'Did not leave—was taken.'"

Hearing this, Paige wrapped her arms around herself, as if a blast of cool air through an open window had sent shivers over her body.

"After eighteen more months in uniform, traveling through Europe to immortalize what we would know as the Holocaust, to record undeniable evidence of what the Nazis did, to take pictures of cities in ruins, lives in ruins, I was finally released to return to the world beyond the horror."

He focused again on Paige, briefly leaving the past, and he saw that she was literally on the edge of her seat, eager for more.

"So now you ask, when did I find her again. And this is too much to believe. I found her again just over three years after I first met her, just after I knocked on the door to my own apartment, our parents' home that Mitchell and I continued to share although they were gone, the home that had been left vacant while we were both in the war. My brother opened the door for me, and immediately, in the foyer, we jumped in a full circle, holding on to each other's arms as if we were young children having just won a baseball game. When we calmed down and could pull ourselves apart, I still reached to tousle his hair in a lovable big-brother way. And then he led me into the living room and proudly introduced me to his wife. He introduced me to my own Celine."

Maxwell stopped talking and took a deep breath to calm himself. "And perhaps this is the last link you needed to know, one link in a family legacy of tragedy that she tried to hide from you, that I wish I could have spared you—that your mother, the beautiful angel Celine, was in the concentration camp in Germany when your father, when Mitchell, arrived with his US army unit."

"Oh my God," Paige gasped, her hand cupping her mouth. "This was never told to us. I pictured them meeting in Europe in a café or in a shop. I know this can't be true." She stopped and thought for a moment. "Wait," she said, her speech almost desperately breathless. "This I know for sure. She had no tattoo…or—oh God. She called it her burn mark and never revealed it under the skin-toned bandage. I always loved the look and feel of her naked arms. They were perfect. They were a dancer's arms. And now from her diary, I know where those arms came from—from a grandmother I never knew."

He shook his head with the dourest expression, as if he wished he could wipe the pain and degradation of those tattoos from all of the victims. "She did. She tried to hide this truth her whole life. But you can only outwardly cover the mark; she couldn't erase its imprint on her soul."

He waited to continue. He wanted to be careful with what he revealed, but he wanted Paige to understand. "And this is what she told me when your father left the apartment and left us alone. This is what she told me when I desperately questioned how it could come to be that she was married to my brother. She said that at Buchenwald, she walked to him when she heard another soldier call out the name 'Noble.' She went to him because she thought she was going to me. In her weakened, emaciated, terrorized state, she fell into his arms. And he took care of her.

"Does any of this make my life clearer to you? Celine, your mother, was my first and only love." In his head, he finished the sentence: *and now I know I was hers.* But he was afraid that might be hurtful to Paige, disrespectful to his late brother, to repeat this truth that Paige had just learned.

He waited to see Paige's reaction to these admissions. She said nothing, her eyes squinting, her forehead wrinkling, as if she were in deep thought. He wasn't sure whether she was truly not being judgmental or she was keeping any judgments to herself. So he continued. "I know how people view me, that I have this reputation as a ladies' man. But this was the problem my whole life. I didn't want to be like that. But, you know, when the one woman I loved turned up on my own doorstep as my own brother's wife, what could I do? What could I do but pretend to get back into the world to search out the someone to replace the someone I could never have?"

The silence that followed between them was unbearable to Maxwell. Finally, Paige simply smiled. She was astonished by the story; she believed that her uncle had finally been open and honest with her. It explained so many of the interactions of the past that she was too young a girl to interpret on her own. "Uncle Maxwell, I understand, and I love you. That's the kind of love I want for myself—the 'once in a lifetime, forever kind of love.'" Suddenly she jumped from her seat with an enormous energy. "Cherise. My mother's baby. Your baby.

My own sister. The baby who is grown now. We have to find her," she said. And then she wondered aloud how old a person they would be seeking, as Maxwell did the same calculations.

"The time we were together was in 1943, and now it is 1970," he said. "She would be around twenty-six or twenty-seven now, I guess. Twenty-six or twenty-seven years old."

Now Paige could not contain her excitement. "We have to find her. Promise me. We have to find her now."

Maxwell hugged Paige as he had never hugged her before. She had lifted from him a great burden, the unbearable secret of his love for her mother. And she had embraced it. He had never felt such respect for her, never felt such pride in her maturity. Had he made good choices in raising her? Had he protected her well enough that now she felt strong enough to protect him? Or perhaps just the timing was right. Paige had continued seeing David Bronstein, even though his own relationship with Florence had ended. It seemed to have blossomed well beyond just a friendship now that David's mother had remarried. Perhaps Paige was ripe for understanding a love story because now she was living her own.

"You bet, we do need to find her," Maxwell finally said. "You bet—we will try our best to find Cherise. This is how we will spend the rest of the summer."

But there was so much more he couldn't tell Paige— like how the young Celine had goaded him to chase her through the fields of the countryside dense with the hues of the spring bounties, running and searching for a new secluded pond or overgrown field, and how they would eventually fall down laughing, overcome by the heat and the exhaustion of the race. He couldn't tell her how he loved the taste of Celine's body, ripe with the sweat of all they had done. How he loved when they were often caught in the briefest of showers, when the water beaded on her skin, catching and preserving whole each raindrop on her face or arm, and he would suck the droplets off her beautiful skin, the most delicious potion to quench his thirst. He couldn't tell Paige how they would lie with their faces toward the sky, challenging each other to make sense of the billowing cloud patterns. He always saw elephants, or rabbits, or trains with the trail of their smoke stacks, and she always saw babies sucking their thumbs or clinging to their mothers' breasts. Thinking back, he wondered, did she know then what was happening to her body, or was it the most innocent of coincidences?

"Do you even have an idea where we could start?" Paige asked, interrupting his encompassing memory.

He literally shook his head to shake off the past. "This is what I am thinking. When I first tried to find her in Europe, I went back to where I last saw her. But there was no trail. So now I will think back to clues from anything she said to me after the time that I found her again, in Chicago."

Chapter 21
She Remains an Enigma

When Mitchell Noble enters the lobby of his co-op apartment, he cannot believe he is finally home. He is trying to contemplate just how many years it has been since he last walked through its strong steel doors, when he is greeted with the booming voice of Elvin Douglass, the building's front-desk concierge. Already an older man when Mitchell left for the service, he now notices that Elvin's hair has further grayed, and what was just a slight bend in his gait is more pronounced. So he is happy to know that the strong, hearty greeting is as familiar as ever.

"Mr. Mitchell Noble," Elvin says. "Wait. Let me help you with that door. And let me just put those bags down for you." He walks as quickly as he can from behind his station. "Please, sir," he adds deferentially, "May I first please shake the hand of a man coming back from his duty to our country. I am proud to know you. Wish I could have been young enough to join you there."

Mitchell is touched by the homecoming. "Elvin, you did your time with the first war. And never be sad you missed this one. I thought you fought our 'war to end all wars.' Well, let's hope this one was. But you forgot to tell me the truth when I left." He pauses and looks right in his eyes. "War is hell," he adds bleakly. And then, although Elvin has extended his hand for a shake, Mitchell turns the handshake into a strong embrace, and the two men hug firmly. "You know, Elvin. You are the closest thing to a father that I am coming home to." Elvin is touched by the comment and takes a handkerchief from his pants pocket to pretend a sneeze and wipe his eyes.

"Now, wait," Elvin says, seeing the shadow of someone not yet emerged from the taxi. "That your brother in the cab? Haven't seen Mr. Maxwell yet."

"Um, no, no…definitely not my brother—you'll see."

"But, Mr. Maxwell, he's coming home, right? I mean he's okay and all, right?'

"Oh, yeah, sorry. Didn't mean to worry you. He should be here within months. They're keeping him on assignments."

"Oh, yes, sir. I'd bet on that. Mr. Meyerson, sir, from Twelve-B, he's been showing some pictures from *Life* magazine that have the name Maxwell Noble under them."

"So you know already. Well, you had better plan a big reception when he returns. I think he deserves balloons in the lobby, at the least."

Although the comment could have been interpreted as a sarcastic remark from a jealous brother, that was anything but the case. Mitchell Noble had lived so long in Maxwell's shadow that he looked at it as the most wonderful, protective place there could be. Even physically, he was just that much shorter, that much thinner than Maxwell, that from the time he was a baby to the time he became a full-grown adult, he would easily be recognized as the younger brother. Maxwell's undeniably more acknowledged assets were his artistry, his creativity, and his social skills, none of which Mitchell had ever claimed to possess. Although there was no doubt that Maxwell was a bright young man, on the intellect spectrum, Mitchell was the one who was "off the charts." He was a math and science genius, a boy who might have been picked on as a nerd by the bullies of his day had he not been able to remain invisible outside of the classroom, quietly glued to his brother's side, hanging out with the acceptable, cool crowd of the grade ahead. No one questioned the presence of the sidekick of a leader. Standing by Maxwell, content not to shine himself, had always worked for the introspective Mitchell. He had no desire to make the effort for other connections. When he was not running with his brother's group, Mitchell would be found in a library or at home on a chair with a book. In fact, his desire to do nothing but study in college, when they were no longer together, had given him the time for graduation with highest honors and distinction and already two articles published in engineering journals.

For their first four months in America, the new Mr. and Mrs. Mitchell Noble are alone in the apartment, Maxwell still not having returned from overseas. Mitchell is lovingly obsessed with his new bride. It is inconceivable to him that he left his home as an educated but awkward, army recruit, almost too uncoordinated to pass his basic-training requirements. So many handsome, self-assured, virile men had easily surpassed him on every physical measure, yet he is the one who returns home with the most entrancing, soft, and sweet French young woman, who sees him as her savior. He remembers eventually being housed with other Counter Intelligence Corps agents in Europe who had not been required to complete basic training, initially. They told him that when they did finally go through the drills because they would be moving from desk jobs or jobs in civilian attire to be attached to fighting units, one camp commander at the 307th CIC had referred to them as "a citizen army of misfits." And Mitchell knew this group of misfits would become the perfect fit for him.

Slowly, slowly, day by day, week by week, Celine's body had filled out to a more normal, though still thin, frame. With nutritional meals, with freshly baked breads, with bounties of fruits and vegetables, with sunlight and warm clothing, and the reemergence of hope, her eyes became brighter, her hair became long enough to be the cutest pixie style, her nails grew beyond the flesh of her fingers, and her lips and cheeks took on a rosier tone, even before gifts of lipstick and rouge were applied.

In his beautiful lakefront residence, she remains an enigma. She will not reveal anything about her past; he knows she even retained her false Christian surname before she took his. Yet where another refugee might be overwhelmed, impressed, and intimidated by her luxurious new surroundings, she blends in easily. She is obviously comfortable with a familiar lifestyle. She will not gawk over a painting but remark on the modern lines, saying her tastes were different and she was always a lover of the Impressionists, or that this one is reminiscent of an early Gaugin. When a classical recording is playing, sometimes she can identify the composer. Or perhaps she always can, he thinks. She is wary to share too much, though she knows he aches to question her. When he catches her moving in cadence to the rhythm of a recording, he will smile at the sight of her so happy and relaxed, and then she will stiffen. If he had found her in another place and time, rescued her on the streets of a city in a normal world, he would have thought she was a runaway and would have known he must reconnect her with her family. But this much he knows to be true: she was torn from a family that has perished, from a way of life that she believes no longer can exist. She does not articulate this, but he knows this. She will no longer accept Judaism. She will not convert to another religion. She cannot believe in any God. And she insists she will not raise children who may one day be forced to wear a yellow star on their clothing and be sent to gas chambers. This demand he agrees to respect so that she will come to America with him: that there will be no religion in their home. He is not afraid that this commitment has compromised his own values because he knows that it will save a life; it will be the only way Celine can survive. And he knows the Jewish Talmudic saying that if you save a single soul, it is as if you have saved an entire world.

For these past months, Mitchell has been working on his future. He and his brother, children of inherited wealth, have never for one moment relied on trust funds to be their livelihoods, perhaps only to be their security. This has been the Noble legacy: a strong work ethic. Mitchell Noble has a plan. He wants to pursue an advanced degree in engineering, and he wants to secure a job that will support the family he envisions. He knows that soon Maxwell will return to live in their co-op, so he feels that he and Celine should consider finding their own home. Following the war, the colleges and universities are inundated with applicants on the new GI Bill. Yet Northwestern University in Evanston, Illinois, with one of the most prestigious engineering programs in the nation and one of the most restrictive Jewish quota policies, has reached out to enroll him. At the same time, the research and development branch of Paquin Laboratories in that same town has offered him a position and is willing to work it around his PhD program schedule. He taps into his personal account for the down payment on a formidable new home under construction in nearby Winnetka. On the morning when he is to drive to the real-estate office and meet his lawyer to finalize the papers, he opens the door to the arms of his brother.

The minute Mitchell has left the apartment for what he says is an important appointment, Maxwell cannot help himself. He needs to touch Celine. "I need to touch you," he says. She looks quickly left and right to see if they are really alone. She actually begins shaking and brings her hands to cover her mouth. When he takes a step toward her, she takes a step back.

He is not prepared for her astonished, almost horrified look. "Oh my God. Did I say that aloud—what I was thinking? What I wanted to say, but I thought I held it in: that I want, that I need to touch you. But your look—did I say it? Can I take it back? I'm sorry. I don't know what to do or say." For a minute, he just stands there and takes her in. She gives him a look he cannot interpret. It is a look of caution, embarrassment, fear, longing...

"I—I don't know how to react," Maxwell finally says. "Because this is how I want to react." He approaches her so that their bodies are no more than a foot apart. It is far too intimate a stance for a brother and a sister-in-law under any circumstances, especially having first been introduced.

"This is impossible. You understand, I am sure. I am married. I am a married woman. I am your own brother's wife."

"Okay, yeah, yeah. I heard that, but I don't understand that. I can't process that. Maybe this was your way back to me. This is what I am praying. That this is some sort of arrangement to work your way back to me...that even my brother, whom I would never want to hurt... knows this and is in on this." He doesn't want to stop talking. He knows that if he stops talking, he may not like what he hears.

She doesn't want to touch him because she is too afraid to mislead him, but she can't stop herself. She puts her hand to his mouth. "Enough," she says. "You must stop. Please, stop." She moves her hand quickly away after it has effectively silenced him, and he keeps looking at her. He says nothing, his expression unreadable.

"You are mad, *non*?" She looks down only, wanting to avoid the eye contact that makes this meeting so hard.

"Mad?" he asks. "Mad at you? Mad that I thought maybe you were dead, murdered, gone—and lost to me forever, and now I find you are alive." His voice rises with each word; he clenches his fists and turns away and then back again. "Are you joking? Are you kidding me?" He is almost crying the words. "I am joyful; I am relieved. I am—" He starts to reach out to touch her face but stops his hand as she steps back to avoid the contact. "And if I am mad," he continues more gently, "it is mad for you. Mad to be with you again, to see you, to hope to touch you."

She does not know what to say, although she can barely stand resisting his moves. "You look well, Maxwell." That is all that she feels she can offer.

He does not answer her immediately. He does not have the right words. This encounter, for which he begins to realize she may have had months to prepare for, has blindsided him. "I look well. Okay." He takes a long pause, bites his lower lip, and lowers his head. "I look well," he repeats. "This is what you say to a man who knows his face is drained of color?" He shakes his head and looks around, as if he is scouting out a companion by his side to help him make sense of this. "I don't know what to do, what to say. My insides are jumping out of my skin."

Maxwell sees she has no answer for him. She just stands still, so he continues. "It was not a coincidence, you know. You married Mitchell. How did this ever come about? Of millions of people in the whole world, you met and married my brother? You knew, yet you married him."

"Stop it. Stop it," she finally says. "You don't know what you are saying. You don't know what I went through. And you—you never came back." She says it softly at first, as if testing the waters of her sentiments. Then she repeats it with greater strength and an almost accusatory tone. "You know what? You didn't come back, and still I was not mad at you. I understood it might have been impossible, or that for you I was but a dalliance. Even in my darkest hours, I was not mad at you. I thanked you. I thanked you from my concentration camp prison. I—"

He grabs her arm, interrupting her in midsentence. Those words, the words "concentration camp," jolt him like a slap across the face. "No, please don't let this be true."

She takes his hand from her arm and says softly, half crying, "I thanked God that he had given me a most wonderful memory to cherish. I had given up on the religion that had only caused me such pain. Yet this one last time, I looked to thank God, even though sometimes I thought you had never been real—that maybe I had dreamed you."

Despite her efforts, he cannot hold himself back from trying to make her understand.

"You think—you can't really think, believe—that I never came back? I was consumed with finding a way back to you. But as you say, there was a war. You knew my orders recalled me to England. And when I finally went back to Derbyshire, I read the note that you were needed. And I was distraught, but I understood. Then I could not get back to you until the armistice was declared. And even for that, I had to plead with an officer to allow me just a week's time before we went on. I searched for you. I went to the very town you had described to me...Pau in France."

"My God. You went to Pau." She cannot believe this—this validation of his love for her.

"Even though the townspeople pretended you never existed, I relentlessly begged them. When finally they told me you had left with a boyfriend, I didn't believe them. I still searched for you."

She cuts in quickly. "You know, of course, there was no boyfriend who came to get me. I had been gone for periods of time working with the resistance on relocating more of the children. There was no longer the window for the safety of England, but we went north through an incredible bridge passage at Château de Chenonceau."

He is intrigued but stays silent so she will continue. "And I am proud of my efforts there. But within a year, when I was helping on a crossing, the other partisans were captured in the woods. And though I thought I was clever in my escape, I was followed back to Pau. They hoped to capture more of the children with me. But our children left in hiding were only the youngest girls whose papers and personal histories did not betray them. They did not even remember a time they were Jewish. So only I was taken." She looks at him forcefully. "Please, you cannot make me go back to the memories of that. The most smugly vindictive Nazi captured me, parading me through the streets as a prize and as a warning to others. We met up with resistance leaders who had also been arrested and beaten, and we were taken on a long transport back to Germany, to Buchenwald, which was specializing in political prisoners. There were horrors there that defy description."

She shakes her head as if that act would rid her of the memories. But it is only indicating that she will not revisit that road immediately.

"But I made it to liberation. I was still alive, though barely, when the Allies came to Buchenwald. Yes, I was there. What is general knowledge now—that I do not know. But I think you, of all people, should understand. I know that you, yourself, took pictures at such camps, that you bore witness. But someday it will all come out, and everyone will see the savagery of the Nazis."

He wants to break in, to put his arms around her, but she waves her hands slightly to stop him. She knows these next words will be impossible for him to comprehend, although the very evidence of it stands before him.

"And then I met Mitchell. And he was good, and he was sweet, and I would have never known that if I hadn't known you. I would never have walked to him if I had not heard the name 'Noble.' I was a broken stick of a person, a wounded, pathetic, emaciated memory of what a human was. But I was alive—alive enough to keep fighting to survive.

"And so, as I wandered around the camp, shocked to be free to do so, but barely with the strength to stay up on my feet, this is what I heard: 'Hey, Noble, come—you have to see this.' He ran to where he was called. It was a column of men laid side by side. They were skeletons with flesh, with bulging eyes—human remains.

"I was no longer soft and beautiful, as you had described me. I was thin, my cheekbones and hip bones protruding—my hair chopped and lice infested, not the hair you ran your hands through to twist into spirals, but hair that would have fallen out with such a move. But I heard this name, and I remembered thinking he is a prince for sure—just like when I first heard the name Noble. I ran to the name, thinking I was running to you—only it wasn't you. But it was someone else who looked at me with grave care and concern, someone who cradled me in his arms, not out of passion— that would come—but out of humanity. He disclosed to me right away that he also was Jewish, but he was not prepared for my response. Instead of the smile he expected, I told him that I would never again believe in God. I told him that I would never again be a practicing Jew. From one country to another, my Judaism has caused me pain and grief. How could a God allow that? He did not try to argue with me. He looked around at the human remains, the walking dead, the barbed wire; he smelled the fetid odor of death, and he could say nothing. He gave me sips of fresh water from his canteen, and then he carried me to an area set up with some food, and he fed me little bits. While I grabbed at what he gave me, looking like a squirrel nibbling on a nut, he sat down next to me, his elbows on the table, his hands over his eyes as if he were praying, and he cried. He had never seen this horror—the horror that was my daily existence. He could not comprehend that such a place could exist. I will speak of this once more only and never again. There were piles of naked, emaciated corpses; there was evidence of the skin of the dead as lampshades, there were the walking skeletons.

"I was taken to a facility for temporary housing for the survivors in the nearby town. The Americans made the townspeople, the citizens of Weimar and surrounding villages, walk through the camps. They made them acknowledge that they were a party to this carnage, even if they did nothing or because they did nothing. They would be forced to bear the responsibility for allowing the atrocities, for seeing the transports to the camp and ignoring them, for smelling the nauseating odors from the crematorium and simply covering their noses with handkerchiefs.

"Mitchell had his assignment, his intelligence to collect and record. But every day when his shift was over, he would come to visit me. He would talk to me and, you understand that no one really in our quarters spoke any English, yet I could converse well. Eventually, his commander gave him extra time so that they could acquire valuable information from me, not unaware that this assignment was a bonus for Mitchell. He began by asking me questions. He was given a special form for me to write any names, even descriptions, of the camp officers and guards and their roles. And then there were questions for me: 'Where is your family from? What route led you to Buchenwald? And can I help you find your family?' I told him what I told you. I answered him, 'I have no family. My mother died before the war. And then my father was taken and killed. Because they needed corroborating information for prosecuting war criminals, I traced my story from my time in hiding. But I will not go back before that. I will not. I cannot talk about my journey. My past is over.' This I said to him, even when I envisioned no future."

For a long time, Maxwell was silent. Within the apartment, the hum of the refrigerator, the hiss of the radiator, the background stereo recording of the Chicago Symphony Orchestra, the wondrous sounds of a life of comfort and culture, contrasted so profoundly to her words redolent of an uncivilized place and time. How courageous she was to have endured all that she had and not be broken beyond redemption. He could not fault her finding any means to return to a world of safety and normalcy.

Finally, Maxwell had to have his turn. "Now, this you don't know," he said. "I could have been there—with a twist of fate and luck, I could have been the one to see you there. My colleague Margaret, Margaret Bourke White, my colleague now when I am working sometimes for *Life* magazine—she took those pictures at Buchenwald that the world first saw. When the war ended, photographers with the military and with the private press were assigned to follow General Patton's Third Army. They rode with them as they made their way through the destruction of Germany. But my assignment was a bit different. They put me with the British 11th Armored Division. I was at Bergen-Belsen. The *Life* photographer there was George Rodger. I worked with him, and I learned from him. My God, the horror we saw. The horror you lived. We understood our responsibility: to document the atrocities, the barbarism, the sick, twisted inhumanity of the Nazi bastards."

This whole time they had been standing and talking, but now Maxwell led Celine to one of the couches, and they sat down. For a moment, he just bent over and rested his head in his arms. She took that opportunity to continue with her story. "And while you took photographs where you were, Mitchell continued to take and record my testimony. After a week, I had the nerve to ask him something. I gathered the nerve to ask him about his family. He told me that his parents had died and that it was just him and his brother. He didn't so much resemble you—not really—you know that. You are the handsome one. But something about the mannerisms, something about the smile prepared me. At first, I didn't want to ask or to even have him say the name. I didn't know how I would react. But he did not know what was in my mind, so he spoke of you. He said these words in an endearing manner, almost envious of you; he had no idea of their impact on me: 'Oh, yes. One brother, Maxwell—my older brother. And now, in the war, he has become famous.'

"'A war hero?' I asked cautiously, fearing to hear of an injury. 'In a different way, a war hero,' he said. 'Among the most revered photojournalists. Not a fighter; a documenter. But what power his pictures have.' Then he was ready to lighten the moment. 'Good thing you didn't meet him first. A real heartbreaker. Handsome as all get-out. A girl in every town, I heard.' He stopped for a minute and said, 'Wait—let me show you some things.' He left the bench we were on to run back to his jeep and retrieve his rucksack. Then when he spoke, not aware that my heart was breaking at his every word, he showed me newspaper clippings. Most you took. In some, you were the subject. 'Look at all the photographs people have sent to me.' This he said with great pride."

Suddenly, and much too late, Maxwell is overcome with regret. He now realizes the folly of his decision not to share his quest for Celine with his brother in their limited communications during the war years. This situation is his own fault. He covers his face with his hands and lets his fingertips massage his temples. He shakes his head sadly, and finally speaks.

"But when you realized who he was—and you said yes to him—what were you thinking?"

She does not hesitate to answer. "I was thinking I would be safe. I was thinking I could go to America and not have fear at every turn. I was thinking I would have someone to count on, someone to care for me."

"And what more? Someone to love?"

Celine reached up for his shoulders, to turn him back to her, so that he would face her again. She looked into his eyes. "Someone to love me," she answered finally.

Chapter 22
An Uncomfortable Situation

Maxwell tried his best to stay away from the Celine who was the wife of his brother. He didn't want to ruin her life or his brother's life or their children's lives—any of their lives. He tried to be content to stay in the background, to rejoice in the unbelievable circumstance that he could be with her once more, in any capacity. He was becoming more and more successful in his profession, and the demands of his travels kept him out of their immediate world for long periods of time.

Sometimes when he visited the home of his brother and Celine, he would take something of hers from a dresser drawer—one silk stocking, one earring—one thing he could touch or smell or study that would be a piece of Celine, that he could own briefly and examine privately. Sometimes it would be a mirror or the lipstick case from her purse. He would take the item home and take it into his bed because he could not take Celine home.

The first time, it was a spur-of-the-moment, spontaneous theft. Celine had not been aware that her handkerchief had not made its way back into her clutch. Discreetly, nervously eyeing the room, Maxwell had folded his hand around it on the side table and slipped it into his pants pocket. But eventually, as the months progressed, it became an obsession with him, and the procurement of each item became a calculated challenge. At a dinner at their home, he would excuse himself to go to the washroom, but he would walk past the nearest one and would continue on to the master bedroom suite farther down the hall of the sprawling ranch-style house. Sometimes, he actually took the book that was on her nightstand. He would keep it turned to the bookmarked page for a month or more before he would return it, replacing it under the bed or behind the dresser as if it had accidentally dropped there, undiscovered. It was easier to remove and hide a paperback than a hard-cover novel under the shield of a sports jacket. He had to hold the book awkwardly against his chest until he could use an excuse to run to the car for something. Initially, the item would find a home in his glove compartment until he took it into his own bedroom, and then eventually it would be returned and replaced with the next trinket. Sometimes, on a subsequent visit, he would make some reference to a scene or character or plot line in the book, and he would savor her look of confusion.

For the first six months of this, Celine had no explanation for the missing items, blaming it on her own absentmindedness or the distractions of everyday life.

She would never look to make culpable their cleaning woman, Sally, who was like a member of the family. But Celine would think about the trustworthiness of an occasional unsupervised workman, the man who was hanging some wallpaper, the electrician rewiring the study. She even wondered if Paige had become curious about her underthings or her jewelry, or her reading materials because she remembered being mesmerized by her own mother's treasures at her age. So when Paige was at school, just a few times, she compromised her daughter's privacy and searched through her drawers for the contraband. There was nothing.

She had wondered how was this happening in her meticulously ordered world. Finally she began to connect the dots. How foolish, how naïve, she realized she was not to have seen the pattern. It was Maxwell. Her inscrutable brother-in-law, Maxwell. The missing items could be linked to his visits. She was sure of it now. The audacity of it was reckless, but surprisingly flattering. Of course, she did not make some discoveries for a week or so after the fact. She would not discover an earring without its pair until she needed it for a special evening out. A pair of missing underpants went unnoticed until the day she selected the matching bra. Emerging from the shower, she would dry herself thoroughly and then wrap the towel around her torso, securing it with a tuck under her arm. She would walk over to her dresser drawer and make her choice of a bra, fastening the clasp on the lacy bandeau, while she allowed the towel to drop to the floor. But as she rummaged through her lingerie, searching for the matching panty, she stood for too long, naked and annoyed. If they'd had no history, she might have been appalled by it, might have run to her husband to handle an *uncomfortable situation*. She saw what it was: an innocent, flirtatious tease—a game, really—and she knew it would be best to ignore it, best for everyone. She would let Maxwell know she was in on the secret. In truth, how often was he really there? Once a month if he was in and out of town. Sometimes three months would pass before they were together if his schedule was full.

Chapter 23
A Promise of Something Good

In 1957, when the children are ten and seven years old, Maxwell calls his brother's house, asking if he might join the family for dinner. He has come back into town after a succession of assignments and almost a month away, and he is feeling quite lonely. Celine answers with her intoxicating French accent and tells Maxwell that her husband is presenting his latest invention at a New York conference, but certainly he is welcome to come.

On the long drive to the Winnetka residence, Maxwell feels an inexplicable elation. There is a word that lingers in his mind: "promise." There is a promise of something good in the air. It is as if he had felt a deep void in his life, and now there is the promise that void will be filled. Perhaps it has to do with these last days spent on an assignment in San Francisco. The *Life* reporter who would be writing the copy for the story he was photographing lived in the Bay area. They would meet each morning at Golden Gate Park, where the writer would gather information for his feature story, explaining the history of the park, and Maxwell's pictures would capture the broad scope of individuals, the melting pot of Americans and foreigners, young and old, who enjoyed the venue. Martin Potter, a somewhat pot-bellied man, would begin the day perfectly put together with a starched white shirt, a meticulously knotted tie, and a bright shine to his shoes—superficial qualities that the rare man like Maxwell Noble did admire. But as the day progressed, Martin's wardrobe would deteriorate dramatically. Wide pink hot-dog juice spots would dot the shirt, and the tie would become a long, loose, hanging noose at the neck and would serve as a mustard napkin. The shoes would have the dust of the dirt paths that somehow Maxwell's shoes could resist. But as Martin's looks faltered exponentially with each hour, all the more his jovial personality emerged, until Maxwell understood the obvious. "Martin, who dresses you in the morning?" he asked, although he guessed the answer from seeing the too-tight wedding band limiting the circulation on the man's chubby ring finger.

"My wife, of course," Martin answered, with an undeniable pride. "Obvious, huh? It's not me, but I let her enjoy trying to reshape my taste, as long as she doesn't try to reshape my body," he said with a laugh.

At first, Maxwell was feeling sorry for the man, obviously so uncomfortable wearing his wife's choices. But then Martin gave Maxwell the biggest grin he had ever seen. "I'm one lucky guy. I don't know where I'd be. God, I don't know who I'd be without my wife behind me, in front of me. Her and the kids." He waved his hands in a "who could ever have imagined" gesture. "Well, I'm one lucky man for a really fat slob of a guy."

Each of the three evenings, Maxwell would invite Martin back to his nearby hotel for a drink, and although he would accept the invitation and they had a great time exchanging professional stories, humorous anecdotes about the wide range of celebrities they had each met, Martin would be checking his watch, anxious to get home to his family before the children were in bed. When he left, Maxwell would move from his deserted table to the bar area to continue a conversation with the bartender. And when the reporter was at home having tucked his son and daughter in bed with a nighttime story, Maxwell was flicking the channels on the television set, continuing his drinking alone in his luxurious suite at the Fairmont.

❧

When Maxwell rings the doorbell, a full bag of treats in the tuck of his arm, he can hear shouting coming from inside. "I'll get it." "No, me!" "No, *me*!" When the door opens, the two children each take a hand to pull him inside, chorusing "What did you bring me?" as he gently kisses Celine on the cheek.

"Okay, calm down. You guessed it. Goodies for everyone." At the top of the sack is a stunning bouquet of purple roses. Celine accepts the gift and holds the bunch in front of her face to take in the fragrance. Easily, he is taken back to their time together in England, to the field of blossoms. "No sneezes?" he asks, very quietly, and it takes Celine a moment to make the connection, although she keeps her smile hidden behind the flowers. Next, he pulls out an intriguing small globe with the Golden Gate Bridge under its dome of glass. When Paige turns it in her hands, sparkling bits of confetti float around in the water, and she asks if this is supposed to be California snow. "Thank you, Uncle Maxwell. It will go right on my shelf with the others." To Roger, he hands a book on the odyssey of the building of the bridge, knowing that his nephew will be fascinated by the engineering feat.

Her children busily examining their gifts, Celine walks back and peeks out the front door. When Maxwell joins her at the entry, he asks, "Looking for something?"

She jumps a bit, not expecting him at her side. "Well, your overnight valise, I guess. Just that you usually have it. You usually don't like to drive back downtown so late after a few drinks, I know." She says this as she innocently passes under the arm he has extended to keep the door open, and she adds, "No matter." He does not tell her that the suitcase is in his trunk.

He is careful not to overinterpret her intent. But her comment is just the kind of encouragement that he needs to wipe away his earlier depression. Like his slovenly working partner he had spent time with the previous few days, he wanted to have that feeling that he belonged somewhere, that someone was waiting for him. And here was that little bit of "promise" he had been anticipating. For a time, he let himself believe that this mind-set wasn't dangerous, pretending that he really belonged here, as if he were the man of the house and not just the visiting uncle, stepping from behind his camera and inserting himself into the frame.

At dinner, the main course is a sumptuous beef brisket, presented in a chili sauce and brown-sugar marinade, served steaming hot over a bed of white mashed potatoes, whipped to a creamy softness. The children talk about their school assignments and after-school activities, much more forthcoming than most their age who would offer only one-word answers that were conversation killers. Roger laughs about his new lab partner—"a girl," he emphasizes, who almost set the science room on fire with a mishandled Bunsen burner. And Paige runs to her room to retrieve and recite the poem that has earned her an "Excellent," a copy of which will be displayed outside the principal's office for a month.

When dinner is over, they form an assembly line to clear the table, rinse the dishes, and load the brand-new electric dishwasher. After a record, lengthy Monopoly game, the males and females paired as partners, there are moans and lingering hugs from children too energized for bed. Eventually, while Celine checks to see that they are each settled in their rooms, Maxwell takes the bottle of red wine he has been sharing with her and moves both of their glasses into the front study.

They spend time catching up on the past few months, comfortably sharing the gold-tufted couch, their bodies angled toward each other, their elbows resting on the back cushions. He pretends not to be drawn to her every movement, the way her fingers comb through her hair, the way she covers her mouth when she laughs, as if she needs to conceal something other than her perfect white teeth. Celine explains that Mitchell has been trying to teach her to play bridge. Her husband is extremely patient with her, she insists. "But his mind runs so many moves ahead, when I am still arranging the cards in suits and counting points." They laugh and nod a mutual understanding of the shared "genius" of their family. "I know he wants us to be more social, but it is like the blind leading the blind. Neither of us is that comfortable in groups. He's doing this now because he doesn't believe I am busy enough at home when he is increasingly away."

"Well, what is keeping you so busy?" Maxwell challenges her.

"Promise not to laugh."

"No promises. But I am intrigued."

She stands up and walks to the center of the room. She holds her hands above her head and then quickly brings them back down. She walks over to one of the two tall and narrow front windows and pulls down the white rolling shade. When she turns back around to him, he thinks she looks like an actress on a movie screen, flanked by the side curtains. He cannot believe that her silhouette is as lovely as the memory of her at eighteen years old, although enhanced by the pleasing curves of a woman. When she moves to the next window to repeat the act, he notices for the first time that the fabric on her shirt dress is opaque. Set against a plain white background, illuminated by the lamps of the living room, the outline of her lower body is detectable. Although she is not tall, her legs are as long and shapely as a swimsuit model's. He can hardly breathe. Celine is still unsure if her actions have afforded her the privacy she desires, so she returns to each window and releases the plush velvet ties of the heavy black- and gold-striped drapery panels.

Maxwell does not understand what he should do now. Is this an invitation to the intimacy he craves? He makes the slightest motion to rise from the couch; he places his hand on the arm of the sofa, but luckily he goes no further.

"Okay, now. Remember, no laughing," she says, resuming her pose in the middle of the room. "You asked what I have been doing to keep busy. Well, I have been attending adult classes at the dance studio in town. It is the same one that the young girls go to after school. I will give you a private ballet recital."

She speaks aloud the moves that she has memorized for her routine. "First position, second position, third position, fourth position, fifth position…plié, plié, jump, jump…" And then she stops. "Well, that is just a taste of it, but you get the idea."

He applauds and stands up, laughing. "Bravo, bravo…more, more."

"Oh, there is not much more. I was never good at dance. My balance has always been poor. I will try my turns, but I will need help." Immediately, he walks toward her. She takes his hands and shows him where to rest them, so that they are barely, barely touching the belt of her dress, but it gives her enough support for a few turns. She has no idea how graceful she appears.

He is intoxicated. "Did you dance when you were a child?" he asks cautiously, risking an unwanted trigger.

"I was never a child," she answers with no emotion. And he knows that the show has ended.

Although it had escaped his vision initially, on the coffee table, he sees they have displayed the newest book of his photographs. The publisher chose the title *The World through the Eyes of Maxwell Noble,* and he is reminded of the discussion about whether the word should be "eyes" or "lens."

Celine reopens the shades and readjusts the draperies to their original positions, and then she moves back to the couch with him for another sip of her wine. When he reaches out for the album, she gets up quickly again and moves to the desk. She handles a shiny silver pen and pencil set, the base engraved with the words "Professor Mitchell Noble." She extracts the ballpoint from its mount and brings it to Maxwell. "That reminds me. You had this first edition sent directly to our home, but you did not sign it for us." She holds the pen out to him and opens it to the first page.

There is barely a pause before he begins his inscription: "To the most important people in my world. Love, Maxwell," he writes. When he hands the pen back to her, it accidentally drops to the floor. They both reach for it, and their fingers touch and remain together an extra few seconds until Maxwell withdraws his. When Celine has the instrument totally in her grasp, she stands back up. She does not look at him but focuses on the book. She sees that the signature is as grand as John Hancock's on the Declaration of Independence.

Celine yawns and stretches her arms back up as if repeating her dancing movements. She gathers up both of their glasses, and Maxwell uses a napkin on the table to wipe away any evidence of the moisture rings. His steps falter a little as he follows her into the kitchen.

"You really should not drive all the way back tonight. It's late, and you are tired and maybe a bit intoxicated, and Sheridan Road is winding and dark. You know that."

"It sounds like you care about me," he responds, still feeling the promise in the air.

"We all care about you. We all worry about you. I would feel responsible if something happened."

Her words are just what he needs. They hit him as soundly as the ice shower he would require if he were to actually make the drive. He was back to reality. This is just a night of hospitality at his brother's home, and he should savor it for what it is and nothing more.

"You know there are extra pajamas and a toothbrush in the guest bedroom. And you know how the children will want you at the breakfast table."

He gives her his most charming smirk.

"You have a suitcase," she said. "Ah-ha. I knew it. In the backseat?"

"The trunk."

"Well, you go get it, and I'll make sure there are extra towels for you in the hall bathroom."

In the bedroom, he changes out of his clothes and hangs them neatly in the closet. He sees a familiar blue shirt on the cedar pole and checks the cuffs for his small monogram. He was wondering where he had left this favorite one, and he remembers contacting a few of the hotels where he had stayed on a European trip more than three months ago to see if it could be found. He puts on his pajama bottoms only. They are a blue and red Scottish plaid in a soft cotton fabric. The matching top would be stifling in the heat of the room. He sits on the edge of the bed and fights his thoughts. He cannot stop envisioning the outline of her body beneath her dress. He cannot stop reliving the feel of her tiny waist as she turned, the smell of her strawberry shampoo as her hair whirred past his nose. He cannot stop remembering how she did not move her fingers away from his when they had touched on the carpet. He cannot stop thinking of her undressing, alone in her bedroom. He pictures her looking in the mirror as she removes her makeup, and he wants to be beside her there. If he stands beside her in front of a mirror, the image will be another photograph in his mind of just the two of them. Twice he leaves the bed and goes to open the door of his room, but then he retreats. A third time, he opens it slightly, not knowing if he will actually proceed down the hall. And this time he sees that Celine is standing before him on the other side, poised to turn the handle, herself, and enter.

They promised themselves this would not happen, that this betrayal would never happen again. Just one time before, they had slipped; just one time they had given in to their tremendous longing. And that had been so gratifying, yet so unsettling to both of them, that Maxwell had known his only option was to distance himself from her. He had taken a yearlong assignment in Japan.

But now no words, discussions, cautions, or sensibilities can keep them apart. When he sees her before him, he pulls her into the room. He does not move himself more than a foot back. He brings her in the room without taking his eyes off of her exquisite face. He has never seen eyes as defined as hers, dark brown orbits floating in the whitest sea. Her lashes are long, curled feathers. He forces her back against the inside of the door and holds her in place with his hands firmly on her shoulders. He wants to stare at her first. Before he touches her further, he wants to inhale her, to consume her. He wants to take her in with all of his senses—sight, touch, smell and taste. He needs to study her before he comes at her with a most voracious appetite, before she moves in rhythm with him to offer herself as the most delicious meal. He releases his grip on one shoulder and moves her arm so that it extends upward. He slides his hand along the flesh of her upper arm, passing the sensitive inside crook of her elbow and resting it forcefully at her wrist. He removes one strap of her nightgown, and it falls to reveal the same fully rounded, but small, perfect breast he has never forgotten. He kisses her shoulder with such an intensity that she is afraid it will leave a mark. She is desperate to have him undress her completely. She wants to use her own hands. But he clasps them still. He is savoring the view of the shadow of her body beneath the folds of light chiffon. Once more, he can only think of the word "promise." There is a promise beneath the pink fabric that will finally become a dream fulfilled. He reaches under her gown and feels every inch of her, moving his hand from her knee and up her thigh until he explores every contour of the space between her legs. And as he becomes familiar with her body again, he places his other hand over her mouth to muffle the sounds he knows to expect. Then he falls to his knees and traces that same path with his mouth until she begs him to let her lie on the carpet. Finally, their lips meet in a kiss as passionate as the act of love to follow. And when they are exhausted and spent, they move to the bed to spoon in each other's arms through the night, intermittently replaying the scenario until the first light of dawn, when she tiptoes back to her own room.

Chapter 24

Innocent Roots

In her Lake Geneva bedroom with her mother's secret diary, Paige cannot stop pacing, although she is imagining that she is floating, that she is lighter than air, and that her feet are barely touching the floor, barely making a sound on the aged wood. This past year has been a remarkable potpourri of emotions and sensations, and they are encircling her now like iridescent, translucent orbs created from the wand of a child's soap-bubble toy. In her mind, she will just reach to touch the globes gently with her fingertips so they will not pop and disappear. She spins in a circle because now she knows that there is the grace and agility of a ballet dancer in her genes; pirouettes and arabesques are running through her veins. She feels as if the heart on the first page of the book has been transported there from her own body and is pulsating in her hand.

It is one more scene in this incredible next chapter of her life that began the previous New Year's Eve. It is as if her life had been an ordinary black-and-white

movie, a *film noir* of deepening plots and denoue-
ments, of joys and tragedies, of interest and intrigue
in ordinary and extraordinary places, but it was waiting for the invention of Technicolor to be complete.
It is as if she was channeling *The Wizard of Oz*. She was
Dorothy in Kansas caught in the monochrome hues
of existence before the tornado and then waking up
to the multicolored vibrancy of a future on the yellow
brick road.

She furtively glances around her room, as if looking for someone hiding behind a curtain or a chaise.
She walks from her bed and turns the old skeleton-key
in the door lock. Then she gathers her abundance of
pillows so she can lean at a comfortable angle while
lying down. From the pocket of her bell-bottom jeans,
she withdraws the group of photographs that she had
appropriated from the basement trunk. She examines
the top one. Immediately, she recognizes the romantic,
passionate look on the face of her mother as a reflection of her own face and feelings the first time she was
in David's embrace.

Since that night just over six months ago, when Paige
had run to the phone, to the distressing news that Maxwell and Florie would not be a couple, to the glorious
realization that she and David would be a couple, she
has felt herself transitioning from a child to a woman.
It is a "metamorphosis"—always a favorite word—and
now it applied to her. But she is not the character in
Franz Kafka's novel, awakening to his repulsive trans-
formation into an insect. She is an insect, a caterpillar,
becoming a butterfly.

From David's perspective on that same night, when he heard her echo, "I love you," when he heard her cry, his heart was already flying toward her over the phone lines. She did not know he was actually holding a plane ticket in his hand. If she had not shared her feelings, or if she had denied them, he would have flown to Chicago to convince her. But no pleas, no convincing was needed, so he simply had to say, "Paige, have your uncle buy you a new dress. I'm coming to Chicago to be your New Year's Eve date this year...and, oh yeah, for the rest of your life."

The next afternoon, when she opened the apartment door to him, he didn't even look to see who else might be around. He left his suitcase in the hall because he needed to be free of encumbrances. He wanted to use both of his hands to circle her waist and bring her to his chest and turn her in a circle. When he was done, he wanted, finally, to lace his fingers through her long, thick, black hair and then lift her face to his, kissing her fully on the lips as he had dreamed of doing for years. Of course, he had so much more in mind; his desire for her had been a consuming passion. Often in the middle of a boring history lecture, he was on the lake path following her into the water. Sometimes under the pressure of a mathematics exam, he would gaze out the window and see her standing there, waving her pouty good-bye. And always, Paige's image would intrude on his intimacies with other young women.

Suddenly, that was all in the past. He had a bouquet of flowers waiting in the hallway for her. This was his plan. He would court her like an old-fashioned gentle-

man because he knew there was time for the relationship to progress properly. Initially, they would visit each
other at their family apartments, staying in guest rooms,
letting the romance blossom with innocent roots, with
the hugs and kisses and teases and touches of dating.
But eventually, she would stay with him in Boston for
weekends, and he would be able to tell her the truth.
His arms encompassing her tightly, their bodies pressed
together so they could each feel each other's heartbeats,
he whispered what she already knew: "For sure from
that first night—you know the night—I have loved you.
That's why I stayed away more than I wanted to, when
I didn't come sometimes to visit when my mother did.
Because I was afraid I wouldn't be able to help myself, to
control myself. That I would picture your bra undone,
and I would want to put my hands under your blouse,
and there would have been some uncomfortable, almost
criminal incident."

Of course now, with the discovery of the diary, Paige's
first thought is to call David. She checks the time. It is an
hour later in New York, and on a midafternoon summer
Saturday, she knows he is most likely jogging in Central
Park or scouting out a pickup game of basketball. She
doesn't remember him mentioning that this would be
a weekend in the Hamptons at one of the megaman-
sions of his grandparents, his cousins, or his friends. But
often their crowd had a spontaneity of entertainment
decisions reserved for those with lives of privilege, and
taking a flight to Bermuda would not even have been
out of the question. She calls, and, as expected, he is
not at home. But her impatience is easily assuaged when

her message prompts a return phone call within an hour. She details for him the "unearthing" of the chest and reads the entire diary letter to him. But when she says there is so much more to the discovery, that Uncle Maxwell has an extraordinary story of his own, David makes her stop.

"This is too big, Paige. This is the buried treasure of your life, and I have to be there to share it with you. You must still be at Lake Geneva, I'm thinking. When will you be back in Chicago?"

"We'll drive back in the morning. We have to. You don't understand; we have a huge mission ahead."

"I'll get a flight to you tomorrow. Whatever this is, I want to be a part of it, okay?"

"More than okay," she says, her angel-winged smile evident in her voice.

Maxwell has no reservations about repeating for David the entire story of his early relationship with Celine, and he knows that Paige craves to devour and digest the details one more time. He watches the two young people holding hands and exchanging glances throughout the story, and he is so pleased—so excited, really—that they are beginning to write their own story now. It will take some pressure off of this quest to find Cherise. If they are unsuccessful in finding her, at least Paige has someone else now in her life, someone who very likely will end up as family for both of them.

He finishes talking once more at the part where Celine is introduced as his brother's new wife, and he repeats her explanation of how she ran to Mitchell Noble at Buchenwald. Paige is a sponge, soaking up every new word or nuance in this retelling, to add more depth to what she already knows. Every time David reacts to a scene unfolding, she nods her head with raised eyebrows and doesn't need to say, "Yes, who could believe this could be true of my quiet, reserved mother."

His narration complete, Maxwell tells them he will be making his first calls to begin their search, and Paige is anxious now to take David's hand and whisk him out of the room.

"Are you okay? This is too much, too unbelievable," he says, and then he sees from her expression that she has something more on her mind.

"Quick, in my room. You have to come in. Close the door."

Although he loves her aggression, he is reticent. "Paige, calm down, Max is right here."

"I didn't mean for that, silly," she begins to say and then reconsiders. "Yes, I actually do need you to hold me immediately," she says with a laugh. He cannot resist pushing her unto the bed, smothering her face and throat with kisses, and messing her perfectly straight hairstyle until she rolls out from under him.

With an animated leap, she bounds from the bed and peeks outside the door. Satisfied that the hall is clear, she sits back down and pats the mattress spot next to her for David. He maneuvers upright from his prone position, but he immediately puts an arm around her and pulls her close. She does not mind because she wants to be able to speak to him quietly, just above a whisper.

"There was something else in the chest that Maxwell doesn't know about, something he's never seen," she says softly.

He tries his best to resist kissing her again, but it is difficult. Her lips are almost touching his ear, her tiny breaths sending slight tremors through his body. She leans back a bit, but only to reach inside her pillowcase to take out the photographs. She hands the group to him, and he sits up straighter, trying to compose himself. "Look at these pictures that my father took. I never thought of my parents as so sensual."

He looks at the first two and is moved by what he sees. This he knows is Paige's beautiful mother. She is exquisite. But within moments, he is a bit embarrassed to be viewing the poses; they are far too intimate. The loosely falling strap of a nightgown, the angle of her mother's chin in a coyly innocent pose, is nothing but seductive, and he feels like a voyeur. He lets go of the images quickly, as if they are on fire, and they fall to the blanket.

"Paige, where did you get these? I am not even sure we should be looking at them. I know what you're saying. Um, wow. She must have really been something..."

"Well, obviously I never saw this side of her. I would have said she was shy, demure. But who knows behind closed doors how anyone would act?" She gives him her most taunting grin. "The pictures were there in the trunk. Right there, hidden within napkins, just like the diary. It's something that you don't think about—your mom and dad acting like lovers."

"Paige, what makes you think your father took those? Is he in some of the pictures? I didn't see him. But I just couldn't look at them all."

"No he's not in any. But I know he took them. The background is the master bedroom at Lake Geneva. You can see her straddling the vanity chair in that room. It kind of makes me cringe to even say it."

David is silent. He is afraid to reveal what he is thinking. The words will have the power and impact of a car crash, and he struggles with his wish to keep quiet and to steer away from an impending disaster.

"What?" Paige asks. "You are keeping something inside. Do I have to pull it from you? I know you're wondering, like mother, like daughter. Do I have this provocative side?"

He knows he must say what he is thinking, what he knows is true. "Paige. Your father didn't take these. You have to know that after what you heard. You have to understand that these are professional photographs. These are Maxwell's photos of your mother."

She is stunned. She slaps him on his chest because she needs to lash out at this egregious statement. "No, you heard the story wrong. That makes no sense. They were only together in Europe before she came to America, before she married my dad."

He holds her arms still so she will not overreact. "Paige, I'm sorry. But think about it. You have to know now. You read me the words."

"Oh my God." She covers her face with her hands. She knows certain passages of the diary by heart: "For my first love...so he will know that I never stopped loving him." She calms herself with deep breaths while she thinks of what to say, what to do.

And then, suddenly, it begins to come back to her. It is an early memory that she knows she has tried to bury or ignore, that she has successfully repressed. She is transported back to their summer home, Weiss House, and she is ten years old. She and her mother had come up to Wisconsin on the train to spend two weeks in Lake Geneva after seeing her brother off on the bus for another session of summer camp in Michigan. They arrive on a Monday, and by midweek, Maxwell has joined them, pulling up in his new car, a sleek white Cadillac convertible, the top purposely down because a tall metal sculpture he is bringing with him is too tall to be transported in a car with a hard top. It is a beautiful work of outdoor art, a boy and a girl reaching upward, their hands connected by a huge crescent moon, as if they are placing it in the sky. From a distance, as Maxwell drove, passersby possibly waved at the two children standing in the backseat while they questioned the judgment of the adult driver speeding along.

Celine and Paige greet Maxwell with much fanfare, and he calls for Augie to gather some of his workers to remove the object from the car and place it in the back garden. Paige thinks it is the most beautiful statue she has ever seen and can't wait to show it to her father when he comes on Saturday to spend the weekend.

On Friday night, her mother encourages Paige to go to bed early. Even at dinner, she is sleepy eyed from a full day of swimming. Although her bedtime is always extended on the vacation nights closest to the peak of the summer solstice, the lingering hours of daylight making it hard to say good night, she goes easily to her room. She turns out her light and closes her book after barely two pages of reading.

She is not sure how long she has been sleeping when she awakens to a loud crash. She can hear a scream and shouting and doesn't know if an intruder has broken a window or if an accident has caused the noise. She sits up, almost paralyzed, for a few minutes, and then decides to run to her parents' room. Halfway down the long corridor, Celine, securing the ties of her scarlet silk robe, catches her and turns her around. "It's okay, sweetheart. A lamp has been knocked over; that's all. I'll take you back to bed." Her mother looks red faced, as if she were crying, which is disturbing to Paige, who wonders if she could be in the middle of a dream.

And a short time later, she senses her door opening. It is her father. He seems oddly disheveled. His glasses are slightly askew, and he has a grim look on his face, which he softens when he realizes her eyes are tiny, open slits. He blows her a good-night kiss.

"Daddy, you surprised me and came back early," Paige says, smiling at him until she involuntarily closes her eyes again.

"Yes, it seems I've surprised everyone," he mumbles.

In the morning, Paige is revitalized from her night's sleep and is eager to share a bear hug with her father. She finds him in the front room sitting alone, looking sullen, barely reacting to her greeting and her news of Uncle Maxwell's new purchase in the yard. When Mitchell comes to the breakfast table, he doesn't take his usual seat and just stands, eating a sweet roll. The catch-up banter that always dominates the weekend morning conversation is missing, and it takes Paige awhile to recognize that she is the only one talking. When she asks where her uncle is, her mother says he had business back in Chicago, and her father simply grabs a cup of coffee and leaves the room.

Many times during the following months, Paige asks her parents when they will see Uncle Maxwell. After six months, she literally cries to her mother how much she misses him. His indomitable spirit had been a vibrant rainbow arched over them whenever he was around. Most times, her mother turns to her in an almost scolding tone and says, "Paige, dear, please. Enough." But once, Celine takes her young daughter and wraps her in her arms and smooths the hair off her forehead and kisses her gently there. "I know. I miss him, too," she says.

When finally Paige thinks she understands the reason for his absence, she goes to her father. "Daddy, I miss Uncle Maxwell so much."

His look, his response, is far less tender. "Paige, you'll be fine without him."

"But Daddy, can't he apologize for what he did? I just don't understand."

"Then there will be things that you will not understand."

"But couldn't Uncle Maxwell just say he's sorry for breaking the lamp, or couldn't he fix it?"

Her father smiles a bit, grateful for his daughter's innocent assessment of the situation. He brings her close and bends to address her so that their eyes are locked on the same level. "Darling, some things are broken beyond repair."

It is only when nineteen-year-old Paige shares this memory with David that she finally understands why the next time she saw Uncle Maxwell was two years later. It was not until after she had lost both of her parents and her brother that Maxwell went to her hospital bed.

Chapter 25
Finding Cherise

Maxwell knew he must approach the task of finding Cherise with the tactical precision of a well-researched and meticulously executed military intelligence operation, although Paige was ready to jump on the next flight to France. She pictured herself on tour buses throughout the country, searching through flea markets and fine restaurants, street fairs in Provence and beaches on the Côte d'Azur, for the sister she sought. The impracticality of it was undeniable, but the scheme was more a reflection of a hopeful heart than a rational mind.

Maxwell's first inclination was to contact a close friend of Mitchell's from the war years. He had been a member of the French equivalent of the American Counter Intelligence Corps. In civilian life, Jonathan Deneau had established a highly regarded international private investigations firm. He was the real-life embodiment of a "private eye" from the various television series that were in vogue. This reuniting of war refugees had

been the crux of his early business, a career of emotional highs and lows, from which he derived the greatest satisfaction whenever the results could at the least
yield closure. But gradually his focus and his finances
had targeted the reuniting of people and possessions.
Displaced survivors, or sadly, more often the relatives of
victims, were desperate to reclaim property, especially
driven when they could not reclaim their loved ones.

"Maxwell, *mon ami*," Jonathan had said when they
first spoke on the phone. "This will be my pleasure, my
gift to you. And I will be discreet, you may be assured."
Of course, Maxwell had to be completely honest with
Jonathan in this search for the child of his brother's
wife, and he was thankful that the French definition of
sexual morality was extremely loose and forgiving.

Together they laid out a logical plan to locate the
young woman who was described. Initially, Jonathan
reached out to French colleagues, who polled their best
contacts, including former members of the WWII resistance. Surely someone must remember the entrancing, young Celine Cheval, the name that had been
on her Christian identification papers and wedding
license. Could she have placed a baby in the town of
Pau, where she lived briefly, or in or around Château de
Chenonceau, where she had aided the underground,
or any villages known to have been receptive to the hidden Jewish children? There was another idea. Just as
the displaced children of the English countryside had
come from the larger cities, especially London, perhaps
Celine had made someone promise that after the war
they would place her child in the city from which most

of the French Jews had fled, Paris. Because she would have delivered the child before her time at the concentration camp, it may have been before her final decision to abandon her faith, when she still would have hoped that her child would find her roots.

Marcel Beauchard was a well-known leader in the French resistance who had retired to the town of Angoulerie, almost halfway between Pau in the south and the town of Chenonceaux. "He does not accept visitors anymore," his daughter had said, sadly, when Philippe Marchand had called her from the investigation firm. She was preparing to deny whatever request he would put forth. But the father had heard her repeat the name "Celine Cheval" into the phone she had grabbed by his bedside. Although he had barely spoken a word in a week, he bellowed in his old, forgotten voice, "Celine, Snow White." And when his daughter turned to him, she saw that his eyes were open and alert and that he had raised his head. "Yes, come and see what he has to say," she offered Monsieur Marchand.

When the investigator came to the door, he said what a privilege it would be for him to meet the legendary hero. But the daughter had her cautions. "I love my father, and I am so proud of him. But he stays in seclusion now. You may be shocked to see his deteriorated state."

"I had no idea," Philippe admitted.

"That is his wish. Both his mind and body are failing. We don't know why—an early dementia, maybe the shocks and shells of the war years taking their toll. But he is cognizant enough to have asked us to protect his privacy. There is the pride of his accomplishments, the wish to preserve the image of his former robust self, but mainly there is guilt for surviving when so many compatriots died."

"But he helped so many," the investigator interrupted.

"He remembers best those whom he could not protect—a group slaughtered while he was scouting ahead for a safer place, for instance. For some years, when I was a young girl, he enjoyed his special status— the honors, awards, and accolades he received, the visits from dignitaries. But by the time I was ten or twelve, he began the shaking, the despair. And we had to shelve away that chapter of his life, as if it were contained in a book in his library. But when he heard this name, part of his old self emerged instantly. He smiled broadly when I invited you here."

As Philippe entered the bedroom, he turned back to the daughter for reassurance. "He is having a good morning," she said. "He is expecting you. He has been waiting for you." She told Philippe to pull the chair close to the bed and to direct his speech mainly to her father's right ear.

"Monsieur Beauchard, it is a pleasure to—" Philippe began but was interrupted by the touch of the man's hand to his arm.

"You know Celine? We called her Snow White. Skin as white as snow, hair as black as ebony."

"I did not know her. I am sorry that I did not. But we have been asked to find someone who might have remembered her from the war years."

"Well, you have found one man." His speech was slow but clear. "She was quite unforgettable. Sweet, quiet, soft...but driven and strong on her missions." Suddenly, the man had a perfect memory. "This was sometime probably in 1942 to 1943. She was with us almost a full year."

Philippe smiled, thinking perhaps he had struck gold. "May I ask something?" he asked. "Might you remember if she had been pregnant or delivered a baby?"

Immediately, the man's face turned angry. "Absolutely not. You have the wrong woman. She was an innocent angel. She was a heartbreaker, not a lover. She waved off any of our advances, and we teased that she slept at night with her gun at her side, not to protect her from the enemy, but from us." He made an agitated coughing sound. Without warning, he closed his eyes, and quickly the snores of sleep could be heard. When Philippe turned to the daughter, she motioned for him to follow her to the front room.

"Thank you for coming," the daughter said sincerely. "I don't know if you have the information you sought. But I am excited to have had my father back for a few minutes."

Some of the leads yielded comical results. There were records of a Cherise Leclaire having been born in the main maternity ward of the Pau community at an appropriate date. But the investigator locating the appropriately aged young woman had opened the door to a redheaded mother and her circle of redheaded children. And when inquiries had been made about the grandmother perhaps originally adopting this mother as a baby, they were led to an upstairs bedroom. There, an older woman was recuperating from a bad cold. Although she was now almost all gray, a few shiny red strands circled her hairline and wove through her eyebrows.

Other clues pointed them toward charming towns and historical sites that were well worth the journey, if not for the disappointment of the quest. While the initial investigation did not uncover information at the Château de Chenonceau that would help their search, Jonathan Deneau encouraged Maxwell to take his niece to that location for their own peace of mind and for the exhilaration of being at such a majestic place. They knew this was where Celine had breathed, eaten, walked, and participated in a heroic operation during the war. Monsieur Deneau had contacted the current owners of the sprawling landmark estate, the Menier family from the chocolate empire, requesting a private meeting and special access for his American friend.

They greeted Maxwell Noble as the celebrity that he was and gave him and his niece full entrée to the buildings and grounds, hoping that Maxwell might be moved to take photographs that would be great publicity abroad for the chateau as a tourist destination. And, of course, they were right. Months after his visit, Maxwell negotiated multipage spreads on the property in both *Look* magazine and *Architectural Digest* that sent droves of Americans their way. After the Palace of Versailles, Château de Chenonceau became the second-most-visited French chateau.

The northeast perspective of the façade was the most breathtaking view and appeared as the cover photo of a coffee-table book that was eventually compiled by Maxwell's publisher. There was hardly a castle in the world that could project such a magnificent architectural integration into its environment. From this angled perspective, the visitor could see how the main entrance was accessible from one bank of the River Cher, and then with a series of arched bridge tunnels at its base, the chateau spanned the entire width of the water. At the right distance, at the perfect light of day, a spectacular duplicate image of the structure was reflected in the rippling mirror of the river itself.

A mixture of Gothic and Renaissance designs, rounded towers, pointed spires, and ornately projecting windows all enticed visitors inside, while elaborate gardens and parks, stone terraces, and spectacular sculptures drew them to the grounds. There were sumptuous floral beds, a Green Garden by the designer Bernard Palissy, and an intricate Italian maze.

As entrancing as the physical structure was, the history behind the Château de Chenonceau was even more fascinating. Although there are references to buildings on the site as early as the eleventh century and knowledge that it had passed through the Marques family in the fourteen hundreds until the owners had to sell it to pay off debts, the true roots of the current version began in the mid-fifteen hundreds. King Henry II presented his mistress, Diane de Poitiers, with the castle, and she would be the first in a long line of women who would lay claim to the famous residence. Diane de Poitiers would be credited with commissioning some of the most important improvements to the castle, including the architect Philibert de L'Orme's river bridge extension. But she would eventually lose her tenure there. Following the death of King Henry in 1559, his widow, Catherine de' Medici, evicted Diane to another chateau and then took her place in the grand bedroom. She expanded the chateau and completed the extension of the bridge to the opposite bank, adding a two-story gallery above the water. On her death, her daughter-in-law became the next in line of a succession of female owners who gave it the moniker "the women's castle" or "Chateau des Dames." By the seventeen hundreds, the estate had passed from royal owners steeped in its debt to wealthy landed gentry.

And still it was women who brought her to life. The beautiful wife of Claude Dupin loved the chateau. Louise Dupin, with a focus and family roots in finance, literature, and theater, held salons that included the noted authors and playwrights of the Enlightenment.

After a succession of owners in the next centuries, Henry Menier purchased Chenonceau in 1913, and it has remained in that family. The interior of the chateau is now a museum showcasing antique furniture, major works of art from the Old Masters, sixteenth-century Flanders tapestries, and priceless carpets. While the much-loved Madam Dupin was able to thwart destruction to the castle during the Revolution, the estate did play a role in both of the wars of the twentieth century. In World War I, the gallery was turned into a hospital facility, and proudly during WWII, the building provided an escape route from the Germans; one side of the bridge structure was in the occupied zone, and the other side was in the free zone. Early in the war, the chateau was hit by the Germans, and then on June 7, 1944, when it was under German occupation, it suffered damage from Allied bombs. In the next decade, architect Bernard Voisin would begin his work to revitalize the jewel from the ravages of time.

Paige was so taken with everything she saw that she spontaneously played with dramatic poses among the flowers, fountains, and statues, and Maxwell couldn't help turning his camera to follow her actions. For the first time, he allowed his beautiful niece to be included in his published pictures, and not only were there rave reviews of his work, but his entrancing model was continually touted as a young Audrey Hepburn. Maxwell's new friend and business associate, Oscar de la Renta, contacted him to allow Paige to be a runway model. But Paige and her uncle both quickly agreed that she would maintain her life of anonymity.

Although it was easy to be caught up in the fairy-tale surroundings of Château de Chenonceau, neither Paige nor Maxwell had forgotten what had taken them there. The current Monsieur Menier had promised to query other family members for memories of a woman named Celine during the war years, but Paige had a feeling that some of the domestic staff could provide answers. Yvette Leland, who was a third-generation housekeeper, said she would discuss the resistance worker with her mother, who had worked during that time and was now retired to a small home in the area. Finally, Celine was placed at the castle, befriended by Madame Leland, who easily remembered her for her strength and sweetness, her fair-skinned beauty, and her perfect figure. "I think she would have confided in me if there had been a baby," the woman had assured her daughter.

So Maxwell and Paige Noble left Chenonceau to travel north to the shimmering capital city of France, to Paris, to pursue a third possible path.

Chapter 26
The Familiar Movements of Her Body

It is a beautiful clothing store—a Paris boutique, just outside of the Marais district. The clothes in the window range from the demurely elegant, which could be purchased by a wealthy, religious Jewish woman living in the quarter, to the edgiest designer cuts for the young, window-shopping tourists. Maxwell is perusing the racks of dresses closest to the door while he waits for a salesperson to respond to the ring of the entry doorbell. He is hoping that this time, his resource has been correct and the trail will not lead to another dead end. He is not sure how much more disappointment either of them can take. When he had shown the picture of Celine at his second café in the district, in hopes someone might identify a person resembling her, but almost twenty years younger, he had been directed to this shop. "The age, *monsieur,* may not correspond to what you say, but the face, *le visage*—more than similar."

And then he hears a shriek. "Oh God!"—not "*Mon Dieu,*" which would have been the words of a French woman, but distinctly "Oh God!" again, and then the word "Maman." This time the word is distinctly French— not the American "mama," but the oval-mouth unfinished "a"—it is the "Maman" that Paige would say. And when Maxwell turns, he sees that the words have come from Paige, who now covers her mouth in astonishment. "Oh my God!" Paige says again. "Maman! It can't be possible." He follows where Paige is looking. And then he sees her as well. It is not a young Celine. It is Celine, as if she had never been hurt, never shot, never buried, never grieved—Celine, as if she had continued living. Celine, not the mother of twelve-year-old Paige, but the mother of the young college student that is Paige today. His own heart leaps, although he does not shout out as his niece did. When he sees the woman, his stomach lifts with the once-familiar butterflies he felt as a young man in love.

They approach her cautiously, together, as she takes an instinctive, protective step backward. The woman cannot take her eyes off of Paige. It is frightening to her. She sees a familiarity in Paige's face that is both unnerving and seductive. Her English is nearly perfect— better than perfect—enhanced by the decorations of her beautiful French accent. "I apologize if I am staring. You remind me of someone," she is compelled to offer immediately. And when she sees them continue to stare at her, examine her, she adds, "Perhaps there is a mutual recognition."

Paige is too paralyzed, unable to respond immediately. Maxwell is regaining his composure. He wonders for a moment if he is actually dreaming. None of this makes sense. This girl/woman could not be his daughter. It is hard to tell how old she is; she has a timeless beauty that belies her age. It is a beauty that has long been imprinted on his own soul. But there is a certain maturity about this woman that would have to make her at least twenty years older than he would have anticipated.

"I apologize for our manners," Maxwell finally says, and Paige, silent now, nods in complicitous agreement. "I should introduce myself. I am Maxwell Noble, and this is my niece, Paige. We have come from America, from Chicago."

"I am pleased to meet you. Please, welcome to my store. I am Risa Solomon."

"Might there be a private space where we could sit and talk a bit?" he asks very respectfully.

The woman calls to someone in another room. "Annette, please. Would you come in front to watch the shop temporarily?" she says in French. A tall and thin beauty, whom Maxwell presumed would be a couturier model on fashion-show days, emerges from behind a silver drapery. Risa is happy that the girl is too preoccupied tending to a run in her stocking as she approaches them to take notice of the visitors she plans to take to the rear salon. She knows Annette would have too many questions about the distinguished man and the enchanting, shy girl. And Risa knows she can provide no answers, yet.

She gestures for Paige and Maxwell to follow her to a private area. The room is also beautifully furnished, with a dark-wood floor partially covered by a yellow and gray area rug and hosting a circle of comfortable chairs in an elegant French toile fabric. Risa offers her visitors tea from a brightly polished silver service, and they are happy to watch her preparations, as if she were putting on a play. Although neither of them voices it, they are each drawn to the familiar movements of her body.

"Now, then," she says when they have each selected their tea bags and sugar cubes. "I feel you have come here for a reason other than to choose the perfect dress for this charming young lady. How may I help you?"

They look at each other, and Maxwell nods to indicate that he will be the one to respond. He is choosing his words carefully. He does not want to scare her away. He does not want her to think they are after something from her. He wants her to understand that maybe, just maybe, they have something mutual to offer. Finally he speaks. "Do you have any idea why we are here?"

"I do not. You have me at a disadvantage."

"But when you first saw us, there was a familiarity?" he questions. "Like you have seen us before."

"Monsieur, I apologize. Not a familiarity with you. But yes, with the young girl."

Paige raises her head. She has been too scared to look at her until now. She didn't want to alert her to her own neediness. If Paige had had her way, she would have embraced this woman and cried into the beautiful, fragile silk of her designer dress. Paige was never so aware of the hunger, the emptiness that has been a part of her life for so long.

"We have come," Maxwell begins, measuring his speech and pressing his feet into the floor, as if he needs to be rooted to the ground. He wants to speak, but his words are very slowly and meticulously being formed. He is embarrassed to seem so inarticulate, but the simplest phrases seem trapped within him. He clears his throat and starts again. "We have come as part of a journey. We are looking for someone. And we have been led to this very location to help solve a puzzle of our lives."

"And you think I may be of assistance in this?"

"Well, actually, we had thought that you might be a very important piece of the puzzle."

"And now?"

"And now we do not know what to think. I do not think anymore that you may be the exact one I was looking for, but I do believe you are a part of the picture."

"You have a story to tell me." There is a self-assuredness about this woman. She rises from her chair, teacup in hand, and very gracefully, with no hesitation to prepare for spillage, submerges the tea bag three times. "This story, I believe, begins in the war."

Paige breaks in now. "How did you know? Do you think you know us?"

Risa recognizes that Paige is pleading with her eyes. She says nothing but raises her hands outward in the universal sign that she does not know. She can only offer her what she does know. If they leave empty handed, she will, at least, not have misled them. She will answer their questions as truthfully as possible. But she has had her own psychological issues lingering from those years.

It is Maxwell's turn to speak again. He gives no prelude and dives right into the story—the story of intertwining lives from two distant continents that has set his heart racing at a maddening pace for the past few decades. "The year was 1942, and I was a young American photographer, part of the US Army. I was just following orders in assignments that would eventually bring the European theater to the homes of American citizens. But this time, it was an easy assignment. I was to go from my base in London to the English countryside, where thousands of children had been evacuated from the danger of German bombs pummeling the big city." He pauses, and a warm smile comes to his lips. "Picture me a different man—many years younger and twenty pounds off my body. I could barely keep my khaki pants held up by my belt. My cheeks are as gaunt as any underfed recruit—I am young and innocent. Even though I am driving around in what could potentially be a war zone, I am naïve enough to be excited. I am in an army jeep with a knapsack, a camera, and a map, and I think I am the luckiest guy in the world. People are acting as if I am important, and I am delighted by this new-found admiration. I am very caught up in myself because residents of each town I am crossing are running to me to be in a picture. They are chasing me to be part of a shot—a picture that most likely they will never see but will be used to document history."

For a moment, he has left the room and is back on the provincial street. "I know I am in England, but somehow a group of young ladies are surrounding me, and I am almost sure they are speaking French. Three beautiful young girls—'teenagers,' as we say at home— are planting red lipstick kisses on my neck and my collar to entice me to snap a shot of them. It is my first taste of the lure of a uniform, and it is still a bit astonishing to me that these giggling girls are paying me such attention. And then I hear a laugh behind me. The laugh is so young and sweet and innocent that it has the song of wildflowers in its notes; it has the smell of the roses in the English fields but the taste of the bubbling wine of France."

Maxwell has been speaking to a spot he has chosen on a floral leaf pattern of the area rug. But now he raises his eyes and looks at the women, eyeing Risa first and then shifting to Paige. "This is how enticing the lyrical laugh is. And when I turn to the laugh, I see the most beautiful of all of the girls of the group. But she is not eager to join her friends in the showering of kisses. Perhaps because she is obviously a bit older and more mature looking, she calls them all silly and berates them for their foolishness. Although I knew no French, I did know the pantomimes of women. When they tease her back, they say her name, and that is all I can understand. But I know that magical name will be my favorite name forever. I want to talk to her, yes, but I want to hold her, too. I want to be the one to plant kisses all over her." He stops from his story and seeks the spot on the floor again. "I am sorry. I am carried away. But I knew immediately that I was in love with this girl."

Risa is intrigued. She takes another sip of her tea and begins to place the cup and saucer on the table, innocently asking, "And this name, this magical name?"

Maxwell pauses and looks directly into Risa's eyes. "It is Celine."

She is startled by the name, as Maxwell hoped, but he does not react quickly enough to stop her hand from shaking and her hot tea from splattering on her foot. He watches her point and extend her foot and blot the liquid with her linen napkin.

He takes his seat again, between the two ladies, and places his hand gently on her arm. The move seems too intimate for people who have just met, but he has the need to make a physical connection with her. Something is going on, but he doesn't understand it yet. On his other side, he reaches to hold Paige's hand. He has unwittingly connected them. He feels that the puzzle pieces will be falling into place soon, that this journey will not be in vain.

"Of course, you know, by then I only wanted to take photographs of that one girl. And when I began to snap my pictures, she was a most willing model." He stands up slowly again. Lost in the memory, he walks over to an exquisite étagère in the room and picks up a framed photograph from one of the shelves. It is a picture of an attractive woman posing on a fashion runway, undoubtedly in one of Risa's designs. He puts the photo down but does not turn back toward the women. "A model, that is, until she grabbed my camera and insisted on taking my picture. And I did not hesitate to release it to her. This, my most precious treasured companion, had become just another object once I saw Celine. I would have given her anything." He faces them now to see that they are following the story, and he can tell they are waiting for more. "Of course, the other young girls just dispersed out of annoyance or respect by the time Celine took over. And I actually had to—and this I am thankful for having the foresight to do—I had to call back one of the girls in the group so that she could take a picture of Celine and me—of us together." He bites slightly on his lower lip and shakes his head. "Do you know the essence of a photographer? Do you understand how we are most comfortable distancing ourselves from life... how we are content to be observers of life? And now, for the first time, I was part of the picture. I was in the moment, not just recording the event."

Paige rises and moves to stand next to her uncle. She takes his hand and balances on her tiptoes briefly, kissing his cheek. She wants him to know that she is open to this love story and doesn't see it as a betrayal of her mother's family, her own family that was to come. He understands that and continues.

"These thoughts, these feelings I am articulating now...you know they are formulated only through the perspective of time. This picture of us together—" Once more, he hesitates, and then he turns directly to Paige. "It is hidden in a drawer. It has always lived in the bottom desk drawer in my study. In the locked drawer that you never discovered, never questioned. And I have opened it to look at the photograph hundreds of times over the years."

Now Risa reaches out for more of the story. "And this girl, this young woman, Celine—what happened with her?"

Maxwell looks over to Paige once more. "Go on. I'm okay," she says, reassuring him that she is mature enough to be comfortable with these revelations.

"What happened to her is what happened to us," he says, turning to Risa. "We spent the most glorious days of my life together. 'Do you want to see the most heavenly place?' Celine had said, taking my hand and pulling me with her. I had to stop her when we had gone barely ten yards. But I didn't let go of that soft and perfect hand. I said, 'Wait. I need my camera—and my knapsack.' I walked her back to the spot where they were. And we had this conversation that I have never forgotten."

"'What else is in there?' she wanted to know, and she started to unbuckle the canvas bag.

"'I don't know—just things.'

"'A picture of your sweetheart back home, perhaps?'

"'No picture of a sweetheart. That I promise,' I said, and she looked pleased. 'No picture, yet, that is, until I develop the ones we just took. And then I will have many pictures to show the girl I meet at my next town when she asks.' The thought line was a bit circuitous for someone tackling the translation of a second language in her head, so Celine appeared confused for a few moments, and then she smiled. 'You are teasing me—this I see now. I will still be your sweetheart.'

"Two young people were drawn together as strongly as if we were polar opposites of giant magnets. We borrowed bicycles and roamed the landscape, the best way to take in the fields of flowers. When the first startling profusion of purple buds came into our view, I jumped from my bike to steal a bunch and present it to her. She brought it to her face and breathed in the pungent scent and then began the cutest sneezing fit I had ever witnessed. I grabbed back the bouquet and flung it into my basket, and then I disentangled her from the bike she was straddling and took her in my arms. We were in love, and we could hardly keep our bodies apart, although we tried to maintain a composure and decorum the first days, as we came to know each other. But, eventually, we could not help ourselves. By the third day, when we were alone, I almost carelessly grabbed my camera by its strap and flung it over my shoulder. And then I scooped her sweet, light body into my arms and carried her to a nearby barn. I laid her down gently on a pile of horse blankets, conveniently placed there as if they were prepared for this moment. Neither of us began the day as experienced lovers. I am being honest now. She had never been with anyone, and I had only the typical experiences for a young man of my age. But, as it turned out, we discovered each other in the most gentle and passionate fashion." Despite what Paige has indicated, he is still careful with his words. "And it was not just our bodies that we discovered were aligned. After we made love the first time, she began to fiddle with the dog-tag chain around my neck. And then she brought it close to her vision and read all of the details. I saw that she had the most incredulous look on her face. 'Maxwell Noble, *Mon Dieu*,' she said. 'I will tell you a secret. You will tell no one, *oui*?'

"'No one,' I assured her.

"She looked around as if scouting to make sure that no farmhand was tending the animals nearby. 'If my secret is out, I will not know where to go. But I will tell you this. I am like you,' she said.

"'What,' I asked, 'a lonely soul who has finally found its mate?' But, no. This is what she said.

"'I have been sent from my home. I am hiding here as a Christian girl. *Mais, je suis en juif.* I am Jewish like you.'"

At this point, Risa cannot keep herself from interrupting. "Please, Maxwell, please I can take no more. Please go forward in the story and then you can go backward again. Please, tell me, what happened with this woman, this girl, Celine? And what has brought you here to me?"

Maxwell becomes optimistic from her impatience, her desperate tone, so he does as she asks and skips forward in his narration. "We were together for less than a month, and then I was called to another location. The army wanted me to proceed back to London. You must understand. London had been my dream at one time, and now I could only wish to think of a way to stay where I was in this quiet, country setting with Celine." He pauses and takes a deep breath.

"And then the war was at its full strength, and I was assigned to follow troops in other locations. I didn't wish to see the sights I once had dreamed about. I only cared to pull from my knapsack the stash of pictures I had eventually been able to develop, and I stared at them many times during my days. Eventually, of course, the war ended, and I ran back to the town of Derbyshire loaded down not just with my photographic equipment, but with some perfumes and French lace. But she wasn't there. I had known that she returned to France to escort more of the children shortly after I was originally called away, but I presumed she had returned. But she was nowhere to be found. And when I went to France, to the town where she said they had been housed, the townspeople there would give me no information."

It is obvious that Risa may begin to cry. "And so you never saw her again—never knew if she survived the war?" she asks, with too much emotion for someone unconnected to the story.

Maxwell looks at her thoughtfully and takes her hand. "But you are wrong. I saw her again and knew her for many years after. By the greatest of coincidences, I was introduced to her back in America. Back in my home town of Chicago. Introduced by my own brother." There is a long hesitation now. "Celine was his new wife."

And now Paige knows she must jump into the conversation. "Celine was my mother." She watches Risa's reaction. It is the emergence of a most enchanting smile that she thought was lost to her forever. She looks over to Maxwell. It has captured him as well. But now they both want her to speak. They are having trouble reading her.

Risa's hand comes up to cover her mouth. "*Mon Dieu.* She survived. Celine survived the war." She sees that her words seem too personal, so she wants to take a step back. "But for you, Maxwell—what a shock."

"She survived the war, yes. And she had a fortunate life in America. She had a husband, two children, and a brother-in-law who loved her with their very souls. But I will skip ahead again. Yes, she survived the war, but she could not survive the random act of violence, the gang shooting in Chicago, that also took the life of her husband, my brother Mitchell, and her oldest child, Roger, and left her daughter, my niece Paige, injured and orphaned. And only these many years later when a diary was discovered did we come to believe that perhaps there was a daughter from our time together."

At this point, Paige breaks in and shows the diary entry to her. On this trip, she carries a copy of it in her purse. She hands it to Risa, who reads it silently. Risa covers her face with her hands and folds her head into her lap, and she sobs. Paige takes the letter from her light grasp and reads aloud one section:

> So many times I have thought of sharing my story with you. But then I am overcome by the threads of a life that include terror, separation, loss, and grief, and I know I cannot tell you only half of a story—only the fairy-tale part. I know you cannot imagine your world changing, and truly that was me at your age. And that is what I want for you always: the cushioning security that the embracing arms of our small family can offer you. That we will always be together.
>
> And so, too, if you had known Cherise—like you, my darling, she was a heart of my heart. Cherise, if you have been renamed, I shall always wonder, but that is who you will always be to me. Our separation was so unbearable, but so necessary for all that the war would bring. What are you doing? What do you look like? I know that I will recognize you any time, and I will pray your fate has been a good one, an easier path than if we had stayed together.

That decision to separate was not a decision of the heart, but of the mind. If people knew what I have done, they would judge me, judge my choice—my abandonment. But people do not know what went on then in a world gone insane that made you feel nothing would ever be easy or normal or safe.

She refolds the note into quarters and puts it back in her purse. "That is all that was written," Paige says. "And I would never have really known what to make of it if I hadn't shared my discovery with my uncle. He thought he knew the answer. He thought he knew what it meant. And he begged me to understand when he told me the story of how he had met and how he had been with my mother, had loved my mother before she was taken to the concentration camp…"

Hearing those words, Risa gasps, but Paige decides to continue. "Before she heard the name 'Noble' again, before she met my father. You have no idea, but this made things clearer to me. I always felt there was something very odd in the relationship of my mother and Uncle Maxwell. This you don't know. When I last saw them together, I was just ten years old. And then he was estranged from the family for the next few years. And then my mother died."

Maxwell is anxious to take over the story. "It was clear to me, although you have to understand that I was stunned by the revelation. I believe that she must have had my baby in France, where she returned to help. How I hate myself now for not making it back to her in time—how much she must have endured, to feel it would be best to give this baby away. Well, now we know more about the horrors of the war. The heart of her heart that she wonders about, wonders if she is safe, wonders if she is renamed—this Cherise, must have been her baby—our baby. Both Paige and I have clung to this hope so that we could find someone to be part of the family we have lost. And so for a month of this summer, we have done nothing but follow clues to find where a baby might have been placed—somewhere between Pau in France where she came from and Buchenwald in Germany, where my brother found her."

Suddenly, Risa stands and turns toward them. "Oh my God—wait. I cannot take this anymore without speaking. What you are saying is shocking to me, and now what I am to tell will be the same for you." She pauses and shakes her head. They cannot tell if she has bad news for them or good news. There is not sadness in her voice, but the look on her face is hard to interpret. Is it a look of contentment, relief, even serenity? "This Cherise she refers to—this Cherise she abandoned—I am this Cherise. You do not know this, although you have heard and said my name. Risa—this is a nickname, as you would call it, for the name Cherise. Celine was my sister. Celine, heart of my heart, was my twin sister."

Maxwell and Paige catch each other with mirrored looks of unmitigated surprise. They squeeze each other's hands as tightly as possible, but they both reserve any speech, waiting for her to say more. Risa sits back down to compose herself, covers her face with her hands, and tries to continue. "In the course of a few minutes only, I have found that Celine survived the war, only to be lost again. I will need to digest this—to come to terms with this. But you have given me a gift. And now, when you tell me the fate of my sister, a sister I had thought perished in the war itself, something else is making sense for me." Deliberately, she reaches to take one of their hands in each of hers. She is clasping them hard as she pulls the hands together to rest on each side of her cheeks.

"The date—the date of the tragedy, this shooting in Chicago—you must tell me." There is desperation in her voice. They are each hesitant to speak the date. It is as if Paige and Maxwell Noble are one mind with con-current thoughts. Neither has the date on the tip of the tongue because they have each tried so hard to bury the horror. They could sooner come up with the date of the Kennedy assassination: November 22 of the next year. But for Risa now, they are each willing to go back to the painful time. The date is in their consciousness and will be spoken aloud by one or the other once more.

"It was April 1962."

For a moment, Paige and Maxwell each think that the other has been the one to speak, not focusing on the speech and accent that neither of them owns.

So Risa repeats. "It was in April. The year was 1962. *Mon Dieu*. It all makes sense now. I am right, *non*?"

"So you knew. You followed the story," Maxwell says.

"No, my new family—I followed only my own story. On that date—for the exact date I will need help…"

"April fourteenth, 1962," Paige and Maxwell now reply, hesitatingly, in unison.

"*Oui.* April fourteenth, I am sure the records will show. On that date, I was taken to the hospital, an excruciating pain in my abdomen. I was alone in the house, so my neighbors helped me. Appendicitis, we thought. None of us were medical people. None of us were thinking about the location of the appendix."

She stops talking for a moment, almost wincing as if the pain were fresh again. "But the diagnosis was unclear. Nothing was revealed. I was sent home." She holds up her finger, asking for another minute to complete her story. "But after that, I felt a lingering emptiness inside, as if an organ had been removed." She pauses again. "And now I know. After all these years, I know I was right."

She walks over to Paige and embraces her. She puts her arms around her and kisses her on each cheek. And then she steps back to just look at her. "Oh, Paige, my dear. You are my precious Celine reborn and delivered to me all grown up—and so close to the age when I last saw her. You are my niece, and Maxwell, I understand you are my family as well." She steps back again. "One second, please, while I compose myself." She moves to a mirror and takes out tissues from a nearby container, wiping away her makeup, smeared from tears welling in her eyes. And then she straightens her dress and approaches them again.

"*S'il vous plait*—you know this one French phrase, I have no doubt," Risa finally says after a long silence. "May I suggest one thing?" She pauses again. "So we may be more comfortable."

But Maxwell breaks in. "Of course. Wait—may I take you somewhere? Perhaps back to our hotel. It is beautiful. We could eat there."

Risa laughs, shakes her head and smiles, and she claps her hands together just one time, ending them in a prayer pose with the tips of her forefingers touching her nose, as if to put an exclamation point on her response. When she does it, her eyes are half closed, so she does not notice Maxwell's reaction to her. He is confused, captivated by this most uncanny memory of Celine's own gestures.

"This I think," Risa finally says. "You are a man used to being in charge, to moving on his own terms. But now you are in my territory, my domain. So I would ask that you come with me to my home. It is only blocks away. Not as lovely, perhaps, as your hotel, but I promise you, it will be worth the short walk."

Chapter 27
Fragile as a Limoges Figurine

When they have each settled into a comfortable chair in the front room of her apartment, Risa begins to speak. "You have told me a story, and now it is my turn. This all eventually found its way into history books. But we were living it. My father, Papa, was the smartest and the dumbest person. He felt the wave in Germany. A scholar, of course, that's what so many of us were—the Jewish people of any country, I believe. They could deal with us first because they were our employers. Scholars work for schools, libraries, governments. Scholars and people of the arts—when you don't value what they have to offer or when you fear it, then those with such talents are most expendable to the state. Even the people they truly needed—the scientists, the engineers, the doctors—they would lose their positions in due time. The businessmen, they would lose their businesses, from the smallest hat store to the largest department store. The state would destroy or confiscate them all.

"But I will back up just a bit. My brilliant father, his head in a book, lifts it once, and there is my beautiful mother—a young ballerina. She had been pulled early from her formal schooling and had been performing with the ballet academy since she was sixteen years old. He is mesmerized when he looks up and sees her at the outdoor café. He uncharacteristically lays his book down, the edge of it catching the saucer's rim, and a drop of his coffee dots the print. He does not care; he does not even blot it. He watches her walk past the café and then retrace her steps. He thinks she is looking for a friend she may be meeting. And then he realizes she is looking at him. He is unnerved as she approaches. He is a professor of literature, a language scholar, yet he can think of no word to describe the way she floats in his direction. He thinks of the thinnest, lightest, most graceful of the animals. She is a gazelle or a doe. And she is prancing toward him.

"'Is this chair available?' she asks him.

"Now it makes sense. She has been walking to and fro to find a vacant seat, and she was eyeing not him, but his solo table. She will no doubt move the chair to another location where her friends are. He can utter no words but motions for her to take it.

"But instead she goes to sit down, to share the spot with him. He is shocked, so he rises, as any gentleman would when a lady is taking an adjacent seat. Her immediate desire is simple and easily fulfilled—to find someone in the busy, popular café who would share a table. And by the most convenient coincidence, his own long-term goal is also seamlessly satisfied. But his desire has broader implications: to have someone with whom to share his life. And that was how they met in 1923. They were married the same year.

"When we were eight years old, in 1933, Adolf Hitler came to power as the chancellor of Germany, and then, of course, the Nazi dictator. And within eighteen months, our bright, pragmatic father—unlike so many of the intellectuals who kept their posts and waited as Hitler marched, marched, marched his men through the streets—left Germany with his young family, not running while looking behind, but leaping while looking ahead. Perhaps he was inspired by the graceful *grand jeté* that was my mother's signature move. English colleagues had helped arrange a position for him at a small college in London. His double advanced degrees qualified him as a professor, not only in German literature, but in the language itself. He was easily placed because he was not pompous, not too self-important to accept a position below his station. He wanted only to be in a large city where my mother might also have a chance to perform, to dazzle. So we were raised first as little German frauleins, and then as English young ladies.

"But my wonderful Papa was not the farsighted man we had thought. As my mother rose to prominence, her reputation grew across Europe. Eventually, the owner of the French ballet was in negotiations for her contract. And in 1937, we were off again, this time to Paris. For Maman, it was a dream, and our Papa, as you can guess, only wished to fulfill her dreams. So now we were little mademoiselles, strolling the streets surrounding our lovely apartment in the Marais. We loved Paris so much.

We hoped to sound as if the beautiful French language was our native tongue. Celine and I worked hard with our linguistic lessons, on erasing the characteristic German patterns from our speech, on making sure that our d's did not sound like t's, that our w's were not v's, that our words were not always accented on the first syllable. Our father's new position was actually at a more prestigious institution than it had been in London. Connections once again had paved his way, but now to the University of Paris, to the *Sorbonne*. So we were in the way again when the Nazis came to that country to expel, and then to exterminate, their Jews.

"By that time, however, as the Nazis moved in to establish their occupation of Paris, Mother's profession had taken its toll on her body. Papa had always worried so much about our mother. She was as strong as a mortar and pestle and as fragile as a Limoges figurine. The physical demands on a dancer of her class are always great, yet she had certain dietary restrictions to maintain her thin, statuesque appearance. The bulkier girls had been weeded out early in the process, first taking smaller parts in the ballet lines and eventually fading back to their hometowns to give lessons to the neighborhood girls. But my mother was a prima ballerina, practicing day after day, performing night after night. This wears on a body.

"Oh, how the Germans enjoyed the spectacle of the ballet, each praising my mother or their own favorite dancer in the various numbers. 'Bravo!' they would shout at the curtain calls. But one day, a disgusting group of officers, drunk with their liquor and their power after leaving their seats and stopping at a nearby bar, saw my mother as she exited the stage door. She knew that her expulsion from the ballet might be imminent, might come with a reluctant call or note to report to the director's office, that it was his great regret that he would have to release her, that he was made to release her from the newest government directives. As it turned out, though, the blow was not as soft and figurative as she might have imagined, but literal. The men baited her, surrounded her, called her 'Jewess,' and spit on her. They knew it was the same angel they had applauded just one hour before, but now, walking on their earthly street, she was as any Jew. They didn't need to strike her—they merely blocked her way to trip her, and their work was complete. The break in her leg, in her already thin tibia, could not heal in her compromised, bilious state. It happened so quickly, moments before any of the male dancers emerged from the same doorway. The arrogant soldiers, proud of their accomplishment, still had the decency to look the other way and allow her horrified colleagues to carry her home. They had lifted her often. She was a bird in their arms, but a bird now whose wing had been clipped. She would never fly again; this they knew. What they could not have imagined, however, was that despite the best efforts of my distraught father and the immediate response of our neighbor, a physician, the break led to an infection, to pneumonia, and to the death of my precious mother.

"And it was not that much later that the terror came once more. It was 1940, and we were sixteen years of age. Finally, we had fallen asleep after an hour of sharing confidences about who we wished to have as our latest boyfriends. It is girl talk and giggling that is the best evidence that we were back to our old selves after an extended period of mourning. But it was a short-lived respite. Celine and I woke up to screams from the floor above. Though the formidable walls of the apartment building usually afforded a respectable privacy between units, sometimes through the vents, we heard the most vociferous emotions of the marriage of our upstairs neighbors, the passionate intimacies, as well as the occasional fights. But what we heard then was more than disturbing, and there were voices that were unfamiliar. They reverberate in my ears even now. 'Out of bed, you whore!' the Germans screamed at poor Mrs. Dresden. And then a grunt from her husband. We heard the foot stamps of heavy boots overhead, and somehow we knew that Mr. Dresden had received a kick in his gut or his chest. 'No, no, please. This is my husband. He can cause you no problem,' his wife pleaded.

"'Just get him dressed, you witch,' they answered. We both had seen our neighbors in the evening, in their bedclothes, occasionally taking them some leftover dinner or dessert our mother had prepared. We knew how Mrs. Dresden looked with her wild hair, grayed before its time, outside of its neat daytime bun. We had laughed and secretly called her 'witch' ourselves. But now we were angered at this same word from the German monster that must be there. And then brave Mrs. Dresden screamed to warn us all: 'They are taking the men! They are taking the men!' And then she was silenced with a horrible thud. We clutched our chests, as we thought we each felt in our own bodies the undeniable impact of the crack of her ribs. We did not call out 'Papa,' although we wanted to. We did not want to alert them that our father was home. But he had heard it all himself. He ran to our room and pushed us into the closet, wedging us behind my mother's clothes that had never been removed. He kissed us and put his hands on our heads and said, '*Shema yisrael Adonai elohanu Adonai echad.*' He wiped the tears from his eyes. 'Take care of each other,' he said. He closed the closet door, and we knew that he stepped into the hall and waited for his turn to be taken.

"All of what had happened to us had brought me further to bond with our community, with Jewish people. But my sister, Celine, became hardened by each move, by each incident. She wanted to live a life without the anxiety of fear, without the constant uprooting. I know now that we describe the same person. This was our conversation in the year 1940. It was the last year I saw her. We were presented with the 'opportunity' to move to the south of France, and we would be placed in convent schools or with sympathetic Christian families. With our own mother gone, the neighborhood women were gracious to watch over us. Gilda Lowenstein, one of our mother's friends, had come to our house, quietly and discretely detailing the plan to send young children and even young women of our age to farming communities in the south. This would be our best chance to escape before the next wave of terror would come. Mrs. Lowenstein said, 'They have taken our men, and next they will take us all. We have made arrangements that a large group will leave tomorrow—and you both must be among them.' When Mrs. Lowenstein left, Celine began packing her bag. But I stood still. I sat on the bed and watched her.

"I could not go. I felt I must stay—perhaps Father would return. But Celine was adamant. I see that you nod, yes. She was quiet and reserved but determined and stubborn when she needed to be, when she felt a threat to her or her family. And that was when she proposed the unthinkable. For three years, I hated her for that decision to separate. And that conversation stays with me as if it were yesterday.

"'If we do what you say, it is madness,' I told her. 'It will be as if we have given our own death sentences. What if we just let the journey unfold? Why do we have to choose the worst destiny? What if nothing bad does happen to us, and this is temporary? What if things go back to normal? We could just live our lives and be together always.'

"The naïveté of my response was unnerving to my sister: 'We are so alike yet so different, my beautiful mirror,' Celine said quietly, brushing aside a long strand of hair covering my left eye, but bothering her as if it veiled her own right eye. 'What if nothing bad happens? You can't mean that—our being Jewish has already been too hard. We have been forced to leave our home country, our mother has been killed, and our father is taken.'

"'But it is what we are. It is who we are,' I said.

"'You are wrong. It is one part of who we are. But sometimes you have to reinvent yourself. What about Maman and Papa? What about their story? Yes, Jewish in a place where that was hard. So they left in time from

Germany. Being Jewish was not their only identity. Papa was a teacher; Maman was a ballerina. If I go to a new place, I can become, or pretend to become, a new person.' Celine was adamant. 'No, I see now that we are so identical and yet so different,' she said to me. 'If you go into hiding, you will put everyone in jeopardy. I can foresee our exile will take two directions. I will be doing as told, pretending to be a Christian girl. And you will be in our room lighting imaginary Shabbas candles.'

"We both knew that she was right. We were identical in so many respects, but I was more spiritual, more devout, more cautious—more trusting. I believed and prayed that our father would return. She would have none of it. But just an hour later, she also could not bear the thought of separation. 'Get your bag. Pack your bag. Pack it, or I will pack it for you!' she cried to me. Still I didn't move. It was as if I was numb or even paralyzed. She called me a fool, and she slapped me. That was how strongly she felt that we needed to leave. She grabbed my arms at my shoulders. She literally shook me, and when I was unmoved, she slapped me again. I did not fight back. I did not have her strength, her courage. Now we know the term—I did not have her 'survivor mentality.' Our last night together could have ended badly, but I thank God that was not the case. Eventually, we sank together to the ground. We could never stay mad at each other. We collapsed together on the floor. And we cried. We cried for our dead mother, our lost father, our vanishing world."

For Risa to offer this insight into her mother's past is astonishing to Paige. And she wants Cherise, her new

Aunt Cherise, to continue. She wants to say aloud those words, "Aunt Cherise," when she asks her question, but she will reserve that for now. "We knew this about my mother—what you are saying. She would having nothing to do with Judaism in America. But you said for three years you were mad about separating, and then you agreed," Paige said. "Can you explain what you meant by that?"

"Yes, sweetheart. Just the next chapter of the terror. I did stay and did wait for Papa, or at least for peace. But once again, the people of a country turned on their Jews. In July 1942, there was the roundup, orchestrated by the Nazis, but our own French police helped them. From our horrifying and humiliating encampment at the bicycle Velodrome, from Vel' d'Hiv on to the internment camp of Drancy, I still had hope, and still I searched for her among the Jews of France who populated that camp. I ran to the fence each time a transport arrived. What did I want to see? Was I selfish enough to wish I would see my own reflection emerge from a cattle car, or did I truly hope that Celine was still safe in the south? Was it disappointment or relief that I felt each time she was not among the new arrivals? I missed her with such an acute pain, as if one of my own limbs had been severed from my body. I could not get a hold on my own emotions. And from Drancy in the year 1944, I went on to Auschwitz, an extermination camp, we had learned, and by then everyone had heard the rumors. A butcher named Dr. Josef Mengele was searching for Jewish twins…for horrible experimentations. And finally, yes, my spirit was broken. I agreed with my sister in thinking that we should not be reunited. I promised myself that if I survived, I would continue to pray for her. But I would never search for her. Even to this day, with betrayals in country after country, I will never have the feeling of innocence and security that I did in my early childhood. On my documents, it was stated that I was a twin. That actually kept me alive, and fairly undisturbed. They were waiting, and they were patient. At the same time that I had stopped looking for Celine, Dr. Mengele was obsessed to reunite us—the beautiful twin daughters of a famous ballerina. Celine's plan had actually saved me. Because the Nazis never located Celine, because her papers must have still carried her Christian name, I was still alive at liberation."

Maxwell and Paige are speechless, using their hands to cover faces wet with tears, mouths frozen in open positions, without the ability to bring forth words. First Maxwell and then Paige stand to give hugs together, and Risa welcomes their embrace. Then Maxwell breaks away from their threesome; he steps back so that Paige and her aunt can have this most exceptional reunion. He watches them together. They are not so much hugging as dancing, not so much dancing as soaring. They are soaring through the memories, embracing Celine at another age, another time. They touch each other's hair, examine their hands, hold each other's faces in their own palms, until the familiarity of Celine that each of them reflects is drawn within them as the spirit of a ghost from a séance, until that ghost disappears and what emerges is a new reality. They can go forward without the shadow of Celine as their only connection.

Without taking her eyes off of her beautiful, newly discovered niece, Risa finally pulls herself away. She needs to return to one part of the story. "But Paige, *ma chérie*, I have something to tell you that perhaps will surprise you. Something you do not know about your mother's observance. Though you tell me that she had denied or ignored our religion, I will need to challenge you on the accuracy of that statement." She rises and walks to a wall of artwork. Nestled among the most enticing street scenes of Paris, all projecting the vibrant pastel colors of the Impressionist school, is a black-and-white, very formal family portrait of Risa sitting in the matriarch's chair, a handsome, older-looking man behind her, his hand on her shoulder, and an adolescent boy at her side. "You see this picture of my family. That is my husband, Etienne. *Alev ha-shalom*, I am a widow now for five years. And this is my son. He is handsome, *non?*"

Paige, whose mind has drifted for just a moment while she focuses on the new surroundings, taking in the beautiful French décor, the stylish pillows and draperies, the pleasing aromas of meals that linger in the plush fabrics, moves quickly to the photograph. She approaches Risa, who removes it from its nail and holds it out to her. She takes it gently, holding it by the ornate wood frame.

"Yes, my lovely Paige, you do have a cousin. And I cannot wait for you to meet him. But it will not be now. It will not be on this trip for you," Risa said. "It will be in the next month, when I am to visit him where he lives. He has not been so far from you for the past few years. He wanted to go to a college with a large Jewish presence.

He is finishing at Brandeis University. He lives in Boston, Massachusetts."

Although it takes a moment to register, Paige grabs her uncle's hands and mouths "Can you believe it?"

"But wait," Risa continues. "Before I tell you about him and call him with the news, I must continue my point. His name—Renaud—just like your brother, Roger, and you, Paige—he was named after our parents, my father, Renee, and my mother, Paulette. May their memory be a blessing. No darling, your mother did not abandon all of our traditions."

Paige cannot stop smiling. This day, though it is not without painful revelations, has been a dream for her. If only she had known of this years ago, how her recurring anxieties could have been alleviated. Now, at almost twenty years of age, certainly she could take care of herself, but how wonderful it would have been to have known this when she was orphaned. It was not that she regretted having spent the years with Maxwell as her guardian. In fact, she understood the magic and privilege, and yes, even the security of it, something her mother would never have believed. But she would have been spared the years of worrying that if something happened to him that she would be alone again. She reaches once more to hug her aunt and then steps back to hold both of her hands and look at her. "May I ask you one favor?" Paige says.

"Of course, my darling."

"May I say something, at least once, and then I will put it back in the chest, in my chest, and the actual treasure chest we found."

"And what is that? I cannot imagine."

"I need to say these words. I need to call you not Aunt Risa, but Aunt Cherise, just one time, if I could. I need to say the words, Aunt Cherise. No—wait. Even I know that doesn't have the right flow, the right rhythm. *Tante Cherise.* That's better. There, I am saying them with no permission."

Maxwell has been listening in amazement. They are his exact thoughts. He needs to call her Cherise, too. As Maxwell watches her, mesmerized by every movement, he understands that Risa, that the Cherise they have found, is not a substitute for Celine. He understands that she is not Celine replaced. He would never want to erase the memory of Celine. But there is much more going on here. Maybe a memory must be given its rest. Cherise is an enchantress in her own right. Her beautiful, luminous complexion is like a porcelain doll, although she does not appear fragile or expressionless. No, perhaps she is not Celine replaced, but Celine enhanced; even the name Cherise has a captivating melody to it, and he hopes she will let it live again. She is lovely, and she is a strong, impressive career woman. Does she not recognize that she is the definition of a survivor?

He cannot stand apart any longer, so he comes closer to them both once more. He takes one of Risa's perfectly manicured hands away from Paige and holds it in both of his. He brings that hand to his lips and tenderly places a kiss just below her knuckles. He hopes she will see it as the formal greeting of the European aristocracy that he had witnessed, not as a prelude to the kiss he could already envision on her lips. He does not say what he wants to say; it is too soon. So he repeats only Paige's request: "May I also call you Cherise—if even just once?"

Now Risa moves the hand that Maxwell has not released and pulls him to her to place a light kiss on his cheek. She is starting to tear up again, although there is the lilt of laughter in her voice. "You two could have had no idea, yet it is as if you have known my own desire, how I have longed to reclaim my birth name. The letters themselves, Celine and I used to say, almost every other one, interwoven into each of our names just like our spirits—more than similar, but not identical. We will start our meeting again from the beginning." She pauses and takes a deep breath. "Welcome, I am Cherise Solomon."

Chapter 28
A Part of Their Family

Each evening of the two weeks she and her uncle had spent in France, Paige had called David in New York with updates on their journey. He wanted more than anything to accompany her, to share this with her. He hated this separation, when he had just become used to alternating weekends with her at one city and then the other. But he couldn't go to Europe with them just now. He was in the final weeks of a coveted internship at a prestigious New York firm, following his first year at Harvard Law School. He had a distinct plan for his future that he knew would be their future. He was just like the Noble men in her life, and just like his own mother, proud and ambitious, wanting to make his own way. And he knew in his heart that it was really for the best that Maxwell and Paige complete this quest together, and alone.

Paige gave a picturesque daily accounting of the adventures of the investigators and their own experiences. Most often, she would begin with, "David, we have to come back to such and such a place together"—especially after her time at the fabulous Château de Chenonceau. One night, she called him with the best news. Initially, he could hardly understand what she was saying, her fast talking and sniffle sobbing interfering with any attempts at already compromised trans-Atlantic communications. But finally, when she composed herself and became coherent, he listened to her descriptions of the Marais district in Paris. He was choked up himself as she spoke of finding Cherise, who was actually her aunt. And when Paige revealed that she had a cousin Renaud at Brandeis, David knew it would not be long before he had his wish. He knew she would soon be transferring to a school in Boston.

When Maxwell and Paige arrived home in Chicago, they were anxious to share their incredible story with Gladys. But, as excited as they were, they were sensitive that the news might be just a bit hard for Gladys to take. They finally, so many years later, were adding to their family. They wished that she could have this same joy. On the plane home, Paige and her uncle had discussed how they would present their news to Gladys. They would be inclusive. They would make her feel that she has always been a part of their family, and now that family was expanding.

They could not have known that Gladys was in the apartment nervously pacing. While she awaited their return, she had set the dining room table with the most exquisite china pattern and the heaviest, most ornate sterling silverware from the Weiss and Noble homes.

She would light the candles on the elegant candelabra as soon as the doorman gave her notice of their arrival.

When Gladys opened the door, Paige enveloped her in her arms with a tremendous hug. "We have a lot to tell you, but first, before we talk, you must unwrap your presents." One beautiful box contained a lavender and white evening dress suit that was obviously of the most luscious couturier fabric and design, and a second box held a gray-and-black silk shawl.

"Oh, my goodness. What beautiful gifts. I love them," she said, modeling the wrap around her shoulders. Paige and Maxwell nodded at each other, proud of their successful choices from Cherise's store. They had each feared that Gladys would not have been able to resist calling them foolish and crazy, throwing them a "Where do you think I would be wearing such items?" attitude.

"Now, just put your things down," she said instead. "There will be plenty of time for unpacking later. I have a special surprise for you in the dining room."

When they walked into the room, their eyes lit up, despite the jet lag of a long flight. And when Paige saw the beautiful table with four place settings, she was even more delighted. "He was just teasing me, then," Paige said. "David told me he couldn't get away midweek, but he just couldn't resist. I knew it."

"Well, honey, I don't mean to disappoint, but I think David was telling you the truth. He told me to expect him Friday night," Gladys answered. "So I am sorry if you are misled."

At this point, even Maxwell was confused. "Okay then, who is our mystery guest?"

Gladys walked over to the butler's cart and filled four glass flutes with the champagne she had just uncorked. She walked out of the room and a minute later returned arm in arm with a handsomely dressed, distinguished-looking black man, possibly just a few years older than she was.

"Mr. Maxwell Noble, Miss Paige Noble," she said. "I would like you to meet Mr. Carter Johnson."

The man extended his hand first to Maxwell and then to Paige. "Please, call me Carter. I brought a nice bottle of champagne for the evening," he said. "And I was hoping you would join me in a toast—to my bright and beautiful bride to be." He raised his glass, nodded at Gladys, and then turned back to Maxwell. "That is, if you give us your blessing. That was Gladys's condition on accepting."

They couldn't have been more surprised or more delighted. They warmed to Carter immediately. And over dinner, Maxwell felt justified giving him the third degree. Gladys said she had met him on campus, but he hardly looked like a student. He said, for him it was "love at first sight."

"But not for you Gladys?" Paige asked. "This guy looks very hard to resist."

Carter spoke up quickly. "Well, you see, she seemed to like me well enough, and I, myself, was very lonely. I had noticed her a few times as I passed by and back, and she wasn't a silly young coed."

"Watch it," Gladys cautioned, for fear he would call her old.

"No, she was a mature student, that much I knew—just a little more seasoned than the others—and so beautiful, I could not believe that her early story had been a hard one when I eventually heard it." He took Gladys's hand in his and kissed it gently.

"He was in my section, three big books on his arms, and he walked back and forth a few times until he took a seat across from me. He started with library small talk: 'What are you reading? What are you studying?' He jumped from his seat when he saw me reach for a book on a shelf a bit too high."

"And then I dropped it on her foot," he broke in.

"I don't know. I thought he was certainly old to be a student himself. I wasn't exactly sure why he was poring through the psychology and sociology texts. Either he was trying to stay close to ask me out, or maybe he was in need of major self-counseling." Gladys looked at her fiancé tenderly. "Finally, he told me. He'd had a brief marriage—'Happy enough'—those were his words—and then she left him, just like that."

"Just like that," he breaks in, repeating the phrase he had obviously told Gladys initially. "I worked too much, she said. I was just not enough fun." He gave an exasperated gasp. "Well, I was trying to get my business going. Isn't that what a husband does? You need to provide."

"He was building his father's small plumbing business into a conglomerate."

"Well, Gladys tends to exaggerate, but I have seven little trucks rolling now with our signage on the side. I've set an apprenticeship program to help employ the local kids."

"You see how suited we are," Gladys beamed, directing a sweet smile in Carter's direction.

"I get it," Paige said. "So Carter, what placed you in the library?"

"Well, this is how we've been growing. The university was calling for bids on some expansion projects, and I was there to check out the current facilities. Most of the time now, I'm in casual or business dress, not decked out like my trade." He moved closer to Gladys and put his arm around her. "I saw this pretty lady out of the corner of my eye and tried to think quickly. I went over to the shelves and saw books on overcoming a loss. Well, I certainly needed that information, so I sat and began reading. From the beginning, though, I was starting to realize something. Although the books were actually helpful, the real answer wasn't in the books. But it was in the library." He paused briefly to send a tender smile to Gladys.

"And then I kept coming by when I knew she'd be there. I wanted to continue sharing her table. Yes, I told her that, even though I know it sounded pathetically needy. I asked her out a few times, but she never said yes. Over the next weeks, I reached into my bag of tricks to dangle her way—tickets to athletic events, tickets to the symphony, seats at a jazz club. I was getting warmer. But here's the thing that held her back: it was my mistake of vanity. A few months before I met her, I decided I would try wearing contact lenses."

"And he didn't wear them very well. You know me. I look right in the eyes and judge the quality of a person. Always have, always will. He seemed bland

and unfocused." She turned to him. "I am sorry, dar-ling. You know I am only speaking the truth."

"And then one day," Carter continued, "I couldn't locate my contact case. I was late getting ready and finally knew I'd just have to give in and wear my glasses."

"Once I saw him in his glasses, I saw the man I would marry. And here you come from Paris with my perfect wedding attire," she said, with fanciful hand movements directed toward the boxes. "Now, was there something that you wanted to tell me?"

Chapter 29
The Lucky One

Ever since Maxwell and Cherise met in Paris, they had enjoyed a special and strong relationship, ostensibly a close friendship, spanning the continents and constantly linking them together. Maxwell orchestrated the pairing as if he were the renowned Sir Georg Solti, conducting the Chicago Symphony. Finally, everything in Maxwell's world was falling harmoniously into place.

Cherise was spending more and more time in the States. It was a sudden brainstorm that had awoken Max in the middle of the night before he and Paige left Europe. If he hadn't thought of this, he swore later, he just never would have left Cherise's city without her. Maxwell would contact Florie's old friend and his newer friend, Oscar de la Renta. They had been sharing great times with Maxwell's foray into the world of fashion, adding his usual creative twist. He was not interested in being a studio photographer. He placed the tall, willowy models out on the street. They would lean against landmark buildings and edifices, their Oscar de la Renta formal ball gowns billowing in the wind at the Empire State Building or at the base of the Statue of Liberty. Surely, Oscar would be impressed enough with Cherise's designs that he could find a place for her in the New York scene.

But he couldn't have imagined Oscar's response: "Are you perhaps speaking of not a Cherise, but a Risa Solomon, with a shop by the Marais?" he questioned.

"Yes, that is the same one. You're familiar with it?"

"Of course. Have you spoken to her about this? I have been courting her for years," Oscar said. "If you can plead my case, I would be most appreciative. The seventies have brought a new set of fashion challenges to the designer world, and Cherise has a pulse on the casual market."

Maxwell couldn't stop smiling as he set the phone down. In his mind, he repeated Oscar's words: "I have been courting her for years," and he hoped his own courtship would be briefer.

Cherise still maintained her Paris boutique while transitioning the daily tasks to new and eager business partners. She was spending an increasing amount of time as a designer in Manhattan. Often Maxwell would come to town, and they would have dinners with Oscar and his wife, and Florie and Maurice Elian Rothschild.

But possibly the main reason that Cherise had decided to shift from Paris as her main residence was to be closer to her son and her newly found extended family. The adorable Renaud Solomon had fallen in love with the America that had fallen in love with him.

His long, wavy, unkempt brown hair, his deep-set eyes, the seductive sounds of his French accent, made him an irresistible playboy, although he was a Brandeis scholar. Young men and young women were both taken with him. The boys wanted to imitate the way Renaud wore an unstructured navy blue or brown tweed jacket with the requisite stone-washed or slightly torn jeans. They wanted the tortoise-shell glasses that made him look like a twenty-one-year-old professor. The college girls wanted to walk with him on the campus; they vied for seats at his library table. But he was quite often seen in the company of a beautiful and slender girl, her thick, black hair cut evenly at shoulder length, not hanging in disarrayed strands like the current fashion, but neatly framing a cameo face. The coeds were not deterred in their pursuit, however, especially when the girl was often seen holding hands with a different handsome young man, sporting a Harvard Law sweatshirt. Eventually, it was confirmed that the girl was Renaud's first cousin, Paige Noble, who was raised by her famous uncle, the photographer, Maxwell Noble. It was rumored that she had turned down modeling contracts.

Even before their trip to France, Maxwell knew that Paige eventually planned to transfer to a school in Boston. He had encouraged Paige and David to let her finish a second year at Northwestern University, although he wasn't exactly sure why it mattered—they were a done deal. But the draw of her boyfriend and her newly discovered cousin out East proved too much for them all. Between the tears of separation and the cost and inconvenience of constant plane flights, Maxwell welcomed the news that she was accepted at Brandeis for the spring term of 1970.

Eventually, when Maxwell received a special call from David Bronstein, he was not incredibly surprised. In the most mature, gentlemanly manner of a nervous suitor, David presented his case for Paige's hand in marriage.

"David, we both love you. Haven't you been part of the family forever? This will be great to make it official, and we'll do it in grand style. You're an impressive young man," Maxwell said, and then he choked up a bit. "She's a great girl, you know. She's been a gift to me. I've been so lucky to have had my time with her."

"That's not ending," David interrupted. "Like you said, we're all family now." He paused and then added, "You know, Paige says the same thing about you, always. She feels she is the lucky one, that you came for her and you never left."

David had told Maxwell he was requesting that both his family and Paige's come to Boston the following week for a few days, although he would not like them to say anything to Paige about the plan. So the next Friday, with Maxwell's permission and blessing, David met Paige after her last class of the day and escorted her to her dorm room to choose her most special outfit. Then he took her to their favorite spot along the banks of the Charles River for a stone-skipping contest.

As he took her hand and led her toward the water, she looked at him incredulously. "I'm a bit confused. For this I needed a nice dress? And nice shoes?" She was walking on tiptoes so her little heels would not sink into the ground.

"Never mind. Just choose your rocks. I've been practicing," he said, calming her.

They each took a few turns that ended in a tie. Although she was annoyed, this was bringing out her competitive side, and she was ready to bend down for a new batch. But when she turned to David, she brought her hands to cover her mouth and whispered, "Oh my God." He was bending down on one knee. In his hand was a small, square, black jewelry box, and when he opened it, he simply said, "I hope this will be the perfect stone for you."

They were all waiting there, anxiously, in the dining room of the elegant Copley Plaza Hotel, waiting to hug and kiss and congratulate the pair and toast them with champagne. It was the group that had spent many wonderful times together over the past year and now would look to an engagement year filled with parties in many locations.

For the next eight months, Maxwell tried to be patient, slowly developing his relationship with Cherise into something more than a friendship, but less than a romance. They interacted as if they were brother- and sister-in-law, each a supportive companion for the widowed spouse. They shared weekends in New York, Boston, Chicago, and Lake Geneva, both with and without any combination of the children, Paige and David and Renaud, and even Florie and Maurice. But more and more lately, he thought he recognized in Cherise his same desire to linger at a hotel door before separating to their own rooms, to unconsciously close her eyes and prolong the parting hug and kiss on the cheek.

Finally, he knew he had to speak to her, privately and honestly. It was at the end of a lovely evening in Boston after taking the three students out to dinner, when they had returned to the Copley. A tremendous self-confidence had been an imprinted part of Maxwell's personality, possibly since his first cry in the hospital at his delivery, his first grandiose announcement that he had entered a room. Yet in all of the relationships Maxwell had pursued over the years, he had never been as nervous about verbalizing his feelings as he was with Cherise.

On the elevator with her, he began the speech he had rehearsed: "Cherise, I need to talk to you about something," Maxwell said, quite proud of his unemotional tone. "Would you join me in my room for a drink?"

"Of course, Maxwell. I'd love that." His confidence was growing because she didn't seem to need any persuading. Had she been waiting for this type of invitation?

"You are beautiful," he said, as he held the door open for her to enter first. He wanted to start with subtle words, but he couldn't help what he was saying. "Wait, turn to me," he continued, shaking his head. "I didn't even see your dress that well with you sitting next to me this evening. It is fabulous. It is elegant and sophisticated. It is designer couture, yet it is young and hippie and ethereal. This is why you are in such demand. You have been able to redefine dressing in this antiestablishment decade."

She laughed. "You sound like a fashion critic. Your next avocation, perhaps?"

Quickly, he moved to the radio. He searched out a station of old standards and held his hand out to her. "It is a dress that says you want to dance." He couldn't have come upon a better tune. It was the Flamingo's revival of "I Only Have Eyes for You." For much of the song, he held her in the ballroom dance school position until he could not help himself and pulled her close, just rocking out the final verses like teenagers at the prom.

When the music stopped, they parted abruptly. He poured them drinks from the little bar. "I want to talk to you seriously about something," he said.

"Is it about the children?"

"It is not."

"Is it about us?"

"It is."

"Funny. I have wanted to talk to you about something as well. In my head, I go over your story, the story of your life that wove through mine." He motioned that they each take a chair in the small sitting room, surprised that she would be the one to begin the conversation, but interested to see where it would lead. "And you know what, Maxwell? In the entire story, who do I feel most sorry for?" She put her drink down and reached across the small table to him. When she held his face with her fingertips, he thought he would jump out of his skin. "It is you, *mon cher*," she said, shaking her head. "To have wasted so much time, so many years, searching to recapture what was lost to you. With your charisma, with your vibrancy of spirit, I could cry for the energy that you reserved in all of your relationships to not forget, to pursue a vanished dream, to—"

"You are so wrong," he said, laughing the words to her. He had a lightness of spirit, as if a tremendous weight had been lifted from him. "It's become so clear to me. You don't understand it at all. But I need you to. I know this now. Remember when I first met you, when I told you we were searching for a missing piece of a puzzle? I could not have imagined the picture that would emerge when the puzzle was completed. You have to believe what I believe. I believe that not one moment of my life was wasted, not one moment of my life was misdirected. Everything that happened before and after meeting Celine, before and after losing Celine more than once, everything that happened just led me down a road and a turn in the road and a detour in the road, until the road led me…to you."

He stopped for a minute and downed the final portion of his drink, as if it would give him courage to continue. "It was not a life wasted. If I may say, it was an incredible life not wasted…not wasted, but waiting… waiting for you. Waiting for the sun and the stars and the moon and the planets to align just so, to place me one day in a beautiful shop, where you were waiting for me." Now he was quiet for a moment and gently placed his hand on her cheek. "What if so much in my destiny kept me parted from Celine because my true destiny wasn't Celine? My destiny was you. Celine, herself, led me here. Not easily, not quickly, not without—not without heartache and drama." He knew his speech to her was gaining in momentum, so he worked to slow himself down. He gave her an almost embarrassed-looking smile. "I know I have a romantic spirit. I know this is not usually a masculine attribute. But I will claim it anyway. I will shout it. I am a romantic, and I believe this no matter how fantastically implausible it seems."

He waited for her to say something, but she remained silent and pensive. "But that was my journey to you. It would be presumptuous for me to think that was your journey as well. I can take it even if your one true love was your husband. Then I'll just have to use my charismatic tricks to win you over, to entice you to open your heart again."

Now she laughed and covered his hand with hers. "My head is spinning. Do you understand? You make me feel like a carefree young girl being asked to a party. Yet you have to realize that I was never that girl. When I was of that age, you heard my stories; my world was changing and breaking apart until it was totally destroyed. There was no young man courting me. We wondered what food we would eat, not what dress we would wear. All of those years were stolen from me. But at liberation, you do not complain about the lost trivialities, the frivolities of the past, when you understand how lucky, how blessed you were to have a future. When we were finally free, there was joy, yes, but mainly confusion, and a lingering fear— where do I go? We had already heard the stories of the displaced Jews of Poland. Anti-Semitism was alive there still. They were not welcomed back to their homes. They could not reclaim what had been stolen from them— physically, spiritually, or emotionally." At this point, she stood up and looked out the hotel window.

"Many people spoke of moving on to America, and others, the Zionists, looked to Palestine. Eventually, I connected with a small group of other French Jews who survived the camps. The draw of our beautiful city was too hard to resist. People tried to dissuade us, but we were determined. And in that group of skeletons with shorn hair, we paired up. My marriage to Etienne was a marriage of convenience, of opportunity, to a sad, lonely widower who watched his wife and daughter as they were selected for the gas chambers. Do you know what it was that depressed me then? I am embarrassed to have been so vain. I was upset because I thought I was not marrying a handsome man, and he probably thought the same of me, not a pretty woman. But as we gained weight and our hair grew back, our features that were almost hideously distorted melded back to normal. We knew nothing of each other. He did not look at me and see the talents of a seamstress, and I did not see in him a respected accountant. He wanted to regain himself, prove that he could protect me when he couldn't protect them. And I craved someone to take responsibility for me. But, surprisingly, love came and grew. And when our real selves emerged over the first years, we knew that the baby we dreamed to have one day would be a bright and beautiful child to begin to replace the families we had lost." She coughed out the last words as she held back her soft sobs.

"You do not know this part, but you can imagine. Etienne could never overcome his depression, his guilt. Renaud and I could never be enough to wipe away the memories. Each time he was ill, he was happy. He would never take his medicine for any of his conditions. Eventually, he had his wish, and he was at peace."

Maxwell, who had moved to stand close behind her as she spoke, now turned her around and held her in his arms. "I don't know what to say except that I will find no peace unless I spend the rest of my life with you."

"I just wondered," Cherise said, her eyes welling with tears, "if you might be interested in kissing me, if we might stop talking long enough to—"

He grabbed her shoulders and pulled her mouth so quickly to his lips that the last words of her sentence bounced on his tongue and disappeared. There was no need for speech.

Chapter 30
My Protector

I became Mrs. David Bronstein, Paige Noble Bronstein, in the summer of 1971. Like any bride, I would have thought my walk down the aisle would have been the highlight of my life. But as it turned out, it was not even the highlight of my day. And my groom would not feel dismissed by that comment. This is what you can say when you marry someone who knows you better than you know yourself, who has seen you at your worst and best, who has been your best friend through the most formative years of your life.

On the morning of my wedding, I woke up to the beautiful sunshine of a mid-July day at our Chicago residence. It was Uncle Maxwell's idea that Gladys return for the prenuptial night and the three of us enjoy a sleepover together this one last time. So that we wouldn't have to cook or clean up, my uncle had arranged for a special catered breakfast. But Gladys would have none of that and canceled the order. "If you've got eggs and pancake batter and orange juice, we'll work together in the kitchen to recreate our best memories," she insisted.

For the previous year, Gladys and Carter had been living near the University of Illinois Chicago Circle. With funding from her best supporter, Gladys had helped open the Bronstein Women's Settlement Home of Chicago at an underserved inner-city location. And Maxwell had endowed two master's degree grants at the university's School of Social Work—one a memorial to Mitchell, Celine, and Roger Noble and one in the name of Darren Barker.

After we ate, Uncle Maxwell called me into the study and led me to sit with him in my favorite alcove. Together, we watched the young families staking out their territory on Oak Street Beach with blankets, picnic baskets, and folding chairs. He put his arm around me and looked at me with a most enigmatic grin. I knew my uncle had asked me there for a special purpose. I was wondering if he might be presenting me with an heirloom necklace to accompany my wedding dress, maybe something from my mother's jewelry collection that he had set aside. I looked around the immediate area to see if there was a small gift box.

"Looking for something, sweetheart?" he asked.

"Well, you're acting funny, like you have a surprise for me. I can read your face like a map."

"You just think you know me so well. What is it you think I might have for you?"

"Well, honestly, don't be mad at me if I'm wrong, okay?"

"Don't be silly."

"Well, I was thinking that maybe you had a necklace or earrings for me. Believe me, I know you've done enough for the wedding. More than enough. But you wouldn't let me choose any jewelry, so that's what I thought."

He smiled slightly again and reached into a pants pocket. He pulled out a small red and yellow jewelry pouch with Oriental lettering. "Open it. It was your mother's. It is yours now."

Impatiently, I fiddled with the knot on the bag. "Wow. Beautiful. Pearls. Pearls interwoven with tiny diamonds." I had never seen this piece before. "From China?" I asked, wrapping my arms around him and giving him a kiss on the cheek.

"I bought them for her. In Japan. I brought them back for her as a present for your birth."

"Always the one to overdo. I can't imagine that my father gave her anything nicer."

"Paige," he said, placing his hand over mine and clearing his throat.

"Do you want to help me clasp them?" I asked excitedly. "I must see them in a mirror."

"Paige."

I turned back to him and stopped what I was doing. I realized he was trying to speak seriously to me.

"Paige, I already told this to David and Cherise, yesterday, so they would be prepared to give you any support you need." He paused again, inhaling audibly. "Paige, I am your father. I am your real father."

"Wait," I said, closing my eyes tightly and placing a hand on my forehead. "I am having trouble understanding this. Remember, I asked you this once and you said no, and I believed you. You don't have to say this. You know how much I love you, as much as a father, anyway."

"Paige, I am your real father. I am not proud of the betrayal that led to that, but I have no regrets that it happened, and I am proud of whom you have become. I know you think I am making this up—that you don't believe it. And it's okay if you want—"

"I do believe it."

"You what?"

"I do believe it. I guess I've kind of thought it for a while."

"But how?"

"In the trunk, with the diary. There were pictures of my mother hidden among the linens. But I thought my father was the photographer."

He shook his head, somewhat embarrassed.

"So how did you connect the dots?"

"It was David who did. Not this whole truth. But when I showed them to David, he knew they were not my father's pictures, that they were professional. He tried not to tell me, but—" I stopped for a moment because I didn't feel comfortable explaining further. "You could have told me, you know. When you told me you had known her before she came to America, you could have told me the rest of the story. I would have still loved you. Uncle Maxwell, you were my savior. You were my protector. To me, the stars and the sun revolve around you. But why tell me now? Why now, when it could have been so important so many years ago?"

"Oh, I wanted to. I wanted to, for sure. But I didn't want to upset you, to hurt you. And I wanted to punish myself, not you. Because it wasn't fair. I didn't deserve to be called your father. My brother, he's the one who raised you, who supported you, who stayed with you when you were sick, who taught you to ride a bike and who read books to you at night. You can't *claim* that label, 'Dad.' You have to *deserve* it. I made this promise to myself: that he would be the only father you would know, and I was lucky to be your uncle."

"But now, why now?"

"But now, my beautiful niece, my precious daughter, you will be married. And a new volume will start—the coffee-table book of your new life. And you and David will begin a family someday. I could step aside as your father because you had a father you knew and loved. Your children-to-be, however, will know only one man as their maternal grandfather, and, of course this is up to you, but I would like to be that man."

By late morning, bellmen had arrived at our apartment and moved suitcases and hanging garment bags with all of our wedding attire to their destination. There had been an engagement party and an assortment of other prewedding celebrations at Weiss House in Lake Geneva that set the property aglow with lights and laughter throughout the previous year. But even before I knew who my groom would be, it had been my dream to walk down the illustrious aisle of gilded columns of the Gold

Coast Room of the Drake Hotel. Over the years, as I dined at the famous restaurants there with Uncle Maxwell, I would always be watching the brides and bridesmaids, the grooms and groomsmen, the little flower girls and ring bearers, as they lined up before the ceremony.

As our own hour approached, David and I were finished with the prewedding formal portraits, and we took a moment to sneak to a side room and enjoy some time alone. I thought he was the handsomest groom of all those I had ever seen, and the tuxedo that Oscar had fashioned for him was exceptional. We allowed each other only the tiniest kisses on the lips; hair and makeup had to remain perfectly in place for another hour. And we knew there would be a lifetime of passion ahead.

As I headed back upstairs for my forgotten purse, I pulled aside the draperies of my hotel suite. I saw the rows of limousines and guests stepping out of them. Mayor Richard J. Daley, of course, was there with his wife, Eleanor "Sis" Daley. Irv and Esther "Essee" Kupcinet were greeting senators and congressmen as they exited cars. Socialites from the East Coast and a few minor members of European royal families mingled with television personalities, fashion designers, models, and athletic icons whom Maxwell had photographed and befriended. Crowds of onlookers were snapping their own pictures, not even realizing that they were capturing some images of the preeminent photojournalists of the time. The Bronstein family had their own entourage from New York arriving from any number of surrounding hotels.

The publicity had made me extremely self-conscious for the previous months. Ours was anticipated to be the "wedding of the year" in magazines like *Town and Country* and the social sections of the New York and Chicago papers. The only reason I could tolerate the attention was my knowing that pictures of the magnificent gown that Cherise had designed for me would enhance her reputation and translate into the career move that could keep her solidly in our country.

Our wedding was a fairy-tale affair, whipped cream on a young life of both deep tragedies and incredible joys. It was a life of privilege, I understood, although I sought a life of privacy. Charitably, I let Uncle Maxwell believe that he still had kept one last thing inside. When he and Tante Cherise escorted me down the aisle, I almost felt the electrical charge between them passing through me, and I found it a most delightful distraction. When we returned from our honeymoon, and Maxwell, holding tightly to Cherise's hand, announced that they were in love, it was hard to do anything but look at David and exchange smiles.

"You knew?" they asked.

"We knew," we chorused.

Then my uncle held out Cherise's hand to us and we saw the brilliant, emerald-cut diamond. Maxwell Noble, whom people identified as a confirmed bachelor, finally would have the true happiness that I knew he really sought; he had finally found his one true love.

Now, in Maxwell's apartment, the most prominent photograph, and the one he loves the most, is not even one of his signature works. It is the photo taken at my wedding. I am in the middle, facing David, and we are surrounded by our families. But even I agree: the eye is always drawn to the distinguished gentleman, the famous photographer, standing proudly as the patriarch, enjoying his position inside the frame. Every family will have its treasured memories. There are family photographs in black and white, and there are color photos. They are lying loose in boxes or hanging on walls in the living rooms and corridors of homes. They are leaning in frames on nightstands so they will never be far from view, and they are sleeping in albums waiting to see the light of day when someone turns a page. And while our story might have played out on a grander scale than most, I have to believe that every family has its own unique history of trials and triumphs, of loves lost and found, of secrets hidden and revealed.

F ollowing the release of her debut novel, *Pictures of the Past*, author Deby Eisenberg joined the Jewish Book Council tour, speaking to book groups, libraries, and organizations across the nation.

A book club leader for over twenty years, Eisenberg is a former English teacher and journalist. She earned her master's degree from the University of Chicago.

Eisenberg and her husband Michael, an obstetrician-gynecologist, live in Riverwoods, Illinois. They have three grown children and seven grandchildren.

To find out more about the author, visit her website at www.debyeisenberg.com.

❧

Also by Deby Eisenberg
Pictures of the Past

When a work of art he had donated to the Art Institute of Chicago decades earlier is challenged as a Nazi theft, the heart-grabbing story of charismatic philanthropist Taylor Woodmere unfolds. Spanning from pre-World War II to contemporary times and sweeping through the European capitals of Paris and Berlin, this compelling historical fiction traces an Impressionist painting and a young love diverted by the Nazis. From a world torn by the horrors of war, a love story emerges that endures through years of separation.

"This novel is one of the most intriguing and beautiful books that I have ever read. The ending of this book will touch your heart... The writing is first class." Mary Lignor, *Book Pleasures*

Notes and Acknowledgments

The writing process for me has taken a similar pattern in my first two novels. It begins with a kernel of an idea sparked by a fascination with a location or an event that I will stumble on through my reading or travels, or my memories that are ripe to resurface. This spark becomes an electromagnetic pull that I will find hard to resist. And so, I will be compelled to envision the people who might have lived in or visited that intriguing place during its heyday or been present and personally impacted by a pivotal historical moment.

I have always been like this. At an art museum, I need to know the stories of the artists' subjects, the people interacting in the paintings. On a tour of any heritage site, I can barely concentrate on the docent's words or the audio narrative streaming into my ear. My mind has drifted to the visitor who had been invited to the venue during its prime. If there is a gift shop, I will need to purchase the guidebook because I will want to know every detail that I have missed.

At a mansion in Newport, Rhode Island, I picture the young college student asked to a dance at a classmate's home at the turn of the century, never imagining the gilded walls, the marble floors, the uniformed staff in attendance whom he will encounter at the formal ball. At Kykuit in New York, a Rockefeller estate, I picture the young craftsman who is completing his assignment, who is envisioning how he can fulfill his own American dream.

Although I had visited the resorts of Lake Geneva, Wisconsin, many times as a child and young adult, it was not until more recently that I discovered the lake path and its fabulous access to the grounds and exteriors of the mansions of the area. I was hooked. This resort community began attracting the affluent leaders in business and industry, most of them from the Chicago area, in the late eighteen hundreds, and it remained a vibrant destination through the early nineteen hundreds and up until the Depression. Classic estates were maintained, refurbished, or razed throughout the years as family ownerships were kept, abandoned, transferred, or bequeathed to organizations. Over the following decades of that century and into the twenty-first century, development experienced its peaks and valleys, as is true of any such venue dependent not only on economic times but also on the passion of a subsequent generation to follow the dream of the original patriarch. But all of the properties have fascinating stories to tell—Loramoor and Galewood, Villa Palatina and Wadsworth Hall, Snug Harbor and Butternuts. So many of the homes have a lineage that follows all or part of the pattern: built, burned, second home constructed, home razed, property subdivided.

Many of my readers have commented on the extent of my historical research, although I have actually tried my best to limit details and maintain the flow of the story. While I have created a world with a fictional estate in Lake Geneva and fictional characters, I am grateful to the true historians of the area who have documented such a wealth of engrossing, rich, and authentic information on the community before and during the time period covered in my novel. *Lake Geneva, Newport of the West, Volume 1*, by Ann Wolfmeyer and Mary Burns Gage, published by the Lake Geneva Historical Society, Inc., provided photographs of the mansions and their residents, accompanied by vignettes depicting life in the era. *Geneva Lake, Stories from the Shore*, edited by Anne Celano Frohna and published by At The Lake, helped guide me along the lake path with Maxwell, Florie, Paige, and David.

Although I did strive to be as true as possible to a region and its people as I developed my characters, my book is a work of fiction. When my characters are at actual historical venues, I strive for descriptions to be as accurate as possible. When they interact with genuine historical figures, I respect the responsibility to stay true to that person's documented personality.

For much of my background research on the *Eastland* disaster, I looked first to the marvelous website of the *Eastland* Disaster Historical Society. Susan Decker,

Barbara Decker Wachholz, and Ted Wachholz have dedicated so much of their time to preserving the history of the tragedy and the memory of the participants. Jay Bonansinga's *The Sinking of the Eastland: America's Forgotten Tragedy,* also provided a wealth of information on the event. Although, of course, the actions of the fictional Weiss and Noble families on board the *Eastland* and on the dock are from my imagination, I tried to follow the timeline and stories of survivors and victims of that fateful July day in 1915.

Although the history of the Western Electric Company is factual, the concept of a Lake Geneva summer retreat for owners and employees is my own design. Similarly, although my chronicling of the history of Lake Geneva is compiled from visits to the area and research, my assertion that my fictional Gables Country Club was "restricted" to Jews is not based on any specific evidence from a real Lake Geneva club. But, in truth, it was very commonplace during that era and throughout much of the twentieth century for the most prestigious country clubs to be exclusive gentile enclaves, if not openly anti-Semitic. Because of this, in the greater Chicago area, very famous and longstanding clubs were established by the Jewish community—among them the Standard Club and the Covenant Club.

I must acknowledge my sister-in-law Cheri Eisenberg, as an inspiration for one of my two main characters, Maxwell Noble. Cheri is a respected freelance photographer, her pictures having appeared in publications such as *Town and Country Magazine, Chicago Magazine,* and *The Chicago Tribune.* Over the years, she has met and mingled with the rich and famous and directed her camera also to the street people she befriended. Her clients have included the Lyric Opera, the Chicago Symphony Orchestra and the Art Institute of Chicago; she has documented events for countless charitable and political functions. Like Maxwell, she has led a most interesting life with assignments in many of the major cities in the United States, as well as in Europe.

And, of course, with love for him and admiration for his delivering thousands of babies in the Chicago area, once again, I must thank my husband, Michael, for his tremendous support throughout this second novel endeavor. And since the release of my first book, *Pictures of the Past*, our grown children and their spouses have increased our joy. So thank you to all of them and their multiplying inspirations for me: Carlee and Keith Londo and Skylar, Jace, and Sage; Rachel and Robbie Eisenberg and Makenzie; Abby and Chad Eisenberg and Laken, Jayden, and Payton.

And special thanks to my forever friends and to the newest friends I made from my journey with ***Pictures of the Past*** for all of their encouragement to write another novel.

Questions for Discussion

1. The bond between Maxwell and Paige was incredibly strong. How could Maxwell emerge as an appropriate and even wonderful guardian for Paige, when he had often been described as a "bachelor vagabond?" Paige's own mother "had referred to Maxwell as a child, himself."

2. If this is a novel of an adolescent's journey for Paige, with its accompanying theme of the "loss of innocence," what were examples of this throughout the story?

3. The plot of *Protecting Paige* centers on three venues and time periods: Chicago in the 1960s and 1970s; Chicago and Lake Geneva in 1915; and France, during WWII. What parallels can be drawn between people and events for these three different eras?

4. Compare and contrast Celine and Cherise in their coping and survival strategies. Was one a stronger individual than the other?

5. How would you describe Maxwell's character? Could you forgive his betrayal, even though it tortured him?

6. Maxwell and Paige searched for one more family member they could embrace. With today's popular websites such as ancestry.com, people are connecting more and more with past generations. What interesting, or even fascinating, connections have you uncovered?

7. Although Florie Bronstein did not emerge as a major character, why was she nevertheless an important figure?

8. With the discovery of Celine's diary, Maxwell and Paige's emotional journey turned into a literal one. How did this impact their lives and set the course of their futures? What else was uncovered in the chest?

9. The author has used a variety of narrative styles and moved from past tense to present tense at times throughout the novel. She felt each change worked best to enhance the story. Did you find this confusing or agree that it helped to draw you into the story and engage with the characters and plot line?

10. A title is so often an author's key to interpreting a novel. Trace references to *Protecting Paige* throughout the story.